CAEDMON'S SONG

Peter Robinson grew up in Yorkshire, and now lives in Canada.

He is renowned for his bestselling Inspector Banks series, which has won numerous awards in Britain, the United States, Canada and Europe.

Peter Robinson's new Inspector Banks novel, *Playing With Fire*, is now available in hardcover, published by Macmillan.

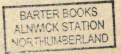

PETER ROBINSON

CAEDMON'S SONG

PAN BOOKS

First published 1990 by Penguin Canada

This edition published 2004 by Pan Books
an imprint of Pan Macmillan Ltd
Pan Macmillan, 20 New Wharf Road, London N1 9RR
Basingstoke and Oxford
Associated companies throughout the world
www.panmacmillan.com

ISBN 0 330 42672 9

Copyright © Peter Robinson 1990

Maps designed by Brian Lehan

3 5 7 9 8 6 4 2

A CIP catalogue record for this book is available from
the British Library.

Typeset by IntypeLibra, London
Printed and bound in Great Britain by
Mackays of Chatham plc, Chatham, Kent

All Pan Macmillan titles are available from www.panmacmillan.com
or from Bookpost by telephoning 01624 677237

For Sheila

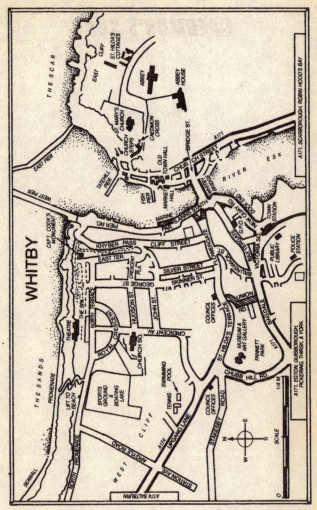

Map by Brian Lehen

CAEDMON'S SONG

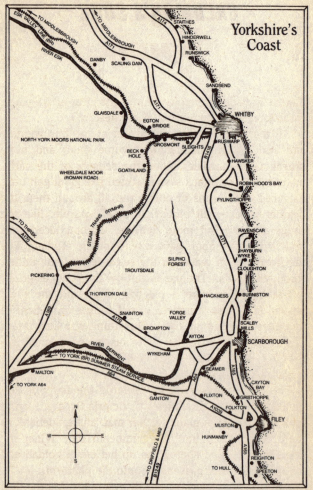

Yorkshire's Coast

Map by Brian Lehen

1

MARTHA

Martha Browne arrived in Whitby one clear afternoon in early September, convinced of her destiny.

All the way, she had gazed out of the bus window and watched the landscape become more and more unreal. On Fylingdales Moor, the sensors of the early-warning missile-attack system rested like giant golf balls balanced at the rims of holes, and all around them the heather was in full bloom. It wasn't purple, like the songs all said, but more delicate, maroon laced with pink. When the moors gave way to rolling farmland, like the frozen green waves of the sea it led to, she understood what Dylan Thomas meant by 'fire green as grass'.

Sea and sky were a piercing blue, and the town nestled in its bay, a pattern of red pantile roofs flanked on either side by high cliffs. Everything was too vibrant and vivid to be real; the scene resembled a landscape painting, as distorted in its way as Van Gogh's wheat fields and starry nights.

The bus lumbered down towards the harbour and pulled up in a small station off Victoria Square. Martha took another quick glance at her map and guidebook as the driver backed into the numbered bay. When the doors hissed open, she picked up her small holdall and followed the other passengers onto the platform.

Arriving in a new place always made Martha feel strangely excited, but this time the sensation was even more intense. At first, she could only stand rooted to the spot among the revving buses, breathing in the diesel fumes and salt sea air. She felt as if she was trying the place on for size, and it was a good fit. She took stock of the subtle tremors her arrival caused in the essence of the town. Others might not notice such things, but Martha did. Everyone and everything – from the sand on the beach to a guilty secret in a tourist's heart – was somehow connected and in a state of constant flux. It was like quantum physics, she thought, at least in so far as she understood it. Her presence would send out ripples and reverberations that people wouldn't forget for a long time.

She still felt queasy from the journey, but that would soon pass. The first thing was to find somewhere to stay. According to her guidebook, the best accommodation was to be had in the West Cliff area. The term sounded odd when she knew she was on the *east* coast, but Whitby was built on a kink in the shoreline facing north, and the town was divided neatly into east and west by the mouth of the River Esk.

Martha walked along the New Quay Road by Endeavour Wharf. In the estuary, silt glistened like entrails in the sun. A rusted hulk stood by the wharf – not a fishing trawler, but a small cargo boat of some kind – and rough, unshaven men wearing dirty T-shirts and jeans ambled around on deck, coiling ropes and greasing thick chains. By the old swing bridge that linked the east and west sides of the town stood a blackboard with the times of high tides chalked in: 0527 and 1803. It was a few minutes before four; the tide should be on its way in.

She walked along St Ann's Staith, sliding her hand on the white metal railing that topped the stone walls of the quay. Small craft lay beached on the mud, some of them not much more than rowing boats with sails. Ropes thrummed and flimsy metal masts rattled in the light breeze and flashed in the sun. Across the narrow estuary, the white houses seemed to be piled haphazardly beside and on top of one another. At the summit of the cliff stood St Mary's Church, just as it had, in one form or another, since Abbot William de Percy built it between 1100 and 1125. The abbey beside it had been there even longer, but it had been crumbling away for over four hundred years, since Henry VIII dissolved the monasteries, and now there was nothing left but a sombre ruin.

Martha felt a thrill at actually seeing these places she had only read about. And she also had a strange sense of coming home, a kind of déjà vu. Everything seemed so damn familiar and *right*. This was the place; Martha knew it. But she'd have plenty of time to explore East Cliff later, she decided, turning her attention back towards where she was going.

The pubs, seafood stalls and souvenir shops on her left gave way to amusement arcades and a Dracula Museum; for it was here, in Whitby, where the celebrated Count was said to have landed. The road veered away from the harbour wall around a series of open sheds by the quayside, where the fish were auctioned before being shipped to processing plants. Obviously, the catch hadn't come in yet, as nothing was going on there at the moment. Martha knew she would have to come down here again and again and watch the men as they unloaded their fish into iced boxes and sold them. But, like everything else, it could wait. Now she had made up her mind, she felt she had plenty of time. Attention to detail was important, and it would help overcome whatever fear and uncertainty remained within her.

She stopped at a stall and bought a packet of shrimps, which she ate as she carried on walking. They sold whelks, winkles and cockles, too, but Martha never touched them. It was because of her mother, she realized. Every time the family had visited the seaside – usually Weston-super-Mare or Burnham-on-Sea – and Martha had wanted to try them, her mother had told her it was vulgar to eat such things. It was, too, she had always believed. What could be more vulgar than sticking a pin in the moist opening of a tiny, conch-like shell and pulling out a creature as soft and slimy as snot? It wouldn't bother her now, though. She had changed. Her mother didn't know it, but she had. Now she could probably even rip apart a lobster and suck out the meat. But her mother's words still stuck in her mind. The more she thought about it, the more she realized that it was not so much the act itself that her mother thought vulgar, but its class associations. Only the lower classes went around at seaside resorts sticking pins in whelks and winkles.

A bingo caller from one of the arcades interrupted her stream of thought: 'All the fives, fifty-five . . . Legs eleven, number eleven.' The amplified voice echoed through the empty auction sheds.

Martha passed the bandstand and took Khyber Pass up to West Cliff. At the top, she walked under the enormous whale's jawbone, set up like an archway into another world. It was a hot day, and by the time she had climbed the steep hill she was sweating. She ran her hand along the smooth, warm, weather-darkened bone and shuddered. If this was just the jaw, how gigantic the creature must have been: a true leviathan. And as she passed under its shadow, she fancied she was like Jonah being vomited forth from its mouth. Or was she going the other way, entering the whale's belly?

She could picture the old Sunday school illustrations of the Bible story: inside the whale had looked as vast and gloomy as a cathedral, with the ribs mimicking its vaulting. And there sat poor Jonah, all alone. She imagined how his cries must have echoed in all that space. But could there really be so much emptiness inside a whale? Wasn't it all a twisted congestion of tubing and swollen, throbbing organs like it was inside people?

She tried to remember the story. Hadn't Jonah attempted to escape his destiny by running off to Tarshish when he was supposed to go and cry against the wickedness in Nineveh? Then a great tempest had raged and the sailors threw him overboard. He spent three days and three nights in the belly of the whale, until he prayed for deliverance and the beast spewed him forth onto dry land. After that, he accepted his destiny and went to Nineveh. She couldn't remember what happened next. There was something about the people there repenting and being spared, which didn't please Jonah much after all he'd been through, but Martha couldn't recall the ending. Still, it seemed remarkably apt. She had struggled against her fate, too, at first, but now she had accepted her destiny, the holiness of her task. She was headed for Nineveh, where evil thrived, and no matter what, there would be no mercy this time.

Captain Cook's statue looked confidently out to sea just beyond the jawbone, rolled-up charts under his arm. Cook had learned his seamanship on the Whitby coal ships, Martha had read, and the vessels he had commanded on epic voyages to the South Seas had been built here, where that rusted hulk lay at anchor in the lower harbour. The *Endeavour* and the *Resolution*. Good names, she thought.

Royal Crescent, curved in an elegant semicircle facing the sea, offered a number of private hotels with vacancies, but the prices were too high. She might have to stay a week or two, and over ten pounds a night would be too much. It was a shame, because these hotels were probably a lot more comfortable than what she was likely to get. Still, a room with a bath and a colour television was too much to ask for. And you always had to pay more if you wanted to see the sea. How often did people on holiday actually sit in their rooms and admire the view? Martha wondered. Hardly at all. But it was the reassurance that counted, the knowledge that it was there if you wanted to look. And that privilege cost money.

The promenade along West Cliff was lined with huge Victorian hotels of the kind that were built in most seaside towns when holidays at the coast came into vogue. Martha knew none of these were for her, either, so she turned down Crescent Avenue to find a cheap bed and breakfast place on a nondescript street.

As it happened, Abbey Terrace wasn't entirely without charm. It sloped steeply down to the estuary, though it stopped at East Terrace before it actually reached the front, and boasted a row of tall guesthouses, all bearing recommendations from the RAC or AA. Many of them even had their rates posted in the window, and Martha chose one that cost nine pounds fifty per night.

Wiping the sweat from her brow with the back of her hand, she opened the wrought-iron gate and walked up the path.

2

KIRSTEN

'Come on now, let's be 'aving yer! Ain't yer got no 'omes to go to?' The landlord of the Ring O'Bells voiced his nightly complaint as he came over to Kirsten's table to collect the glasses. 'It's half past eleven. They'll have my licence, they will.'

'Pray cease and desist,' said Damon, holding up his hand like a stop sign. 'Dost thou not ken 'tis the end of term? Know'st thou not 'tis the end of our final year in this fair city?'

'I don't bloody care,' the landlord growled. 'It's time you all pissed off home to bed.' He snatched a half-empty glass from the table.

'Hey, that was my drink!' Sarah said. 'I haven't finished it.'

'Yes you have, love.' He stood his ground, not a big man, but quick and strong enough to outmanoeuvre a bunch of drunken students. 'Out, the lot of you. Now! Come on!'

Hugo stood up. 'Wait a minute. She paid for that drink and she's got every bloody right to finish it.' With his curly blond hair and broad shoulders, he looked more like a rugby player than a student of English.

Kirsten sighed. There was going to be trouble, she could sense it. Damon was drunk and Hugo was proud and foolish enough, even sober, to start a fight. Just what she needed on her last night at university.

The landlord tapped his watch. 'Not at this time, she hasn't. Not according to the licensing laws.'

'Are you going to give her it back?'

'No.'

Behind him, the cellarman, Les, an ex-fighter with a misshapen nose and cauliflower ears, stood poised for trouble.

'Well, fuck you, then,' Hugo said. 'You can have this one too.' And he threw the rest of his pint of Guinness in the landlord's face.

Les moved forward but the landlord put out an arm to stop him. 'We don't want any trouble, lads and lasses,' he said in an icily calm voice. 'You've had your fun. Now why don't you go and have your party somewhere else?'

'Might as well, Hugo,' said Kirsten, tugging at his sleeve. 'The man's right. We'll get nothing more to drink here and there's no sense starting a fight, not tonight. Let's go to Russell's party.'

Hugo sat down sulkily and frowned at his pint glass as if he regretted wasting the stout. 'All right,' he said, then glared at the landlord again. 'But it's not fair. You pay for your drinks and that bastard just snatches them off you. We ought to get our money back, at least. How long have we been coming here? Two years. And this is how we get treated.'

'Come on, Hugo.' Damon clapped him on the shoulder and they all got up to leave. ' 'Twould indeed be a great pleasure to drown yon varlet in a tun of malmsey, but . . .' He pushed his glasses back up the bridge of his nose and shrugged. '*Tempus fugit*, old mate.' With his short haircut and raddled, boyish complexion, he looked like an old-fashioned grammar-school kid. He whipped his scarf dramatically around his neck and the end tipped over a glass on the table. It rolled towards the edge, wobbled back and forth there, undecided, then stopped for a moment before dropping to the floor. The landlord stood by patiently, arms folded, and Les looked ready for a fight.

'Fascist bastards,' Sarah said, picking up her handbag.

They beat a hasty and noisy retreat out of the pub, singing 'Johnny B. Goode', the song that had been playing on the jukebox when the landlord unplugged it.

'Russell's is it, then?' Hugo asked.

Everyone agreed. No one had any booze to take along, but good old Russell always put on a good spread. He had plenty of money, what with his father being such a whiz on the stock market. Probably a bit of insider-trading, Kirsten suspected, but who was she to complain?

And so the four of them walked out into a balmy June evening – only Damon wearing a scarf because he affected eccentricity – and made their way through the deserted campus to the residence buildings. There were Hugo, Sarah, Kirsten and Damon, all of them final-year English students. The only person missing from the close-knit group was Galen, Kirsten's boyfriend. Just after exams, his grandmother had died and he'd had to rush down to Kent to console his mother and help out with arrangements.

Kirsten was feeling a little tipsy as they hurried to Oastler Hall and up the worn stone steps to Russell's rooms. She missed Galen and wished he could be here to celebrate, too – especially as she had got a First. Still, she'd had enough congratulations to make her thoroughly bored with the whole business already. Now it was time to get maudlin and say her farewells, for tomorrow she was heading home. If only she could keep Hugo's wandering hands away . . .

The party seemed to have spilled over into the corridor and adjoining rooms. Even if they wanted to, which was unlikely, Russell's neighbours would hardly have been able to get to sleep. The newcomers pushed their way through the crowd into the smoky flat, calling greetings as they went. Most of the lights were off in the living room, where The Velvet Underground were singing 'Sweet Jane' and couples danced with drinks in their hands. Russell himself leaned by the window talking to Guy Naburn, a trendy tutor who hung around with students rather than with his colleagues, and welcomed them all when they tumbled in.

'Hope you've got some booze,' Hugo shouted over the music. 'We just got chucked out of the Ring O'Bells.'

Russell laughed. 'For that, you deserve the best. Try the kitchen.'

Sure enough, half-finished bottles of red wine and a couple of large casks of ale rested on the kitchen table. The fridge was full of Newcastle Brown and Carlsberg Special Brew, except for the space taken up by litre bottles of screw-top Riesling. The four latecomers busied themselves pouring drinks, then wandered off to mingle. It was hot, dim and smoky. Kirsten went to stand by an open window to get some air. She drank cold lager from the can and watched the shadows prance and flail on the dance floor. Smoke curled up and drifted past her out of the window into the night.

She thought about the three years they had spent together and felt sad now they were all going their separate ways in the big, bad world beyond university – the *real* world, as everyone called it. What an odd bunch they'd made at the start. That first term, they had circled one another warily and shyly, away from home for the first time, all lost and alone, and none of them willing to admit it: Damon, the witty eighteenth-century scholar; Sarah, feminist criticism and women's fiction; Hugo, drama and poetry; herself, linguistics, specializing in phonology and dialects; and Galen, modernism with a touch of Marxism thrown in for good measure. Through tutorials, department social evenings and informal parties, they had made their tentative approaches and discovered kindred spirits. By the end of the first year, they had become inseparable.

Together, they had suffered the vicissitudes, the joys and the disappointments of youth: Kirsten consoled Sarah after her nasty affair with Felix Stapeley, her second-year tutor; Sarah fell out with Damon briefly over a disagreement on the validity of a feminist approach to literature; Galen stood up for Hugo, who failed his Anglo-Saxon exam and almost got sent down; and Hugo pretended to be miffed for a while when Kirsten took up with Galen instead of him.

After being close for so long, their lives were so intertwined that Kirsten found it hard to imagine a future without the others. But, she realized sadly, that was surely what she had to face. Even though she and Galen had planned to go and do postgraduate work in Toronto, things might not work out that way. One of them might not be accepted – and then what?

One of the dancers stumbled backwards and bumped into Kirsten. The lager foamed in the can and spilled over her hand. The drunken dancer just shrugged and got back to business. Kirsten laughed and put her can on the window sill. Having got the feel of the party at last, she launched herself into the shadowy crowd and chatted and danced till she was hot and tired. Then, finding that her half-full can had been used as an ashtray in her absence, she got some more lager and returned to her spot by the window. The Rolling Stones were singing 'Jumpin' Jack Flash'. Russell sure knew how to choose party music.

'How you doing?' It was Hugo, shouting in her ear.

'I'm all right,' she yelled back. 'A bit tired, that's all. I'll have to go soon.'

'How about a dance?'

Kirsten nodded and joined him on the floor. She didn't know if she was a good dancer or not, but she enjoyed herself. She liked moving her body to the beat of fast music, and the Stones were the best of all. With the Stones she felt a certain earthy, pagan power deep in her body, and when she danced to their music she shed all her inhibitions: her hips swung wildly and her arms drew abstract patterns in the air. Hugo danced less gracefully. His movements were heavier, more deliberate and limited than Kirsten's. He tended to lumber around a bit. It didn't matter to her, though; she hardly ever paid attention to the person she was dancing with, so bound up in her own world was she. The problem was, some men took her wild gyrations on the dance floor as an invitation to bed, which they most certainly were not.

The song ended and 'Time Is on My Side' came on, a slower number. Hugo moved closer and put his arms around her. She let him. It was only dancing, after all, and they were close friends. She rested her head on his shoulder and swayed to the music.

'I'll miss you, you know, Hugo,' she said as they danced. 'I do hope we can all still keep in touch.'

'We will,' Hugo said, turning his head so that she could hear him. 'None of us know what the hell we're going to be doing yet. On the dole, most likely. Or maybe we'll all come out and join you and Galen in Canada.'

'If we get there.'

He held her more closely and they stopped talking. The music carried them along. She could feel Hugo's warm breath in her hair, and his hand had slipped down her back to the base of her spine. The floor was getting more crowded. Everywhere they moved, they seemed to bump into another huddled couple. Finally, the song ended and Hugo guided her back towards the window as 'Street Fighting Man' came on.

When they'd both cooled down and had something to drink, he leaned forward and kissed her. It was so quick that she didn't have time to stop him. Then his arms were around her, running over her shoulders and buttocks, pulling her hips towards him. She struggled and broke away, instinctively wiping her mouth with the back of her hand.

'Hugo!'

'Oh, come on, Kirsten. It's our last chance, while we're still young. Who knows what might happen tomorrow?'

Kirsten laughed and punched him on the shoulder. She couldn't stay angry with him. 'Don't pull that "gather ye rosebuds" stuff with me, Hugo Lassiter. I'll say this for you, you don't give up trying, do you?'

Hugo grinned.

'But it's still no,' Kirsten said. 'I like you, you know that, but only as a friend.'

'I've got too many friends,' Hugo complained. 'What I want is to get laid.'

Kirsten gestured around the room. 'Well, I'm sure

you've got a good chance. If there's anyone here you haven't slept with already.'

'That's not fair. I know I've got a reputation, but it's completely unfounded.'

'Is it? How disappointing. And here was me thinking you were such an expert.'

'You could find out for yourself, you know,' he said, moving closer again. 'If you play your cards right.'

Kirsten laughed and wriggled out of his grasp. 'No. Anyway, I'm off home now. I've got to be up early to pack in the morning, especially if I'm to have time for lunch.'

'I'll walk you.'

'No you won't. It's not far.'

'But it's late. It's dangerous to walk out by yourself so late.'

'I've done it hundreds of times. You know I have. No thanks. You stay here. I don't want to end up fighting you off out there. I'd rather take my chances.'

Hugo sighed. 'And tomorrow we part, perhaps forever. You don't know what you're missing.'

'Nor do you,' she said, 'but I'm sure you'll soon forget all about it. Remember, tomorrow for lunch in the Green Dragon. Remind Sarah and Damon, too.'

'One o'clock?'

'That's right.' Kirsten pecked him on the cheek and skipped out into the warm night.

3

MARTHA

The room was perfect. Usually, a single room in a bed and breakfast establishment is nothing more than a cupboard by the toilets, but this one, clearly a converted attic with a dormer window and white-painted rafters, had been done out nicely. Candy-striped wallpaper brightened the walls, and a salmon-pink candlewick bedspread covered the three-quarter bed. Just to the left of the window stood the washstand, with clean white towels laid neatly over a chrome rail. The only other furniture consisted of a small wardrobe with metal hangers that jangled together when Martha opened the flimsy door, and a bedside lamp on a small chest of drawers.

The owner leaned against the door jamb with his arms folded while she made up her mind. He was a coarse man with hairy forearms and even more hair sticking out over the top of his white open-necked shirt. His face looked like it was made of pink vinyl, and six or seven long fair hairs curled on his chin.

'We don't get many girls staying by themselves,' he said, smiling at her with lashless blue eyes. It was obviously an invitation to state her business.

'Yes, well I'm here to do some research,' Martha lied. 'I'm working on a book.'

'A book, eh? Romance, is it? I suppose you'll find plenty of background for that here, what with the abbey

ruins and the Dracula legends. Plenty of romance in all
that history, I'd say.'

'It's not a romance,' Martha said.

He didn't pursue the matter further, but looked at her
with a fixed expression, a mixture of superior, mocking
humour and disbelief that she had often seen men use on
professional women.

'I'll take it,' she said, mostly to get rid of him as quickly as possible. She didn't like the way he leaned against
the doorway, arms folded, watching her. Was he hoping
she'd start taking out her underwear to put in the drawers? The room began to feel claustrophobic.

He stood up straight. 'Right. Well, here's the keys.
That big one there's for the front door. Come in any time
you want, but try not to disturb the other guests. There's
a lounge with a colour telly on the ground floor. You can
make yourself a cup of tea or instant coffee there, too, if
you like. But be sure to wash out your cup afterwards.
The wife has enough on. Breakfast's at eight-thirty
sharp. If you want an evening meal, let the wife know in
the morning before you go out. Anything else?'

'Not that I can think of.'

He closed the door behind him as he left. Martha
dumped her holdall on the bed and stretched. The slop-
ing ceiling was so low at that point that her fingers
touched the plaster between the beams. She poked her
head out of the window to see what kind of view you got
for nine pounds fifty a night. Not bad. On her right, very
close, at the top of the street, loomed St Hilda's Church
with its high, dark tower, like one of the monoliths
from *2001*; to her left, on the opposite hillside over the
estuary, stood St Mary's, built of lighter stone, with a
smaller, squarish tower and a white pole sticking up

from it like the mast of a ship. Beside it stood what was left of the abbey, where, according to her guidebook, the Synod of Whitby took place in 664 AD, when the churches in England dumped their Celtic ways and decided to follow Roman usages. The poet Caedmon had lived there at the time, too, and that was more interesting to Martha. After all, Caedmon was the one who had called her here.

She unpacked her toilet bag and went over to the sink to brush her teeth. The shrimp had left fibres between them and a salty taste in her mouth. As she spat out the water, she glimpsed her face in the mirror. It was the only part of her that hadn't changed much over the past year or so.

She wore her sandy hair cut short more for convenience than anything else. As she never had any reason to do herself up to look nice for anyone, it was far easier just to be able to wash it and forget about it. She didn't have to wear any make-up either, and that made for less fuss. Her complexion had always been clear anyway, and the smattering of freckles across her nose was hardly a blemish. Her eyes were a little Oriental – slanted almonds, and about the same light brown colour. Her nose tilted up slightly at the end – snub, they called it – and revealed the dark ovals of her nostrils. She had always thought it was her ugliest feature, but someone had once told her it was sexy. *Sexy!* Now *there* was a laugh! She had her mother's mouth: tight, thin-lipped, downturned at the edges.

All in all, she thought she looked haughty, stiff and aloof – prissy, in fact – but she knew well enough that her appearance had diverse effects on men. Not so long ago, she had overheard a conversation in a pub between two lads who had been giving her the eye all evening.

'Now there's a bird looks like she needs a bloody good fuck,' the first one had said.

'Rubbish,' his mate had replied. 'I'll bet she's had enough cock to pave the road from here to Land's End – ends up!' And they had laughed at that.

So much for her looks. Perhaps men just saw in her what they wanted to see. They used her as a mirror to reflect their own vile natures, or as a screen onto which they projected their obscene fantasies.

She put her toothbrush in the chrome holder on the wall and turned away from the mirror. It was early evening now. The tide would be on its way in.

She had enough money with her to survive away from home for far longer than she needed to, and though she was almost certain that this was the place where she would find what she was looking for, she knew there was always a chance she could be wrong. It might be one of the smaller fishing villages along the coast: Staithes, Runswick Bay or Robin Hood's Bay. No matter: she would check them all out if she had to. For now, Whitby felt right enough.

She was tired after her long journey. Maybe later, around sunset, she would go out and explore the town and find something to eat, but for now a nap was her best bet. First, though, she took what clothes she'd brought with her out of the holdall and put them in the drawers by the bed. There wasn't much, all of it casual: jeans, cords, denim shirts, a jersey, underwear. The grey quilted jacket in case of chilly evenings, she hung in the wardrobe.

Finally, she took out the most important thing she'd brought and smiled to herself at how it seemed to have become a ritual object, a talisman, and how simply handling it gave her a sense of awe and reverence.

It was a small, globe-shaped glass paperweight, flattened at the bottom, smooth and heavy on her palm. Ten pounds she'd paid for it at the craft centre. For ages she had stood there in the heat of the kilns and watched the man making the glassware he sold, explaining the process as he went along. He thrust the long blow-pipe into the white-hot heart of the furnace and brought out a blob of molten glass. Then he dipped this in the dishes of bright colours: vermilion, aquamarine, saffron, indigo. Martha had always thought you were supposed to keep blowing down the tube, but he had simply blown into it quickly and then covered the end with his hand. When the air heated, it expanded and puffed out the glass. She never did find out how he got the colours inside the paperweight, though, or how he made it so heavy and solid. This one was all dark shades of red: carmine, crimson and scarlet. The folds and curves they made looked like a rose. When Martha turned it in the light, the rose seemed to move slowly, as if under water. If ever she felt herself slipping away from her mission, denying her destiny, she knew that all she had to do was reach for it, and the smooth, hard glass would strengthen her resolve.

She placed it beside her on the bedspread and lay down. The rose seemed to open and pulse in the changing light as she stared into it. Soon she was sleeping soundly beside it.

4

KIRSTEN

Kirsten lingered on the pavement outside Oastler Hall and took a deep breath. She could still hear the music – Led Zeppelin's 'Stairway to Heaven' – above the muffled talk and laughter behind her. Taking stock of herself, she found that she didn't feel any more tipsy than she had earlier – less so, if anything. At the party she had drunk only about a can and a half of lager, and the dancing seemed to have driven much of the alcohol out of her system. She must have sweated it out, she supposed, considering the way her blouse was sticking to her.

The night was warm and muggy. There was no breeze to speak of, just an occasional breath of warm air such as one feels on opening an oven. Everything was still and quiet.

Kirsten headed for the park. She had crossed it plenty of times before, day and night, and never had any cause to worry about the journey. The worst that ever happened was that the gang of skinheads who hung out there early in the evening might hurl an insult or two at passing students. But the skins would all be tucked up safely in bed at this time of night.

Most of the houses in the area were old and far too large for one family these days, so they had been bought by landlords and divided into flats and bedsits for the students. It was a comfortable neighbourhood, Kirsten thought. No matter what time of day or night, if you had a problem or just wanted a cup of tea and a chat, there was always likely to be someone you knew burning the midnight oil not much more than five or ten minutes' walk away. Like a village within the city, really. Even now, soft, inviting lights burned behind many of the windows. She would miss it all very much. This was the place where she had grown up, lost her virginity, changed from a shy, awkward teenager into a wiser, more confident woman.

The park was a large square bordered on all sides by well-lit roads. Tree-lined avenues criss-crossed the cropped grass. In the daytime, students would lie out in the sun reading or playing makeshift games of cricket or football. Up near the main road were the public toilets – said to be a favourite haunt of local homosexuals – and colourful flower beds. At the centre of the park, thick shrubbery grew around the bowling green and the children's playground.

At night the place felt a little spookier, perhaps because there was no lighting in the park itself. But you could always see the tall, amber street lights on the roads, and the sound of nearby traffic was comforting.

Kirsten's trainers made no sound on the tarmac as she followed the path under the dark trees. There was very little traffic about. The only thing she could hear was the odd car revving up in the distance and the sound of her shoulder bag brushing against her hips. Somewhere, a dog barked. The sky was clear and the stars, magnified by the haze, looked fatter and softer than usual. How different from winter stars, Kirsten thought, all cold and sharp and merciless. These ones looked like they were melting. She looked up and turned her head in all directions but couldn't find a moon. It had to be there somewhere – perhaps behind the trees.

Yes, she would miss it all. But Canada would be exciting, especially if Galen came, too, as he intended. Neither of them had ever crossed the Atlantic before. If they could save enough money, they would take a few months after completing their courses and travel the continent together: Montreal, New York, Boston, Washington, Miami, Los Angeles, San Francisco, Vancouver. Even the names sent shivers of excitement up Kirsten's spine. Three years ago she could never have imagined doing such a thing. University hadn't only given her a first-class education, it had given her freedom and independence, too.

Soon she got to the centre of the park, near the bowling green. The whole tract of land was slightly convex, and this was the highest part. She could see lights in all directions, defining the valleys and hillsides upon which the city was built. Because of the warm, moist air, the far-off street lights all had haloes.

Just off the path stood a statue of a lion with a serpent coiled around it. Kirsten had noticed the other day that some idiot – perhaps the skinheads – had spray-painted its head blue and scrawled filthy graffiti in red all over its body. That didn't matter in the dark, though, and she decided to give in to an impulse she had often felt.

Swishing over the grass, she went up to the statue and ran her hand over the still-warm stone. Then, with sudden resolve, she jumped astride it.

The lion was small enough that her feet easily touched the ground. Down the path, she could see through the trees to the lights on the main road and the turning into her own street, only a few hundred yards away. To think she had been here all this time and had always wanted to sit on the lion but hadn't done so until now, her last night. She must have passed it at least a thousand times. She felt silly, but at the same time she was enjoying herself tremendously. At least nobody was watching.

She gripped the smooth mane and pretended she was riding through the jungle. In her mind, she could hear screeching cockatoos, chattering monkeys, humming and clicking insects, and snakes slithering through the undergrowth. She raised her head to look for the moon again, but before she could find it, she noticed a strange smell and, a split second later, felt a rough hand cover her mouth and nose.

5

MARTHA

The tide was in when Martha walked back under the whale's jawbone to Pier Road, and the small fishing boats bobbed at their moorings in the harbour. The sun was going down behind West Cliff, and, at the top of the hill opposite, St Mary's Church shone warm gold in the last rays.

There was still nothing happening in the auction sheds, but some of the locals seemed to be pottering around on their own small boats.

Martha leaned against the railing on St Ann's Staith and watched two men in navy-blue jerseys washing the deck of a red sailboat. She had brought her quilted jacket with her, but the air was still so warm that she carried it slung over her shoulder. As night came in, the fishy smell of the place seemed to grow stronger.

Something about the air made her crave a cigarette. She had never smoked before the past year, but now she didn't care one way or another. Whatever she felt like, she would do, and damn the consequences.

She went into a small gift shop near the Dracula Museum and bought ten Rothmans; that would do for a while at least. Then she went back to the railing and lit a cigarette. One of the men down in the boat glanced up at her admiringly from time to time, but he didn't call out or whistle. She was waiting for them to speak. Finally, one said something technical to the other, who replied in equally incomprehensible jargon, and Martha moved on.

She was hungry, she realized, dropping the cigarette and grinding it out with the ball of her foot on the stone quay. Down by the bridge she saw people ambling along, eating from cardboard cartons of fish and chips. She hadn't noticed any other kind of food available so far; the place was hardly crammed with French, Italian or Indian restaurants, and she hadn't even seen a McDonald's or a Pizza Hut yet. Clearly, it was a fish-and-chips-or-nothing kind of town.

At the first fish bar she found, she bought haddock and chips and wandered around by the bus station as she ate. The fish was fried in batter, of course, and had a kind of oily taste because the skin had been left on. It was good, though, and Martha licked her fingers when she'd finished, then carefully dumped the carton in a litter bin.

It was almost dark now. She stood on the bridge for a while, smoking another cigarette to take away the greasy taste. In the lower harbour, the rusted hulk she had seen earlier was still at dock. On the north side of the bridge, where the estuary widened towards the sea, strings of red and yellow quayside lights reflected in the dark water, twisting and bending as it lapped, like people's reflections in funfair mirrors. On its cliff-top, St Mary's stood floodlit against the dark violet sky.

Martha walked over the bridge to Church Street, in the oldest section of town just below East Cliff, stopping to buy a newspaper on her way, just before the shop closed. It was that quiet time after dinner and before bed. Places like Whitby shut down early. Martha was thirsty, but already the Monk's Haven cafe was shut; there was nowhere you could just drop in for a cup of tea or coffee. She also needed to sit down and think for a while.

The Black Horse pub across the street looked inviting enough. Martha went in. Antique brass fixtures attached to the walls shed real gaslight on the small, wainscoted room. The lounge was cosy, with narrow, pew-like wooden benches and scored oblong tables. It was also quiet.

Martha bought a half of bitter and found a free corner. A few years ago, she would never have thought of even entering a pub by herself, let alone sitting in one. But this place felt safe enough. The few people who were there seemed to know each other and were already involved in conversation. There were no lone wolves on the lookout for female flesh; it clearly wasn't a pick-up joint.

She glanced quickly through the copy of the *Independent* she'd bought. Finding nothing of interest, she folded the paper and put it aside. What she really had to do, she thought, was work out some kind of plan. Nothing too detailed or elaborate, because she had recently learned that serendipity and intuition played a greater part in events than anyone imagined. And she had to remember that she wasn't alone in her task; she had spirits to guide her. Nonetheless, she couldn't just wander the place aimlessly for days. Right now, it was all right; she was finding her way around, becoming familiar with the environment. There were certain spots she needed to know about: sheltered places, isolated paths, the shadows of the town. But she needed a plan of action.

Taking out a small notebook and her guidebook, she set to work. First of all, she scanned the map and made a note of places that looked like they were worth exploring: the beach area, St Mary's graveyard, the abbey grounds, a long cliff walk towards Robin Hood's Bay.

Then she turned her mind to a more serious problem: where could she find someone who actually *lived* and worked in Whitby? Where would he be likely to live, for example? So far she had seen no one but holidaymakers and those residents who ran guesthouses, pubs and shops. Nobody else actually seemed to live around the harbour area, where the men worked on their boats.

She flipped back to her map to see how far the town spread. It was small, with a population of about thirteen thousand, and East Cliff didn't seem to extend much at all beyond St Mary's. That left the southern area, further inland along the Esk estuary, and West Cliff itself. Up there, according to her map, housing estates seemed to stretch almost as far as Sandsend. And then there were smaller places nearby, like Sandsend itself, and Robin Hood's Bay. They weren't exactly suburbs, but it was possible that some people lived there and commuted to and from Whitby.

At one time, she might have felt as if she was looking for a needle in a haystack. After all, she had so little to go on. But she trusted her instincts now. There could be no doubt about it; she would know when she had found the one she was looking for. Her spirits would help guide her towards him. And Whitby felt like the right place; she could sense his nearness.

Martha sipped her beer. Somebody put an old rock and roll song on the jukebox and it reminded her of something a long time ago, another evening listening to old songs on a jukebox. She shut it out. Memories and sentiment were luxuries she couldn't afford these days. She stuck her hand in her holdall and felt for the smooth, hard sphere.

6

KIRSTEN

A long, oily blackness punctuated by quick, vivid dreams. A figure hunched over her, dark and hooded, and a blade flashed. It seemed to slice at her skin. Long cuts flapped open and blood welled, but there was no pain. She saw, as if from a great distance, the sharp steel pierce the pale flesh of her thigh. It went in deep and when it slid out, blood oozed around the edges of the gash. But she felt nothing at all. Then the darkness came again.

This time it was a figure all in white, a human shape with no face. The same things happened. The knife was different, but it cut just like the other, and again there was no sensation.

They were all just dreams. She couldn't possibly see these things, could she? Her eyes were closed. And if they had really happened, then she would have screamed out in agony from the pain, wouldn't she?

7

MARTHA

A loud shrieking woke Martha at four o'clock in the morning. She turned over in bed and frowned as she looked at the luminous dial of her watch. The row went on. It sounded very close. Finally, she realized it was the seagulls. They must have found a shoal of fish, or perhaps a cat had spilled the dustbin at the back of one of the fish bars and they had zoomed in on that. It was a terrible noise: the sound of raw hunger and greed. She pictured the gulls ripping dead fish apart, blank white faces speckled with blood.

She sighed and turned over again, pulling the sheet up around her ears. The gulls had woken her from a dream. Maybe she could get back to it. All her dreams were good these days – technicolour jaunts of indescribable beauty, full of ecstasy and excitement, visits to alien worlds, flying easily through space and time.

They hadn't always been like that. For a long time she had suffered from terrifying nightmares, dreams of blood and shadows, and then for a while she hadn't seemed to dream at all. The good dreams only started when the dark cloud in her mind disappeared. At least, she had always thought of it as a cloud, or perhaps a bubble. It was opaque, and whichever way she looked at it, it always deflected the light so that she couldn't see inside. She knew it was filled with all her agony and anger, yet it refused her entry.

For so long she had walked around on the edge because of that cloud inside her. Always on the verge of violence, despair or madness. But then one day, when she found the right perspective, she saw inside and the darkness dispersed like a monster that vanishes when you discover its true name.

The seagulls were still wailing over their early breakfast when Martha drifted off to sleep again and dreamed about her secret lake. Its waters flowed from the fountain of youth, clear and sparkling in the sun that never stopped shining, and she had to swim through narrow coral caverns to get to it. Only she knew about the lake. Only she could swim so effortlessly so far without the need for breath. And as she swam, the sharp, pinkish coral cut thin red lines across her breasts, stomach and thighs.

8

KIRSTEN

The first thing Kirsten saw when she opened her eyes was a long curving crack in the white ceiling. It looked like an island coastline or the crude outline of a whale. Her mouth was dry and tasted bad. With difficulty, she swallowed, but the vile taste wouldn't go away. Around her she could hear only quiet sounds: a steady hissing; a high-pitched, rhythmic bleeping. She couldn't smell anything at all.

She moved her head and glimpsed shadowy figures sitting beside her bed. It was difficult to focus from so close, and she couldn't make out who they were. Then she became aware of muffled voices.

'Look, she's coming round . . . she's opened her eyes.'

'Careful . . . don't touch her . . . she'll wake up in her own time.'

And someone bent over her: a faceless figure all in white. Kirsten tried to scream, but no sound came out. Gentle hands touched her brow and pushed her shoulders firmly back onto the hard bed. She let her head fall on the pillow again and sighed. The voices were clearer now, like a finely tuned radio.

'Is she all right? Can we stay and talk to her?'

'She'll talk if she wants to. Don't push her. She's bound to be feeling disoriented.'

Kirsten tried to speak but her mouth was still too dry. She croaked, 'Water,' and someone seemed to

understand. An angled straw neared her mouth and she
sucked greedily on it. Some of the water dribbled down
the edges of her dry, cracked lips, but she managed to
swallow a little. That felt better.

'I must go and fetch the doctor.'

The door opened and hissed shut slowly.

'Kirstie? Kirstie, love?'

She turned her head again and found it easier to focus
this time. Her mother and father sat beside her. She tried
to smile but it felt like it came out all crooked. Her teeth
felt too big for her mouth. Her mother looked beside herself, as if she hadn't slept for days, and her father had
dark heavy bags under his eyes. He looked down on her
with a mixture of love and relief.

'Hello, Daddy,' she said.

He reached out and she felt his soft hand close on
hers, just like when they used to go for walks in the
woods when she was a child.

'Oh, Kirstie,' her mother said, taking out a handkerchief from her handbag and dabbing her eyes. 'We were
so worried.'

Her father still said nothing. His touch told Kirsten all
she needed to know.

'What about? Where . . .'

'Don't try to speak,' her father said softly. 'It's all
right. It's all over now. Everything's going to be all right.'

Her mother was still patting away at her eyes and
making little snuffling noises.

Kirsten rolled onto her back again and stared at the
scar on the ceiling. She licked her dry lips. Sensation was
returning to her bit by bit. Now she could catch the
clean, white, antiseptic smell of the hospital room. She
could also feel her body. Her skin felt taut, stretched too

tightly over her flesh and bones. In places, it pinched at her as if it had snagged on something and puckered.

But worse than that was the burning ache in her breasts and in her loins. She had no sensation of the tight flesh there, just of a painful, throbbing absence.

The door opened and a white-coated man walked over to her. She flinched and tried to roll away.

'It's all right,' she heard someone say. 'The doctor's here to take care of you.'

Then she felt her sleeve pulled up, and a cool swab touched her arm. She didn't feel the needle going in, but it made a sharp prick when it slid out. The pain began to recede. Warm, soothing waves came to carry it far out to sea.

Her senses ebbed and the long darkness advanced to reclaim her. As she slipped away, she could still feel her father's hand in hers. She turned her head slowly and asked, 'What's happened to me, Daddy? My skin feels funny. It doesn't fit right.'

9

MARTHA

When Martha got downstairs for breakfast the next morning, the other guests were already seated. Only one small table, set for two, remained. Beyond the bay window, the sun was shining on Abbey Terrace, and the sky was blue again.

By the door stood a help-yourself trolley: jugs of orange or grapefruit juice; milk and miniature packets of Corn Flakes, Special K, Rice Krispies, Alpen and Frosties. Martha took some Alpen, poured herself a glass of juice and sat down. She helped herself to a cup of tea from the stainless-steel pot on the table. Judging by its colour, the tea had been stewing too long. She looked at the place opposite her and hoped that no one would join her for breakfast. Never very cheerful first thing in the morning, she had just about managed to nod and say hello to the others. Conversation would be out of the question.

As she sipped the bitter tea, she cast her eyes around the room. In the bay window sat an old couple. The man's dark brown hair was swept straight back from his wrinkled forehead and plastered down with Brylcreem. He had smiled when she came in, showing a set of stained and crooked teeth. His greyish face had the lined and hollow look of a fifty-a-day man, and his breath came in short emphysematic gasps, confirming the diagnosis. His wife hadn't smiled. She had simply stared at Martha with suspicious, beady eyes, as if to say, 'I know your type, young lady.' Blue-grey hair hovered around her moon-shaped head like mist.

By the opposite wall sat a young couple, probably on their honeymoon, Martha guessed. They both looked very serious. The man was thin, swarthy, bearded, and precise in his tea-pouring; the woman's face, as she sat bowed forward, was almost completely hidden by a cascade of glossy black hair. When she looked up at him, a shy, secret smile lit her eyes. They hadn't even noticed Martha come in.

Most of the noise came from the third table, near the serve-yourself trolley, where a tired-looking young woman and an equally exhausted man both struggled to put on a brave face as they tried to control two finicky youngsters. The children looked like twins: same blond colouring, same whiny voices: 'I don't *like* Shreddies, Daddy! Why aren't there any Sugar Puffs? I want Sugar Puffs!' 'Have some Frosties,' the pale mother said, trying to placate them, but to no avail. She glanced up and smiled weakly at the others. The father, dressed for a day on the beach in white slacks and a pale blue sports shirt showing the curly ginger hairs on his forearms, looked over and gave Martha a what-can-you-do-with-them shrug.

The owner's wife came in to take their orders. Not that there was much choice: you could have your eggs soft or hard, your bacon medium or crispy. There was a determined set to the woman's mouth, and she moved about her business with a brusque, no-nonsense certainty, all the while managing to smile and respond to small talk about the weather. Perhaps if anyone wore the pants around here, Martha thought, it was the wife. Her husband probably had a day job and only happened to be around because Martha had arrived late in the afternoon. Perhaps he was even a fisherman. If she could get a chance to chat casually with him, she might be able to find out something about how the local operation worked.

Just after she had given her order for crispy bacon and medium-poached eggs, the final guest came down, ordered and helped himself to cereal and juice, which he brought over to Martha's table and plonked down opposite her. He was tall and athletic-looking, probably a jogger, with a deep suntan, thin face, aquiline nose and lively blue eyes. His short, curly black hair still glistened from the shower. He smelled of Old Spice aftershave.

He poured some tea and grinned broadly, showing a perfect set of dazzling teeth, the kind one rarely sees in English mouths. My God, Martha thought, a morning person. Probably been for a run around the town before breakfast. She managed to muster a tiny, brief smile, then looked away again to see how the couple were coping with the two kids.

'Sleep well?'

'Pardon?'

The young man leaned forward again and lowered his voice. 'I said, did you sleep well?'

'Fine, thank you.'

'I didn't.'

'Oh?'

'Just put me right next to the bathroom, didn't they? Six o'clock the blooming parade starts – one after the other – and they all have to flush the loo. I think the pipes run right through my bed. Talk about clatter and bang. Keith's the name, by the way.' He stuck out his hand and smiled. 'Keith McLaren.' His accent was

Australian, certainly, Martha thought, but as she had specialized only in regional British accents, she couldn't pin it down to any specific area.

Martha took his hand reluctantly and gave it a quick, limp shake. 'Martha Browne.'

'And before you ask, yes, I'm an Aussie. I'm just taking a little time off from university to travel this lovely country of yours.'

'You're a student?'

'Yes. Master's degree in surfing and sunbathing at Bondi Beach University.' He laughed. 'Not true. Wish it were. I'm studying law, not half as interesting. I'm making my way up the coast to Scotland. Got some family there.'

Martha nodded politely.

'Seagulls, too,' Keith said, apropos of nothing, as far as Martha could make out.

'What?'

'Bloody seagulls kept me awake too. Didn't you hear them?'

'Seagulls, you say?' The owner's wife arrived at their table and set down two plates, which she held with worn oven gloves. 'Mind, they're hot. Seagulls, eh? You get used to them if you live here. Have to.'

'They never wake you up?' Keith asked her.

'Never. Not after the first couple of months.'

''Fraid I won't be here that long.' He looked at Martha again. 'Moving on tomorrow. Travelling by local buses whenever I can. Walking or hitching if I can't.'

'Well, good luck to you,' the woman said, and moved on.

Keith stared at his plate and prodded a dark medallion of reddish black stuff with his fork. 'What's that?' he asked, turning up his nose and leaning forward to whisper. 'Whatever it is, I don't remember asking for it.'

Martha examined the contents of his plate. They were the same as hers: bacon, egg, grilled tomato and mushrooms, fried bread, and the thing that Keith was pointing to. 'Black pudding, I think,' she said. 'Must be today's special.'

'What's it made of?'

'You don't want to know. Not at this time in the morning.'

Keith laughed and tucked in. 'Well, it sure tastes all right. That's what I like about staying at these places. They always give you a breakfast that sets you up for the entire day. I won't need much more than a sandwich till the evening meal. Are you eating here?'

'Not in the evenings, no.'

'Oh, you should. I usually come back. Well, I say usually, but this is only my third day. They do a decent spread. Good value, too.'

When he went back to his food he stopped talking and left Martha in peace. She ate quickly, hoping to get away before he started up again, even though she knew a rushed meal would give her indigestion. Across the room, one of the children flicked a slice of tomato at the wall with his spoon. It splattered on the faded rose-patterned paper and slithered down, leaving a pink trail behind. His father reddened and took the spoon from him angrily, and his mother looked as if she was about to die from embarrassment.

Martha pushed her chair back and stood up to leave. 'Excuse me,' she said to Keith. 'Must be off. Lots to do.'

'Aren't you going to finish your cup of tea?' Keith asked.

'I've had two already. Anyway, it's stewed.' And she hurried upstairs to her room. There, she locked the door, opened the window and enjoyed a cigarette as she leaned on the sill and looked at the small white clouds over St Mary's.

After she'd finished the Rothmans and paid a visit to the toilet, she picked up her holdall and set off down the stairs again. At the first-floor landing, she bumped into Keith coming out of his room. Just my luck, she thought.

'Want to show me around?' he asked. 'What with both of us being alone here . . . Well, it seems a shame.'

'I'm sure you know more about the place than I do. I've just arrived, and you've been here three days already.'

'Yes, but you're a native. I'm just a poor ignorant foreigner.'

'I'm sorry,' Martha said, 'but I've got work to do.'

'Oh? What would that be, then?'

'Research. I'm working on a book.'

They were walking down the last flight of carpeted stairs to the hallway. Martha couldn't just break away from him. She wanted to see which way he turned in the street so that she could walk the other way.

'Well, maybe we can have a drink this evening, after you've finished work and I've worn out my poor feet?'

'I'm sorry, I don't know what time I'll be finished.'

'Oh, come on. Say seven o'clock, all right? You know what they say: "All work and no play . . ." There's a nice, quiet little pub just on the corner at the end of the street. The Lucky Fisherman, I think it's called. Is it a date? I'm away tomorrow anyway, so you'll only have to put up with me the once.'

Martha thought quickly. They had passed the door

now and were already walking down the front steps to the path. If she said no, it would look very odd indeed, and the last thing she wanted was to appear conspicuous in any way. It was bad enough being a woman by herself here. If she acted strangely, then this Keith might just have cause to remember her as some kind of oddball, and that wouldn't do at all. On the other hand, if she did agree to have a drink with him, he would no doubt ask her all kinds of questions about her life. Still, she thought, there was no reason why she couldn't tell him a pack of lies. That should be easy enough for a woman with her imagination.

'All right,' she said as they reached the gate. 'Seven o'clock in the Lucky Fisherman.'

Keith smiled. 'Great. See you then. Have a good day.'

He turned left, and Martha turned right.

10

KIRSTEN

When Kirsten drifted out of the comforting darkness for the second time, she noticed the vases of red and yellow flowers and the cards standing on her bedside table. Then she turned her head and saw a stranger sitting at the other side of the bed. She gripped the sheets around her throat and looked around the rest of the room. The white-smocked nurse still hovered in the background – that, at least, was reassuring – and sitting against the wall by the door was a man in a light grey suit with a notebook on his lap and a pencil poised, ready to write. Kirsten couldn't focus all that clearly on him, but he looked too young to be as bald as he seemed.

The man beside her leaned forward and rested his chin on his fists. He was about her father's age – early fifties – with short, spiky grey hair and a red complexion. His eyes were brown, and a tiny wen grew between his right eye and his nose. Wedged between his left nostril and his upper lip was a dark mole with a couple of hairs sprouting from it. He wore a navy-blue suit, white shirt and a black and amber striped tie. His expression was kindly and concerned.

'How are you feeling, Kirsten?' he asked. 'Do you feel like talking?'

'A bit groggy,' she replied. 'Can you tell me what's happened to me? Nobody's told me anything.'

'You were attacked. You've been hurt, but you're going to be all right.'

'Who are you? Are you a doctor?'

'I'm Detective Superintendent Elswick. The bright young lad over by the door there is Detective Sergeant Haywood. We're here to see if you can tell us anything that might help us catch whoever did this.'

Kirsten shook her head. 'It's all dark . . . I . . . I can't . . .'

'Stay calm,' Elswick said softly. 'Don't struggle with it. Just relax and let me ask the questions. If you don't know the answers, shake your head or say no. Don't get worked up about it. All right?'

Kirsten swallowed. 'I'll try.'

'Good. You were at a party the night it happened. Do you remember that?'

'Yes. Vaguely. There was music, dancing. It was the end of term bash.'

'That's right. Now, as far as we can gather, you left alone at about one o'clock. Am I right?'

'I . . . I think so. I don't remember the time. I did go out by myself, though. It was a lovely warm night.' Kirsten remembered standing by the door of Oastler Hall and breathing in the honeyed air.

'And then you walked through the park.'

'Yes. It's a short cut. I've done it lots of times. Nothing ever—'

'Relax, Kirsten. We know. Nobody's blaming you. Don't get upset about it. Now, did you notice anyone else around at all?'

'No. It was quiet. There was no one.'

'Did you hear anything?'

'Only the cars on the road.'

'Nobody left the party and followed you?'

'I didn't see anyone.'

'Were you aware at any time of someone following you?'

'No. I suppose I might have run if I had been. But no.'

'What about earlier in the evening? As I understand it, you were at a pub with some friends: the Ring O'Bells. Is that right?'

Kirsten nodded.

'Did you notice anyone taking an unusual interest in you, anyone who seemed to be watching you closely?'

'No.'

'Any strangers there?'

'I . . . I don't remember. It was busy earlier, but . . .'

'There was some trouble, wasn't there? Could you tell me about it?'

Kirsten told him what she could remember about the incident with the landlord. It seemed so silly now; she felt embarrassed to think of it.

'So you and your friends were the last to leave?'

'Yes.'

'And you didn't see anyone hanging around outside?'

'No.'

'What about the attack itself? Do you remember anything about how it happened?'

Kirsten closed her eyes and confronted only darkness. It was as if a black cloud had formed somewhere in her mind, and inside it was trapped everything that this man wanted to know. The rest of her – memories, feelings, sensations – could only circle the thick darkness helplessly. It was a chunk of her life, a package of pain and terror that had been wrapped up and hidden away in the dark. She didn't know if she could penetrate it, or if she wanted to; inside, she sensed, lived horrors too monstrous to confront.

'I was looking for the moon,' she said.

'What?'

'I sat on the lion – you know, that statue in the middle of the park – and I threw my head back. I was looking for the moon. I know it sounds silly. I wasn't drunk or anything. It's just that it was my last night and I'd always wanted to . . . to just . . . sit. That's all I can remember.'

'What happened?'

'When? What do you mean?'

'You were sitting on the lion looking for the moon. What happened next?'

Superintendent Elswick's voice was soft and hypnotic. It was making Kirsten feel sleepy again. Now that she had come round fully, she could feel her aching body with its tight skin, and she wanted to sail out on the tide again and leave it behind.

'A hand,' she said. 'That's all I remember. A hand came from behind, over my nose and mouth. I couldn't breathe. And then it all went black.'

'You didn't see anyone?'

'No. I'm sorry . . . I . . . There was something . . .'

'Yes?'

Kirsten frowned and shook her head. 'It's no good. I can't remember.'

'Don't worry about it, Kirsten. Just take it slowly. You can't remember anything at all about the person who attacked you, no matter how insignificant it might seem?'

'No. Only the hand.'

'What was the hand like? Was it big or small?'

'I . . . I . . . it's hard to say. It covered my nose and mouth . . . It was strong. And rough.'

'Rough? In what way?'

'Like someone who's done a lot of hard work, I suppose. You know, lifting things. I don't know. I've never felt a hand that rough before. We had a gardener once, and his hands looked like this one felt. I never touched them, but they looked rough and calloused from doing manual work.'

'This gardener,' Elswick said, 'what's his name?'

'It was a long time ago. I was just a little girl.'

'Do you remember his name, Kirsten?'

'I think it was Walberton. My daddy called him Mal. Short for Malcolm, I suppose. But I don't see why—'

'At this point, Kirsten, we know nothing. We need everything we can get. Everything. No matter how absurd it seems. Is the gardener still around?'

'No, not any more. Daddy knows. He'll tell you.'

'All right. Is there anything else?'

'I don't think so. I can't remember what happened after the hand grabbed me. How long have I been here?'

'Ten days. That's why we have to act as quickly as we can. The more time goes by, the harder it is to pick up a trail. Can you think of anyone who might have wanted to harm you? Any enemies? An angry boyfriend, perhaps?'

Ten days! It was hard to believe. What had she been doing here for ten days? Just sleeping and dreaming? She shook her head. 'No, there's only Galen. There's no one who'd do something like this. I don't understand it. I never did any harm to anyone in my life.' Tears began to trickle from the corners of her eyes into the fine hair above her ears. 'I'm tired. I hurt.' She felt herself fading again and didn't want to stop.

'That's all right,' Elswick said. 'You've been very help-ful. We'll go now and let you get some rest.' He stood up and patted her arm, then nodded to Sergeant Haywood that it was time to go. 'I'll come back and see you again soon, Kirsten, when you're feeling better. Your mother and father are still here, waiting outside. Do you want to see them?'

'Later,' Kirsten said. 'Wait. Where's Galen? Have you seen Galen?'

'Your boyfriend? Yes,' Elswick said. 'He was here. He said he'd come back. He left those flowers.' He pointed to a vase of red roses.

When Elswick and Haywood left, the nurse came over to straighten the bed. Just as the door was closing, Kirsten could hear Elswick saying, 'Better keep a man here twenty-four hours a day . . . Might come back to finish what he started.'

Before the nurse could move away, Kirsten grabbed her wrist.

'What's happened to me?' she whispered. 'My skin feels tight and twisted. Something's wrong.'

The nurse smiled. 'That'll be the stitches, dearie. They do pull a bit sometimes.' She ruffled the pillow and hurried out.

Stitches! Kirsten had had stitches before when she fell off her bicycle and cut her arm on some broken glass. It was true, they did pull. But those stitches had been put in her arm; she had felt only very minor, localized pain. If stitches were the cause of her discomfort this time, then why did her whole body feel as if it had been sewn tightly and ineptly around its frame?

She could have a look, of course. Ease down the covers and open her nightdress. Surely nothing could be simpler. But the effort was too much for her. She could manage the movements all right, but what really stopped her was fear: fear of what she might find. Instead, she welcomed oblivion.

11

MARTHA

There were no names on the gravestones. Martha stood in the cliff-top cemetery by St Mary's and stared in horror. Most of the stones were blackened around their edges, and where the chiselled details should have been, there was just pitted sandstone. On some of them, she could see faint traces of lettering, but many were completely blank. It must be the salt wind, she thought, come from the sea and stolen their names away. It made her feel suddenly and inexplicably sad. She looked down at the ruffled blue water and the thin line of foam as waves broke along the beach. It didn't seem fair. The dead should be remembered, as she remembered them. Shivering despite the heat, she wandered over to the church itself.

It was an impressive place inside. She skipped the taped lecture and, instead, picked up a printed guide and wandered around. At the front stood a huge, three-tier pulpit, and below it stretched a honeycomb of rectangular box pews said to resemble the ''tween-decks' of a wooden battleship. Some of the boxes had engraved brass nameplates screwed to their doors, marking them out as reserved for notable local families. Most of these were at the back, where the minister would have a hard time seeing because of all the fluted pillars in the way. The rich could sleep with impunity through his sermons. But at the front, right under his eyes, some boxes were marked FREE, and others, FOR STRANGERS ONLY.

That's me, Martha thought, opening the catch on one and stepping inside: a stranger only.

When the latch clicked behind her, the small enclosure gave her an odd sense of isolation and sanctuary within the busy church. All around her, tourists walked and cameras flashed, but the box seemed to muffle and distance the outside world. A fanciful idea, to be sure, but it was what she felt. She ran her finger along the worn green baize that lined the sides of the box and the pew bench itself. There was even a red carpet, and patterned cushions to kneel on. Martha's knees cracked as she knelt. Now she was even further away from the world outside. It would make a good place to hide, if things should ever come to that, she thought. Nobody would be able to find her in a box pew marked FOR STRANGERS ONLY. It was just like being invisible. She smiled and let herself out.

Through the car park by the abbey ruin was a footpath, part of the Cleveland Way. According to Martha's map, it would take her all the way from East Cliff to Robin Hood's Bay. For the moment, she decided to explore just a short stretch of it. As she walked, she kept her eyes open for Keith McLaren, just as she had done while touring the cemetery and church. She already had a good idea of the story she would tell him that evening, and if he did happen to see her walking around St Mary's and the cliff-top, then her lies would gain even more credibility. She didn't want to run into him by accident, though.

A narrow boardwalk ran right along the edge of the high cliffs. In places, some of the cross-boards were missing, and erosion had eaten away the land right up to the path itself. There was a fence between the walk and the sheer drop, but even that was down here and there, and signs warned people to tread carefully and to walk in single file. It was dizzying to look down on the sea swirling around the sharp rocks way below.

When she got to Saltwick Nab, a long knobbly finger of rock jutting out into the sea, Martha noticed ramshackle wooden stairs and a path leading down. Slowly, she made her way to the pinkish-red rock. It started near the base of the cliff as a big hump, then dropped so that it was hardly visible above the water for a short distance, and finally rose to another knob – rather like a submerged camel with a long way between humps, she thought – further out to sea. There was nobody else around, so Martha sat down on the sparse grass for a rest. In the distance, between the humps, a white tanker was slowly making its way across the horizon. Waves caught the low section of the nab sideways on and spray cascaded over it in a shower of white.

Martha lit her second cigarette of the day. It tasted different out in the fresh, salt air. She crossed her legs and contemplated the rhythms of the sea as it swelled and slapped against the rock. Soon, she could see the waves coming and predict how hard they would break.

She had got the feel of the place now; so much so that she felt quite at home. There were no problems as far as she could see – except perhaps for the Australian. But even he seemed naive and harmless enough. She could string him along over a couple of drinks, and tomorrow he'd be gone. All she had to do now was find the one she was looking for. It might take a day or two, but she would succeed. He was close; of that there could be no doubt. Again, she felt a shiver of fear, and her confidence wavered. When the time came, she would have to summon up the nerve and do what had to be done. She slipped her hand into the holdall and felt for her talisman. That would help her, of course – that and her guiding spirits.

After a while, she flicked her cigarette into the sea and stood up. Fear is for the passive, she told herself. When you act, you don't have time to feel afraid. She brushed the grass and sand from her jeans and headed back towards the footpath.

12

KIRSTEN

The nurse popped her head around the door. 'A visitor for you, dearie.' Beyond her, Kirsten could make out the shoulder of the uniformed policeman sitting outside her room. Then the door opened all the way and Sarah walked in.

'Sarah! What are you doing here?'

'Some welcome! Actually, it wasn't easy. First I had to get permission from that bloody detective superintendent. And as if that wasn't enough, I had to get past Dixon of Dock Green out there.' She jerked her thumb towards the door, then pulled up a chair and sat beside the bed. For a long moment, she just looked at Kirsten, then she started to cry. She leaned forward and the two of them hugged as best they could without dislodging the intravenous drip.

'Come on,' Kirsten said finally, patting her back. 'You're hurting my stitches.'

Sarah moved away and managed a smile. 'Sorry, love. I don't know what came over me. When I think of everything you must have been through . . .'

'Don't,' Kirsten said. The way she felt, she needed Sarah to be her usual self: outrageous, down-to-earth, solid, funny, angry. She was sick of sympathy; even less did she want empathy. 'It's no wonder you had a hard time getting in, dressed like that,' she hurried on. Sarah wore her usual uniform of jeans and a T-shirt. This one bore a logo scrawled boldly across the front: A WOMAN NEEDS A MAN LIKE A FISH NEEDS A BICYCLE. 'They probably think you're a terrorist.'

Sarah laughed and wiped her eyes with the back of her hand. 'So how are you, then, kid?'

'I'm all right, I suppose.' And it was partly true. That day, Kirsten did feel a bit better – at least physically. Her skin felt more like its old self, and the frightening internal aches had diminished during the night. She felt numb inside, though, and she still hadn't found the courage to look at herself.

'Do I look a mess?'

Sarah frowned and examined her features. 'Not so bad. Most of the bruises seem to have gone, and there's no permanent damage to your face, no disfigurement. In fact, I wouldn't say you look much worse than usual.'

'Thanks a lot.' But Kirsten smiled as she spoke. Sarah was clearly back to normal after her brief bout of tears.

'You must have taken a hell of a beating, though.'

'I must?'

'You mean you don't know?'

'Nobody's told me what happened.'

'That's typical of bloody doctors, that is. I suppose he's a man?'

'Yes.'

'Well, there you are, then. What about the nurse?'

'She seems too timid to talk much.'

'Frightened of him, I should think. He's probably a real tyrant. Most of them are.'

'The police have been, too.'

'They're even worse.'

'Do *you* know what happened?'

'All I know, love, is what it said in the paper. You were

attacked by some maniac in the park and stabbed and beaten.'

'Stabbed?'

'That's what it said.'

Perhaps that explained the stitches and the way her skin had felt puckered and snagged. She took a deep breath and asked, 'Did it say if I was raped as well?'

'If you were, the newspaper didn't report it. And knowing the press, they'd have made a field day out of something like that.'

'It's just that I feel so strange down there.'

'Really!' said Sarah. 'Bloody doctors act like they own your body. They ought to tell you what's wrong.'

'Maybe I haven't pushed hard enough. Or maybe they don't think I'm strong enough yet. I've been feeling very weak and tired.'

'Don't worry, love. You'll soon get your strength back. You know, I'm sure if you refuse to take your pills or start screaming in the night, they'll tell you what's wrong. Would you like me to tackle the doctor for you?'

Kirsten managed a weak smile. 'No, thanks. I need him in one piece. I'll try later.'

'All right.'

'You didn't answer my question.'

'What question's that?'

'What are you doing here? I thought you were going home for the summer.'

Sarah reached out and took Kirsten's hand. Her own was small and soft with long fingers and short, bitten nails. 'Someone's got to look out for you, love,' she said.

'But seriously.'

'Seriously. That's the main reason, I tell no lie. Oh, it'd only be rows at home anyway. You know how much my parents approve of me. I lower the tone of the neighbourhood. Besides, who wants to spend a bloody summer in Hereford, of all places.'

'Lots of people would,' Kirsten said. 'It's in the country.'

Sarah shrugged. 'Maybe I'll pay a brief visit, but that's all. I'm here to stay. We're getting a feminist bookshop together where that old second-hand record shop used to be. Know what we're going to call it?'

Kirsten shook her head.

'Harridan.'

'Harridan? But doesn't that mean—'

'Yes, a bad-tempered old bag. Remember all that fuss when Anthony Burgess said Virago was a poor choice of name for a woman's press because it meant a fierce or abusive woman? Well, we're going a step further. We'll show them that feminists can have just as much sense of irony as anyone else.' She laughed.

'Or bad taste,' Kirsten said.

'Often the same thing. Now what are we going to do about you?'

'What do you mean?'

'When you get out of here.'

'I don't know. I suppose I'll be going home. I don't really feel right, Sarah. My mind . . . I'm very mixed up.'

Sarah squeezed her hand. 'Bound to be. It'll pass, though. Probably the drugs they're giving you.'

'I have terrible nightmares.'

'You don't remember what happened, do you?'

'No.'

'That'll be it, then. Temporary amnesia. The brain blanks out painful experiences it doesn't like.'

'Temporary?'

'It might come back. Sometimes you have to work at it.'

Kirsten looked away towards the window. Outside, beyond the flowers and the get-well cards on her table, she could see the tops of trees swaying slowly in the wind and a distant block of flats, white in the July sun. 'I don't know if I want to remember,' she whispered. 'I feel so empty.'

'You don't have to think about it yet, love. Rest and get your strength back. And don't worry, I won't be far away. I'll take good care of you, I promise.'

Kirsten smiled. 'Where's Galen? The police said he'd been here.'

'Yes. I phoned him and he dashed up to see you as soon as I told him the news. He stayed for three days. He'd have sat by your bedside all the time if they'd let him. Anyway, his mother's having a really hard time getting over his grannie's death so he had to go back. Apparently she's on the edge of a nervous break-down. Very highly strung woman. He said he'd come again, though, when you regained consciousness. He's probably on his way right now.'

'Poor Galen.'

'Kirsten.'

'What?'

'I wouldn't expect too much. I mean . . . Oh, shit, never mind.'

'What? Tell me.'

'All I mean is that, sometimes, when things like this happen, men go funny.'

'How?'

'They can't deal with it. They just act strange . . . ashamed, embarrassed. They get turned off. That's all.'

'I'm sure Galen will be all right.'

'Of course he will, love. Of course he will.'

'Sarah, I'm thirsty. Will you pass me some water please? I've got these damn tubes in one arm and the other's just too tired.'

'Sure.' Sarah picked up the plastic bottle from the bedside table and held it for Kirsten, tilting it so that she could suck on the straw easily. 'Like being a bloody baby again, isn't it?'

Kirsten nodded, then removed the straw from her mouth. 'Okay, that's enough. Thanks. I hate feeling so helpless.'

Sarah put the bottle back and took her hand again.

'What's been happening in the outside world?' Kirsten asked.

'Well, we haven't had a nuclear war yet, if that's what you're worried about. And the police came and questioned us all about you.'

'How did they find out who I am?'

'They found your bag. Look, you don't know any of this, I can see, so I might as well tell you what I know. Do you want me to?'

Kirsten nodded slowly. 'But not about . . . you know . . . the attack.'

'All right. Like I said, I don't know what actually happened, but apparently a man taking his dog for a walk found you in the park and acted quickly. They reckon he saved your life. As soon as the police found out who you were from your student card, they were round at the university asking questions about your friends. It didn't take them long to find out about the party, so we all got a visit from PC Plod the next day. I suppose they thought one of us might have followed you and tried to do you in, but no one left the party for a long time after you. I stayed till two, and Hugo was still there trying to put his hand down my knickers. They even found out about the row in the Ring O'Bells. I'll bet that fascist landlord and his simian sidekick got a good grilling, too.'

Kirsten nodded. 'Yes, the superintendent mentioned that. The police moved fast, didn't they?'

'Well, what do you expect? You *are* a poor, innocent student, and your father *is* managing director of that hush-hush government electronics firm. Connections, love. It's not as if you were just some street tart touting for rough trade, is it?'

'Don't be so cynical, Sarah.'

'I'm sorry. I didn't mean to sound callous. But it's true, isn't it?'

'I don't know. I'd like to think they do everything in their power to catch someone who does things like this, no matter who to.'

'So would I, but dream on, kid.'

'What about the others? How are they?'

'Hugo dropped by a couple of times, and Damon put off his summer job for a week to come and see you, but you were out to the world then. They left flowers and cards.' She gestured towards the bedside table.

'Yes I know. Thank them for me, will you?'

'You'll be able to thank them yourself. I'm sure they'll be back now they know you're in the land of the living again.'

'Where are they now?'

'Hugo dashed off home to Bedfordshire, no doubt to sponge off his parents and bonk the local milkmaids for the rest of the summer, and Damon's going hop-picking in Kent. Imagine that, poor Damon getting those lily-white hands dirty!'

'So they're all gone.'

'Yes, love. All but me. And you won't get rid of me that easily.' Kirsten smiled and Sarah squeezed her hand again. 'They'll be back. Just wait and see. Anyway, I think I'd better go now. You look all in.'

'You'll come again soon?'

'Promise. Get some rest.' Sarah bent and kissed her forehead lightly, then left.

As Kirsten lay there, she tried to take in all that Sarah had told her. Of course, she couldn't expect the others to stick around for so long, and a visit from the police must have given them a scare. Hugo probably thought they were after that gram of coke he'd bought to celebrate the end of term. But all the same, she felt deserted, abandoned. She knew they all had to go their separate ways. In fact, she remembered, that had been very much on her mind that last night. (Why did she call it her 'last' night? she wondered.) But it wasn't as if she had the plague or anything. Was there something in what Sarah had hinted? Were Damon and Hugo embarrassed by what had happened to her? Ashamed even? Afraid to face her? But why should they be? she asked herself. They had work to do. They would be back as soon as they could get away, just as Sarah had said. And Galen was probably on his way right now.

Sarah's visit had renewed her spirits a little. It had also inflamed her curiosity. Obviously, there was more to this whole business than she was aware of. Could she really get the doctor to open up if she kept nagging at him or having screaming fits?

At least there was one thing she could do right now.

Tentatively, she pushed down the bedclothes and started to unbutton the top of her nightgown. It was a slow job, as her good arm was hooked up to an IV machine and she had to fumble with the weak and awkward fingers of her left hand, the one she hardly ever used. She didn't really believe that she'd get very far, but, to her surprise, she found once she'd started she couldn't stop, no matter how difficult and painful the movements were.

Finally, she managed to get the first four buttons undone. It was hard to bend her head forward and look down, so she shuffled herself back against the pillows and slumped against the headboard. From there, she could just tilt her head forward without straining her neck too much. At first, she couldn't see anything at all. The nightgown still seemed to cling around her breasts. She rested a moment, then pulled at it with her free hand. When she looked down again, she started screaming.

13

MARTHA

The Lucky Fisherman, a bit off the beaten track, turned out to be an unpretentious little local frequented mostly by townspeople. Martha didn't notice any real difference between the public bar and the lounge; both had the same small round tables and creaky wooden chairs. The woodwork was old and scratched, and one of the embossed glass panels in the door between the bars was broken. At one end of the room was a dartboard, which no one was using when she walked in at five past seven.

There were only a few other customers in the place, most of whom leaned easily against the bar chatting to the landlord. Keith was sitting at a table in the far corner under a framed photograph, an old sepia panorama of Whitby in its whaling days, with tall-masted ships in the harbour and chunky men in sou'westers – like the man on the packets of Fisherman's Friend cough lozenges – leaning against the railing on St Ann's Staith and smoking stubby pipes. The fence had been made of wood in those days, Martha noticed: one long beam held up by occasional props.

'Good day?' Keith said, standing as she came up to him.

'Good day,' Martha answered.

He laughed. 'No, I mean did you *have* a good day? We don't all talk like Paul Hogan, you know.'

Martha put her holdall on a vacant chair and sat down opposite him. 'Who?'

'Paul Hogan. *Crocodile Dundee*. A famous Aussie. Lord, don't you ever go to the movies or watch television?'

Martha shook her head. She vaguely remembered the name, but it seemed centuries ago, and she could recall no details. Her mind seemed to have no room left for trivia these days.

'What *do* you do for entertainment?'

'I read.'

'Ah. Very sensible. Drink?'

'Bitter. Just a half, please.'

Keith went to the bar and returned with her beer and another pint for himself.

'So how *was* your day?' he asked again.

'Good.' It was a long time since Martha had talked like this with a boy – a man, really – or conversed with anyone, for that matter. She seemed to have lost all her skill at small talk. She must have had it once, she assumed, though she couldn't remember when. All she could do was let Keith take the lead and follow as best she could. She dipped into her bag for her cigarettes and offered him one.

'No, I don't,' he said. 'But please go ahead.'

She lit the Rothmans, noting that she would soon need another packet, and reached for her drink again.

'Well . . .' Keith said.

Martha got the impression that she was supposed to say something, so she forged ahead. 'What about you? Where did you go?'

'Oh, I just walked around, visited the usual places. Sat on the beach for a while. I even went for a dip. I'm not used to it being so warm over here.'

'It is unusual,' Martha agreed.

'I'm making my way up the coast to Scotland. I think I told you.'

Martha nodded.

'Anyway, it's a complete holiday. No papers, no radio, no TV. I don't want to know what's going on in the world.'

'It's not usually good,' Martha agreed.

'Too true. And what about you? I'm curious. Why are you here all by yourself, if it's not a rude question?'

Martha thought of saying that yes, it was a rude question, but that would only get his back up. It was much easier to lie. She realized that she could tell him anything she wanted, anything under the sun – that she lived in Mozambique, for example, and was taking a rest from organizing safaris, or that she had run away from her husband, an Arabian prince to whom she had been sold as a young girl and shut away in a harem. She could tell him she was travelling around the world alone, as stipulated in the will, on a legacy left by her billionaire arms-dealer father. It was an exhilarating feeling, a feeling of tremendous power and freedom. Best keep it simple and believable, though, she decided, and told him she was doing research for a book.

'You a writer, then?' he asked. 'Silly of me, I suppose you must be, if you're working on a book.'

'Well, I'm not famous or anything. It's my first one. You won't have heard of me.'

'Maybe one day, who knows?'

'Who knows? It's a historical book, though, more of an academic study, really. I mean, it's not fiction or anything.'

'What's it about?'

'That's hard to say. It's partly about early Christianity, especially on the east coast here. You know, Bede, Caedmon, St Hilda, the Synod of Whitby.'

Keith shook his head slowly. ''Fraid you've lost me. I'm just a simple Aussie law student. Sounds fascinating, though.'

'It is,' Martha said, glad to have lost him. With luck, there would be no more questions about what she was doing. She finished her cigarette, then drained her glass. Keith immediately went for refills.

'Do you know anything about the fishing industry here?' Martha asked when he came back.

He squinted at her. His eyes really were a sharp blue, as if he had spent so much time staring into blue skies and oceans that they had taken their colour from the water and air. 'Fishing industry? That's a funny question. No, I can't really say I do.'

'I just wanted to see them bring in the catch, that's all,' she said quickly. 'It's supposed to be very interesting. They take them to that long shed down by the harbour and auction them off.'

'That'll be on Friday,' Keith said.

'Fish on Friday? Is that a joke?'

Keith laughed. 'No. What I mean is, I heard they go out on a Sunday and come back Friday, so that's when the catch comes in. That's the big boats. Little boats, like keel boats and cobles, come and go every day, but they've so little to sell it's all over before the sun comes up.'

Martha thought for a moment, making mental calculations, trying to remember what happened on which day. The person she was looking for must have a small boat of his own, she concluded. That might be easy to trace if she knew where to look. There should be a register of some kind . . .

'It's only a couple of days,' Keith said. 'Pity I won't be here. You'll have to get up early in the morning to see the boats come in, but the auctions go on for quite a while.'

'What? Sorry.'

'To see the boats come in. I said you'll have to get up early. They come in before dawn.'

'Oh, well, I'm sure the seagulls will wake me.'

Keith laughed. 'Noisy little blighters, aren't they? Tell me, do you come from this part of the country?'

'Yorkshire? No.'

'I thought your accent was different. Where you from, then?'

'Exeter,' Martha lied.

'Never been there.'

'You've not missed much. It's just a city, like all the rest. Tell me about Australia.'

And Keith told her. It seemed to suit both of them. Keith could find suitable expression for his homesickness in talking about Sydney life, and Martha could pretend to be interested. The whole evening was beginning to seem like a farce to her, and she wondered why she had bothered to agree to meet him at all. It brought back disturbing memories, too, mostly of her years as a teenager, pretending to be interested in what the boys said as they showed off, and then, later, fending off their wandering hands for as long as it seemed proper to do so. Would Keith turn out to be just like the rest, too? She put that last thought right out of her head.

'. . . as flash as a rat with a gold tooth,' Keith was saying. 'But that's just what people from Melbourne say.

It's hardly surprising Sydney's like a flashy whore to them. Melbourne's more like an old maid in surgical stockings . . .'

The place was filling up. Already most of the tables were taken, and three men had just started to play darts. Martha nodded in all the right places. She soon found that she'd finished her second half-pint.

'Another?' Keith asked.

'Are you trying to get me drunk?'

'Why would I want to do that?'

'To take advantage of me.'

Keith blushed. 'I wasn't . . . I mean I—'

She waved dismissively. 'Doesn't matter. Yes, I'll have another, if you like.'

It was while he was away at the bar that Martha first heard the voice. It made her hackles rise and her throat constrict. Casually, she looked around. Only two men were playing darts now, and it was one of them who had spoken. He was small and swarthy and wore a navy-blue fisherman's jersey. He looked as if he hadn't shaved for a couple of days, and his eyes seemed to glitter unnaturally, like the Ancient Mariner's, under his ragged fringe. He caught Martha looking and returned her gaze. Quickly, she turned away.

Keith came back with the drinks and excused himself to go to the gents.

Martha turned her head slowly again, trying to catch the man in her peripheral vision. Had he recognized her? She didn't think so. This time he was so absorbed in throwing the dart that he didn't notice her looking. Could it really be him?

'Do you know him?'

Martha almost jumped at the sound of Keith's voice.

She hadn't seen him come back. 'No. What makes you ask that?'

Keith shrugged. 'Just the way you were looking at him, that's all.'

'Of course I don't know him,' Martha said. 'This is my first day here.'

'You just seemed to be staring rather intently, that's all. Maybe it's someone you thought you recognized?'

'I've told you, I don't know what you're talking about. Just drop it, will you?'

'Are you sure you're all right?'

'Yes, I'm fine,' Martha said. And it was probably the truest thing she'd said to him all evening. Now she had something concrete to work on, her mind seemed more able to focus and concentrate. On the other hand, she felt herself drifting further and further away from Keith. It was becoming harder for her to follow his conversation and respond in the appropriate way at the right time. He began to seem more like an irritating fly that she kept having to swat away. She needed to be alone, but she couldn't escape just yet. She had to play the game.

'You a student, then?' he asked.

'Yes. I'm doing postgraduate work at Bangor.'

'And this book, is it your doctoral thesis?'

'Sort of.'

It was excruciating, like some awful interview she had to go through. As she answered Keith's inane questions, Martha was conscious all the time of the darts match going on behind her. Her skin was burning and her pulse beat way too fast.

Finally, the game drew to a close. The man she had been watching walked over to the bar, where she could see him out of the corner of her eye, and put his empty glass down on the counter. 'Well, that's my limit for tonight,' he said to the barman. 'See you tomorrow, Bobby.' The accent was right, the voice hoarse.

'Night, Jack,' said the barman.

Martha watched Jack walk towards the exit. He glanced briefly in her direction before he opened the door, but still showed no sign that he recognized her. She looked at her watch. It was a quarter to ten. For some reason, she got the impression that what had just happened was a kind of nightly ritual: Jack finishing his game, putting his glass on the counter and making some remark about the lateness of the hour. If he was a fisherman, then he would probably have to be up early in the morning. But shouldn't he already be out at sea? It was all so confusing. Still, if it was his habit to do this every night, she could come back tomorrow, when Keith was out of the way, and . . . Well, the next move would take careful planning and a lot of grace, but she had plenty of time.

'Want to go?'

With difficulty, like focusing on something from a great distance, Martha turned her attention back to Keith. She nodded and reached for her holdall. Outside, the warm fresh air felt good in her lungs. A bright half-moon hung high over St Mary's.

'Want to go for a walk?' Keith asked.

'Okay.'

They walked along East Terrace by the row of tall, white Victorian hotels, towards the Cook statue. As they passed the whale's jawbone, Keith stopped and said, 'That must have been exciting, setting off after whales.'

'I suppose I'd have been one of the waiting women,' Martha said, 'hoping to see the jawbone of a whale nailed to the masts.'

'What?'

'It was a sign. It meant everyone was safe. The women used to walk up here along West Cliff and look out for the ships coming home.' Martha looked at the huge arch of bone. From where she stood, it framed the floodlit St Mary's across the harbour as perfectly as if the whole set-up had been contrived by an artist.

'It's hard to imagine you doing that,' Keith said, moving on slowly. 'Pacing and waiting.'

'Why do you say that?'

'Well, I can't really say I *know* you of course, but you give me the impression that you're a modern woman, liberated or whatever. You'd have been more likely to be out there on the ships.'

'They didn't take women.'

'I don't suppose they did. But you know what I mean.'

Martha didn't. It had been his first really personal remark and it took her aback. How could someone just sit and talk about inconsequential things for an hour or two and then come out with a statement like that? She hadn't even been paying attention to him most of the time. Could he really see into her character? She hoped not. He wouldn't like what he saw.

By the Cook statue, they sat on a bench and looked out to sea. A cool breeze ruffled her hair and the moon's reflection seemed to float somewhere far in the distance, yet its eerie white light spread over all the ripples and billows of the water as far as the eye could see.

Martha thought of the passage from Lawrence's *Women in Love*, where Birkin threw pebbles at the moon's reflection in a pond. It was supposed to symbolize something, or so her English teacher had said, but nobody really knew what. Symbols, to her, had always stood for things you felt but couldn't explain. And now she felt like throwing pebbles at the rippling white sea.

'Do you have a boyfriend?' Keith asked.

'What do you think? You seem to know what kind of person I am. What would you say?'

'I'd be surprised if you didn't. But if I was him I wouldn't let you go away by yourself like this.'

'Why not?'

'Stands to reason, doesn't it? A pretty girl like you . . .'

A pretty girl! Martha almost laughed out loud. From where they sat, at the top of the cliff and back a little bit from its fenced edge, she couldn't see the waves break on the beach below. She could hear them though, and the deep grumbling hiss as one withdrew filled the silence before Keith spoke again.

'There's something disconcerting about you, though,' he said.

'Oh? What's that?'

'Well, for a start, you're not easy to get to know.'

Martha looked at her watch. 'We've been together about three hours,' she said. 'How much do you expect to get to know about someone in that time?'

'It's not time that counts. Some people you can get to know real quickly. Not you, though. There's hidden depths to you.'

'Why am I disconcerting?' Martha asked. Despite herself, she was becoming interested in his perception of her.

'Oh, I don't know. You seem so distant. And you don't get my jokes. It's like you've spent the last few years on another planet. I mean, if I make a little joke, you don't laugh, you ask a question.'

'Like what?'

Keith laughed. 'Like that!'

Martha felt herself blushing. It wasn't a feeling she enjoyed. She smiled. 'I suppose you're right. It's just curiosity.'

He shook his head. 'No, it's not. It's more like a form of defence. You're very evasive. You've got a lot of defences, Martha. You're hiding in there somewhere, behind all the walls and barbed wire. Why?'

Martha became aware of Keith's arm slipping around her shoulder. It made her stiffen. Surely he must sense her resistance, she thought, but he didn't remove it. 'Why what?' she asked.

'Why do you need to protect yourself so much, to hide away? What's there to be afraid of?'

'There's a lot to be afraid of,' Martha said slowly. 'And what makes you think I'm protecting myself from the world? Maybe I'm protecting the world from me.'

'Now that really is choice. I'm not sure I understand you, not at all. But I do find you intriguing, and very attractive.'

A ship's light blinked far out to sea. Keith leaned over and kissed her. Martha managed to contain her boiling rage and let him. It was a soft, tentative kiss, not a violent, tongue-probing attack. A small price to pay, she told herself amid her anger, for appearing normal. She knew she wasn't responding with the enthusiasm he expected, but there was absolutely nothing she could do about that.

'It's a shame I have to go tomorrow,' he said, breaking away gently. Clearly her response, or lack of it, didn't mean very much to him. 'I'd like to spend more time with you, get to know you a bit better.'

Martha said nothing. She just stared out at the rippling moon on the water and watched the ship's light move across the horizon like a star through the sky. He kissed her again, this time more passionately, exploring her teeth with his tongue. When she felt his other hand slip up over her side and reach for her breast, she pulled away.

'No,' she said, as calmly but firmly as she could. 'What do you think I am? We've only just met.'

'I'm sorry,' Keith said, 'really I am. I didn't mean to offend you. I just thought . . . I mean I hoped. Oh God, you can't blame a bloke for trying, can you?'

Martha could, but she didn't say so. Instead, she tried to placate him despite the rage she felt. 'It's not that I don't like you,' she said. 'It's just too soon. I guess I'm not the kind of person for a holiday quickie.'

Now Keith seemed offended. 'That's not fair. That's not what I had in mind.'

But it was, Martha knew. Oh, Keith was a nice enough boy, not too pushy, but all it came down to was that he wanted to go to bed with her. He would make out that he didn't usually do such things, and she was supposed to say the same. Then he would tell her how it was different with her, really special. He was a wolf, all right, but a tame one. Getting the brush-off just made him sulk and become petulant. They weren't all as easy as him to fight off.

'Come on,' Martha said. 'Let's go back. It's getting chilly.'

Hands in pockets, head down, Keith walked beside her back to the guesthouse.

14

KIRSTEN

'It's *my* body. I have a right to know.'

Kirsten leaned back on the pillows. Her eyes were puffed up, and the tear-tracks had dried on her cheeks. The doctor stood by the bottom of the bed, and her parents sat beside her.

'You were in no state to be alarmed,' the doctor said. 'You've been suffering from severe trauma. We had to avoid upsetting you.' For the first time, Kirsten actually looked at him. He was a short, dark-skinned man with a deeply etched frown that converged in a V between his thick black eyebrows. Somehow, the lines made him look like a short-tempered person, though Kirsten had seen no evidence of this. If he had tried to keep the full extent of her injuries from her, he had at least been gentle.

'I'm already alarmed,' she said. Her nightgown was buttoned up again now, but the memory of what she had seen still frightened her. 'Look, I'm not a little girl. Something's wrong. Tell me.'

'We didn't want to upset you, dear.' Her mother echoed the doctor. 'There's plenty of time to go into all the details later, when you're feeling better. Why don't you just rest now? The doctor will give you a sedative.'

Kirsten struggled to sit up. 'I don't want a bloody sedative! I want to know now! If you don't tell me, I'll only imagine it's worse than it is. I feel awful, but I don't think I'm going to die, am I? What else could be so bad? What could be worse than that?'

'Lie back and keep calm,' the doctor said, gently pushing her down. 'No, you're not going to die. At least not until you've had your three-score and ten. If you were, you'd have done so before today.' He moved back to the end of the bed.

'So tell me what's wrong.'

The doctor hesitated and looked towards her father. 'Go on,' he said quietly. 'Tell her.'

Kirsten wanted to let him know that his permission wasn't required. She was twenty-one; she didn't need his approval. But if this was the only way to find out, so be it.

The doctor sighed and stared at a spot on the wall above the top of her head. 'What you saw,' he began, 'is the result of emergency surgery, the sutures. It looks bad now, but when they heal, it will be better. Not like new, but better than now.'

Anything would be better than now, Kirsten thought, picturing her red and swollen breasts covered with stitch marks like zips, like something out of a Frankenstein movie.

'When you were brought in,' the doctor went on, 'one breast was almost severed. We counted thirteen separate stab wounds to the mammary region alone.' He shrugged and leaned forward, gripping the metal bedframe. 'We did the best we could under the circumstances.'

'Alone? You said *alone*. What else was there?'

'You'd been beaten around the face and head and, all in all, you had thirty-one stab wounds. It's a miracle that none of them hit a major artery or organ.'

Kirsten gripped the top of the bedsheet and held it

tight across her throat. 'What did they hit then, apart from my tits?'

'Kirsten!' her mother gasped. 'There's no need to speak like that in front of the doctor.'

'It's all right,' the doctor said. 'I suppose she has every right to be angry.'

'Thank you,' Kirsten said. 'Thank you very much. You were saying?'

The doctor fixed his gaze on the wall again. 'Most of the other entry points were in the region of the abdomen, thighs and vagina,' he went on. 'It was a vicious attack, one of the worst I've ever seen – at least on a victim who survived. There were also shallow slashes across the stomach, and something that looked like a cross with a long vertical had been cut from just below the breasts to the pudenda. The cuts weren't deep, but they needed stitching nonetheless. That's why your skin feels so tight.'

Kirsten lay silent and relaxed her grip on the sheets. It was even worse than she had thought. Thirty-one stab wounds. That terrible ache between her legs. She gulped and struggled to force back the tears. She was damned if she was going to prove them right and react like a baby. 'If I'm not going to die,' she said, 'why are you all look-ing like undertakers? What's the bad news you're hiding from me? What is it you're all trying to save me from? Am I disfigured for life? Is that it?'

'There will be some disfigurement, yes,' the doctor said, glancing at Kirsten's father again for the go-ahead. 'Chiefly of the breasts and the pubic area. But that's not the main damage. There's always the possibility of further surgery to correct some of the disfigurement. The real problems are internal, Kirsten,' he said, for the first time using her Christian name, and saying it softly. 'When you came in, you were unconscious. We had to operate immediately to put things right, to save your life, and we had to do it quickly, because there's always considerable anaesthetic risk when a patient is unconscious.'

'Well?'

'You were suffering from severe internal bleeding, and there was a strong chance of infection, of peritonitis. We had to perform an emergency hysterectomy.'

'I know what that means,' Kirsten said. 'It means I can't have children, doesn't it?'

'It means surgical removal of the uterus.'

'But it means I'll never be able to have babies, doesn't it?'

The doctor nodded.

Kirsten's mother began to sob into a handkerchief. Her father and the doctor looked solemn. One machine beside her bleeped rhythmically, another hissed, and colourless fluid dripped into her arm from the IV. Everything in the room seemed white, apart from her father's charcoal-grey suit.

'It wasn't something I'd planned for the immediate future anyway,' she said with a little laugh, showing them she could put a brave face on things. But this time she couldn't stop the tears from flowing. Her father and the doctor were both staring down at her.

'Why are you looking at me like that?' she shouted, turning her face to the wall. 'Go away! Leave me alone.'

'You insisted I tell you everything, Kirsten,' the doctor said, 'and you'd have to have been told eventually. I said I thought it was too soon.'

'I'll be all right.' Kirsten reached for a Kleenex. 'How

did you expect me to react? Jump for joy? Is there anything else? Now you've started, you might as well get it all over with.'

There was a short pause, then the doctor said, 'Some of the stab wounds perforated the vagina.'

Her mother turned away to face the door. Such frank talk was clearly too much for her. Vaginas, breasts, penises and the rest had always been forbidden subjects around the house.

'So?' Kirsten said. 'I'm assuming you patched *that* up as well.'

The doctor nodded. 'Oh, yes. We had to close the lacerations, stop the bleeding. But as I said, it was an emergency patch-up.'

'Are you trying to tell me you made some kind of mistake because you were in a hurry? Is that it?'

'No. We followed standard emergency procedure. I told you. You were unconscious. We had to act fast.'

'So what *are* you trying to say?'

'Well, there was some tissue loss, and the damage could be serious enough to cause permanent problems.'

'*Could* be?'

'We just don't know yet, Kirsten.'

'And where does all this leave me?'

'Intercourse might be a problem,' the doctor explained. 'It could be painful, difficult.'

Kirsten lay silent for a moment, then she laughed and said, 'Oh, wonderful! That's just what I was feeling like right now, a really good fuck.'

'Kirsten!' her father snapped, showing the first signs of anger she had seen in him in years. 'Listen to the doctor.' Her mother started crying again.

'There's a chance that reconstructive surgery sometime

in the future might help,' the doctor went on, 'but there are no guarantees.'

It finally dawned on Kirsten what he meant – more from his tone than what he actually said – and she felt a chill shoot through her whole being. 'This could be for ever?'

'I'm afraid so.'

'And a hysterectomy can't be reversed, either, can it?'

'No.'

Kirsten turned towards the window and noticed it was raining outside. The tree-top leaves danced under the downpour and the distant flats had turned slate grey. 'For ever,' she repeated to herself.

'I'm sorry, Kirsten.'

She looked at her father. It was odd to be discussing such things as her sex life in front of him; she had never done so before. She didn't know what he assumed about her activities at university. But now here he was, looking sad and sympathetic because she couldn't make love, perhaps never would again. Or maybe it was the bit about no children that hit him the hardest, she being an only child.

She didn't know which was worse herself; for the first time in her life, the two things converged in a way they never had before. She had been on the pill for two years and had slept regularly with Galen, only her second lover. They had never thought about children and the future, but now, as she remembered their gentle and ecstatic love-making, she couldn't help but think of new life growing inside her. How ironic that it took the loss of the ability both to enjoy sex and to bear children to make her see how intimately connected the two functions were. She laughed.

'Are you all right?' her father asked, coming forward to take her hand. She let him, but hers lay limp.

'I don't know.' She looked at him and shook her head. 'I don't know. I feel sort of empty inside, all dried out and dead.'

The doctor was still hovering at the foot of the bed. 'As I said, there is a chance that reconstructive surgery might help. It's something to think about. I don't know if you understand this, Kirsten,' he said, 'or at least if you realize it yet, but you really are very lucky to be alive.'

'Yes,' said Kirsten, rolling on her side. 'Lucky.'

15

MARTHA

The next morning the honeymooners were gone, leaving one empty table, but Keith sat with Martha anyway. He made polite conversation over breakfast but demonstrated none of the ebullience and energy he'd shown the previous day, when he had first found himself at the table with her. Enforced celibacy, she guessed, had seriously dampened his spirits. It would be best to say nothing about last night, she decided. After all, it *was* Keith's last day; perhaps tomorrow she would be able to eat alone.

A particularly near and noisy flock of seagulls had awoken most of the guests at about three-thirty in the morning, and that provided a safe and neutral topic of conversation over the black pudding and grilled mushrooms that again augmented the usual bacon and egg.

Martha ate quickly, wished Keith a good journey, and hurried upstairs. She hadn't slept well. It wasn't only the scavenging gulls that had disturbed her, but thoughts and fears about what she had to do next. For weeks she had planned it and dreamed of it, gone over it all so often in her mind that she could perform the act in her sleep. Now that it was close, she felt terrified. What if something went wrong? What if, when the time came, she couldn't go through with it? Even the holiest have their doubts, she reminded herself. Faith would see her through.

Across the harbour, a few woolly clouds hung over St Mary's, but they were drifting slowly inland. The sun lit up the cottages that straggled up the steep hillside. Beyond St Hilda's, closer at the other end of the street, the sky was clear. A light breeze wafted through the window, bringing the salt and fishy smell of the sea.

Martha didn't know what to do with herself all day. She couldn't act until after dark, and she had already got the lie of the land. It would look suspicious if she stayed in her room, though, especially on such a lovely day at the seaside. Spells of warm, sunny weather were rare on the Yorkshire coast. Whatever she did, she would have to go out.

She waited until she had heard the other guests leave for the day, hoping that Keith was among them, then crept down the stairs and out into the morning sun. Already, courting couples strolled hand in hand along Skinner Street, content after a night of love set to the music of screeching gulls. Families paused and glanced idly at the racks of postcards and guidebooks outside the gift shops. Children in shorts and striped T-shirts, swinging bright plastic buckets and spades, demanded ice creams. Babies slept in their prams, oblivious to the noise and bustle of life going on all around them.

Martha went into the first newsagent's she came across and bought *The Times* and a packet of twenty Benson and Hedges. The ten Rothmans, a brand she hadn't liked all that much anyway, hadn't lasted very long, and she had a feeling she wouldn't want to be caught without. For twenty-one years she hadn't smoked a single cigarette. Now, within about a year, she had become addicted.

She wandered down busy Flowergate, a narrow street

crammed with shoppers, towards the estuary. Overhead, flocks of gulls screamed and flashed white in the sun. When she reached the bridge, she checked the high-tide times chalked on the board: 0639 and 1902. It was ten o'clock now; that meant the tide would be well on its way out. She jotted the times down in her notebook in case she should forget.

One problem with the guesthouse was that the manager's wife made awful coffee. Martha would have preferred it to tea in the morning, but she had no stomach for a pot of powdered Nescafé. Now she craved the caffeine that only a cup of strong, drip-filter coffee could provide.

She crossed the bridge and turned left along Church Street, joining the procession heading for the 199 steps up to Caedmon's Cross, St Mary's and the abbey ruin. A short distance along the narrow cobbled street, just before the marketplace, she found the cafe she had noticed before, the Monk's Haven, near the Black Horse pub. The cafe was meant to look very olde worlde. A painted sign, much like a pub sign, in Gothic script hung above the entrance, and pots of bright red geraniums ranged along the top of the frontage above the mullioned windows with their white-painted frames.

Martha ordered a cup of black coffee and sat down to struggle with *The Times* crossword. While mulling over clues, she watched the ebb and flow of people beyond the windows: more couples pushing babies in prams; toddlers hanging onto mummy's hand; stout old women with grey hair and sensible shoes. Outside the music shop opposite, a skinny young man clad in jeans and a checked shirt, who looked like he hadn't slept for a month or combed his hair for at least as long, started singing folk songs in a nasal voice. Some people dropped coins into the hat that lay on the pavement beside him.

When she had done as much of the crossword as she could, Martha read through the paper. She found nothing of interest. Waiting was no fun. It must be like this for soldiers, she thought, just before they know they are going into action. They sit around in the trenches, or on landing craft, smoking and keeping very quiet. She had no idea what she would do when it was all over. That was an aspect of the business she had left completely to instinct. Because she didn't know how she would feel when it was done, she couldn't make any plans about what to do. She just hoped that possibilities would present themselves when the time came.

She wandered up and down Church Street gazing at the displays of jet-ware, beautiful polished black stones set in gold and silver, or larger chunks carved into ornamental chess pieces and delicate figurines. By noon she was hungry again. So much for the staying power of black pudding and bacon. Desperate for an alternative to fish and chips, she nipped into the Black Horse and ordered a steak and kidney pie, which she washed down with a half of bitter. Then she smoked a cigarette and struggled for a while longer with the crossword. By half past one she was out on the street again wondering what to do with the rest of the day. She didn't want to go up to St Mary's again, and there was no sense in simply tramping the streets all day.

Close to the junction of Church Street and Bridge Street stood a small bookshop. The bell pinged as Martha went inside, and a plump, bespectacled girl smiled at her from behind a counter stacked with invoices and orders. The place had a large and comprehensive paperback fiction section, which Martha browsed through methodically, starting with A: Ackroyd, Amis, Austen, Burgess, Chatwin, Dickens, Drabble, Greene, Hardy . . .

'Can I help you?' the assistant asked, coming out from behind her counter and raising her glasses.

'No,' Martha said, flashing her a quick smile. 'Just browsing. I'll find something.'

The woman went back to her paperwork and Martha carried on scanning the titles. She wanted an ordered world she could lose herself in for a while. Nothing modern would do; twentieth-century literature, with its experiments in style, its self-conscious artistry and its lack of morality and order, had never much interested her. At one time she had liked to escape into the occasional crime novel – Ruth Rendell, P. D. James – but such things held no appeal for her now. For a moment she considered *Moby Dick*. She had never read it, and the seaside, especially an old whaling centre, would be the ideal place to start. But when she got to the Ms, she found they hadn't a copy left in stock. The only Melville book they had was *Pierre*, and she was in no mood for that. Finally, she settled for Jane Austen's *Emma*. She had read it at school, for her A-Levels, but that seemed a lifetime ago. With Jane Austen, you could count on nothing more to ruffle the ordered surface than an occasional social gaffe or mistaken romantic intentions.

What better to do, then, than spend an afternoon on the beach reading *Emma*? She just hoped Keith wasn't there. He had said he was moving on, but he could have changed his mind.

She made her way back over the bridge. With the tide out, the River Esk was reduced to a narrow channel in the sand. Boats leaned in the silt at odd angles. Martha walked along St Ann's Staith, thinking of the old days in the photograph when the railing was made of wood. She passed the amusement arcades, seafood stalls and Dracula Museum, then at the end of Pier Road she took the steps down to the beach.

Whitby Sands runs below West Cliff, and over the centuries, the sea has carved small caves and caverns in the sheer rock wall. Martha poked her head inside one. It didn't go very deep, but it was a dank, gloomy place, full of slimy rocks, smelly seaweed and dead, dried-out molluscs that crunched underfoot. She shivered and turned away.

The beach itself was crowded – only to be expected on such a fine day – but Martha managed to find a spot where she could lean back against the rock and stretch her feet out. Children screamed and splashed in the water, bravely taking it in turns to stand fast as waves came in and bowled them over. Anxious parents kept one eye on the knitting or the newspaper, and the other on the kids. Some children were busy constructing elaborate sandcastles with turrets, battlements, moats and drawbridges.

Some people were even sunbathing. A couple of teenage girls wearing skimpy bikinis lay flat out on towels. A group of boys about the same age, playing cricket nearby, kept hitting the ball in their direction just to make an excuse to chat the girls up.

What Martha was watching, she realized, was another way of life, another world completely – or one she had once known but lost. If she felt like a visitor from outer space when she watched lovers walk hand in hand, parents push babies in prams, and children play in the foam, she felt even more so when she watched the elaborate contact and courtship rituals of these teenagers bursting with hormones.

The first couple of times the cricket ball kicked up a little sand on the girls' bare stomachs, they responded with abuse. Anyone watching would think they didn't like getting sand in their navels. After a while, though, they started to join in the spirit of the game. They would pick up the ball and throw it towards the sea, or run off and bury it in the sand, laughing and making fun of the boys. Martha had never before noticed the importance of sheer repetition and persistence in the human mating ritual.

It was like watching a species of animal or insect, Martha thought, putting Jane Austen aside and lighting a cigarette. No matter how much progress we seem to have made, we still dance to primitive patterns so deeply imprinted that we wouldn't recognize them if they tripped us up in the street. Which they often do. Though we have the miracle of language, we still make more sense with meaningless sounds, gestures, looks and silences.

And beneath all the elaborate courtship rituals, Martha thought, lay pure animal desire and the scarcely recognized impulse to perpetuate the species. Just like Keith last night. He had wanted Martha. He had wanted to take her to his bed naked and enter her for the pleasure it gave him. All that fuss over five minutes of grunting sounds – or was it squelching sounds? – someone had once said. People would do anything for it: lie, cheat, steal, maim, kill, even die.

The whole human drama seemed so sad and pointless to Martha that day on the beach. People amounted to nothing more than puppets manipulated by forces they didn't understand or, worse, even perceive. Shakespeare was right, as usual— 'As flies to wanton boys, are we to th'gods; They kill us for their sport.' Martha included herself, too. Hadn't she experienced the 'sport' of the gods? And just how much choice did she really have in this tragedy or farce she was acting out? She was jumping to strings as much as anyone else. Different strings, perhaps, with more sinister pullers, but beyond her control nonetheless. Despite the heat, she shivered.

Finally, she managed to pull herself out of the philosophical gloom. She told herself she was just getting nervous, that was all, and that the weak and cowardly part of her nature was trying to sap her confidence. She had to be strong. It was no good giving in to a sense of futility; only one thing kept her going, and until that was done, she couldn't afford to reflect on life. Besides, who was she to make such judgements anyway?

She crossed her legs and picked up Jane Austen. It was a hot day on the beach, and there she lay in jeans and a shirt buttoned up to the neck. She was too warm, but she couldn't take her clothes off and lie almost naked like the teenage girls in their bikinis. And the rituals and consummation of courtship were beyond her, too. But for her, she thought, there was another kind of consummation devoutly to be sought. And seek it she would. Tonight.

16

KIRSTEN

Like most people who hear bad news, Kirsten went through all the textbook stages, including the belief that a second opinion would prove the doctor wrong, and that what he had told her was gone forever would somehow be miraculously restored. The first night, she convinced herself that it was all a bad dream; it would pass. But it didn't. Even in the mild light of the next morning everything was the same: her stitches, her aches, her wounds, her loss.

The nightmares of painless, almost bloodless, slashing and slicing continued. She never woke up screaming, but sometimes she would open her eyes suddenly at some ungodly hour of the morning to escape the relentless images and to puzzle over them.

Other times, she lay awake all night. Especially when it was raining. She liked to try and empty her mind and pretend that her hard hospital bed was really a pallet of pine needles deep in the woods behind her parents' house in Brierley Coombe. The rain pattered gently on the leaves outside her window, and for short periods she could imagine it falling, soft and cool, on her eyelids, and she could almost escape the horror of her condition.

At least she wasn't dead. In a way, the doctor had been right: she was lucky. If that man hadn't been walking his dog so late and hadn't got curious when it started to growl and scratch around in the shrubbery, then she would have simply bled to death on a summer's night out in the park, only a hundred yards or so from home. But the man had stopped, and for that she should be grateful.

Now she was a cripple with all her limbs intact – external limbs, anyway. Her sense of violation and loss was almost unbearable at times; that most intimate part of herself had been stolen and destroyed. She cried, prayed and even, at one time, fell into a fit of hysterical laughter. But ultimately, she accepted the truth, and depression bore down on her. At its heart was that thick cloud, an opaque mass swelling like a tumour in her mind, repelling all light and taunting her with its darkness and its heaviness.

The doctor and nurses ministered as best they could to her healing body. The stitches dissolved, leaving the flesh bunched up and corrugated around her breasts. Livid scars quartered her, like the doctor had said, in the shape of a cross with a long vertical bar and a short horizontal, from just below the breasts to her pubic hair – at least to where that hair *had* been, for the nurse had shaved her down there and now all she had was itchy stubble. Externally, the pubic region didn't look too bad. She glimpsed it for the first time when she was able to walk to the toilet alone. It was red and sore, covered in a lattice of fading stitchwork, but she had expected worse. It was inside where most of the damage had been done.

Her parents came in and out, her mother still too upset to say very much and her father taking the burden stoically. Superintendent Elswick dropped by again, but to no avail. She still couldn't remember what had happened or give them any information about her attacker, beyond the feel of his calloused hands.

Sarah visited again, too. She said she'd take on the small flat if Kirsten was going home to convalesce. Kirsten agreed. It would save a lot of trouble moving stuff when her parents took her home. She didn't tell Sarah about the full extent of her injuries. Maybe later. At that time, she couldn't bear to talk about it. She did, though, ask her to try and keep the others away for a while.

And then, a full week after she had been given the news, Galen turned up, breathless, from the station, lank dark hair flopping over his ears, concern etched in every feature of his thin, handsome face. He sat beside her and grasped her hand. At first neither of them knew what to say.

'I came before,' Galen told her, finally. 'They said you were unconscious and they didn't know when you'd come round. I phoned every day. I couldn't stay. My . . .'

Kirsten squeezed his hand. 'I know. I understand. Thank you for coming back.'

'You look a lot better. How are you feeling?'

'I can get up and walk around now. They tell me I'll be able to go home soon.' She touched her face gingerly. 'The bruises have all gone now. The swelling's gone down.' How much did he know about what had happened to her? She didn't want to give anything away.

Galen lowered his head and shook it, his face darkening. He smashed his fist into his palm. 'If I could get my hands on the bastard—'

'Don't,' Kirsten said. 'Just . . . don't. I'd rather not talk about it.'

'I'm sorry. You can't imagine how I feel. I've been blaming myself ever since it happened. If only I'd been there, like I should have been.'

'Don't be silly. It's not your fault. It could have happened to anyone at any time. You can't be expected to guard me night and day.'

Galen looked into her eyes and smiled. His grip tightened on her hand. 'I will from now on,' he said. 'After you've recovered and all that. I promise I won't let you out of my sight.'

Kirsten turned her head aside and looked out at the dazzling tower blocks rinsed by last night's rain, and the sunlight dancing in the polished leaves. 'What are you going to do?' she asked.

Galen shrugged. 'I don't really know. I suppose I'll just hang about at home for the rest of the summer. Mother's still taking it very badly – grandmother's death. And I'll come and visit you in Brierley whenever I can. It's not too far away and I'll have the car.'

'It might be better if you didn't visit me,' Kirsten said slowly. 'At least, not for a while.'

Galen frowned and scratched his earlobe. 'Why? What do you mean?'

'Just that I need some time by myself, to recover.' She managed a smile. 'Call it post-operative depression. I wouldn't be very good company.'

'That doesn't matter. You'll need me, Kirstie. And I want to be there for you.'

She rested her free hand on his forearm. 'No. Not for a while. Please. Just let me get myself sorted out.'

Galen got up and wandered over to the window, hands in pockets. His shoulders slumped the way they always did when he was disappointed about something. Just like a little boy, Kirsten thought.

'If you say so,' he said, with his back to her. 'I suppose it's the . . . er . . . the psychological effects that are worse than even the physical ones, is it? I mean, I don't know. I couldn't know, could I, being a man? But I'll do my best to understand.' He turned around again and looked at her.

'I know you will,' Kirsten said. 'I just think it's best if we don't see each other for a while. I'm all confused.'

She still wasn't sure how much they had told him. He knew that she'd been attacked, that was clear enough, but had they been vague about the nature of the assault? Perhaps he assumed that she'd been raped. Had she been? Kirsten wasn't too sure about that, herself. As far as the doctor had been able to make out, there had been no traces of semen in the vagina. It had been such a mess, however, that she didn't see how he could possibly be so certain. Did penetration by a short, sharply pointed metal object count as rape? she wondered. In the end, she just had to settle for the general opinion that people who do what this man did to her are usually incapable of real sexual intercourse.

'What about Toronto?' Galen asked, returning to the chair and hunching over her.

'I don't know. I just can't see myself going, not the way things are now. Not this year, at least.'

'But it's still a month or so off. You'll probably feel better by then.'

'Maybe. Anyway, you go ahead. Don't worry about me.'

'I wouldn't go without you.'

'Galen, don't be so stubborn. There's no point sacrificing your career because of me. I can't promise you anything right now. I can't even—' And she almost told him then, but pulled herself back just in time. 'I just don't know how things are going to go.' She started crying. 'Can't you understand?'

The effort of letting him down gently and hiding her feelings and her disability from him at the same time was proving too much. She wished he would just leave. When he bent down to comfort her, she felt herself freeze. The reaction surprised her; it was something she'd never done before. And it came from deep inside; it was completely involuntary, like a twitch or a reflex action. Galen felt it, too, and he backed off, looking wounded.

'I understand,' he said stiffly. 'At least, I'll try.' He patted her hand. 'Let's just leave it be for now, okay? Plenty of time to think about our future later on, when you're fully recovered.'

Kirsten nodded and wiped the tears away with the backs of her hands. Galen passed her a Kleenex.

'Is there anything you want,' he asked, 'anything at all I can bring you?'

'No, not really.'

'A book?'

'I've not felt much like reading. I can't seem to concentrate. But thank you very much. You'd better go, Galen, go back home and take care of your mother. I'm glad you came. I know I don't seem it, but honestly I am.'

He looked disappointed, as if he had been summarily dismissed. Kirsten knew she hadn't managed to sound very convincing. Her breasts ached and she felt close to tears again. He took hold of her hand, with that little-boy-lost expression on his face, and didn't seem to want to let go.

'I'll come again,' he said. 'I promise. I'll be up here for a couple of days sorting things out, anyway.'

'All right. But I'm tired now.'

He leaned forward and kissed her gently on the lips. She caught the toothpaste smell on his breath. He must have brushed his teeth on the train, she thought, or as soon as he got to the hospital.

When he left, she gave in and let the tears fall. There just seemed to be no future. Certainly there would be no life for him with her. If he was lucky, they would drift apart and he would go to Toronto in September. He might even meet someone else.

Kirsten had no idea what her full recovery would feel like, or even if such a thing were possible. The doctor hadn't sounded very hopeful about reconstructive surgery. Presumably, she would feel fine on the outside, though the scars would remain and have to be covered up. Was she just supposed to get used to her new state, put her past behind her and get on with life? Go to Toronto with Galen, even?

He would be very understanding about her disability, at least for a while. Perhaps he would even marry her out of love and pity, and as time went on she would considerately turn a blind eye to the bits on the side he needed to give him what she could no longer supply. She would be grateful just because he was self-sacrificing enough to love a cripple.

No. It didn't sound right. Such a life could never be, *should* never be. Without really telling him why, she would have to ease Galen out of her life for his own good.

The depression was on her, in her, a kind of numbing fatalism that would admit no light, no comfort. She couldn't imagine it ever ending, things getting back to normal. Already the carefree, cheerful young graduate who had stepped out of Oastler Hall, enjoyed the warm air and scanned the night sky for the moon as she sat on the stone lion was gone. Utterly. Irredeemably.

And who or what was going to take her place? Kirsten wondered. She felt vague and disturbing forces moving inside her, like flitting shadows in places so deep and dark she had not known they existed. And she felt powerless to do anything about them, just as she had when Galen had tried to hold her and she'd frozen on him. She was no longer in control.

But it was more, even, than that. She knew she only controlled enough of herself to give the comforting illusion of being in command. At best, like most people, she could control certain aspects of her behaviour. It was mostly a matter of manners, like not burping at the dinner table. But her habits and mannerisms shouldn't change so dramatically unless she made a great conscious effort to alter them. She surely wouldn't just wake up one morning and no longer bite her nails under stress or stop blushing when she overheard someone talking about her. No more than Galen could stop his shoulders slumping when he didn't get what he wanted, or Sarah sucking on her upper lip with deceptive calm before responding sharply to a remark that had offended her.

Yet that seemed to be just what had happened. What Kirsten had done when Galen had reached for her – before she had even had time to think about it – was something that had never been in her repertoire of responses. It was her habit always to return the embrace of a friend or a loved one. But that part of her – the part, perhaps, that responded to affection and love – was gone now, changed. She no longer recognized herself.

It would be typical of the doctors, she thought, to put it down to what had happened to her. It's like, they would say, touching a hot coal and flinching the next time the hand nears another. Once bitten, twice shy. Conditioning. One of Pavlov's dogs. Naturally, they would go on, anyone who has suffered and survived such a vicious attack is bound to react with suspicion when another man, however familiar, approaches her in any intimate way.

Well, maybe they were right. Perhaps it would pass in time. Animals and humans who are used to being ill-treated often strike out at first when someone finally offers them love, but in time they come to accept it and trust those who give it. Surely she, too, could re-learn the right responses? But Kirsten wasn't convinced. For some reason, she believed that this new instinctive and frightening reaction to her lover's concern was only the beginning, that there were other changes going on, other powers at work, and that she had no control over any of them.

What was she going to become? All she could do was wait and see. Even then, she realized, she would probably be none the wiser, for she would have shed her old self and would have nothing left to compare the new one with. After all, she wondered, does a butterfly remember the caterpillar it used to be?

17

MARTHA

Martha found a pizza place to eat in that evening. Oddly enough, instead of giving her butterflies in her stomach, nervousness was making her hungry. Upstairs was a take-away, where busy white-jacketed cooks prepared orders, but downstairs was a tiny cellar restaurant with only four tables, each bearing a red-checked tablecloth and a candle burning inside a dark orange glass. Very Italian. Martha was the only person in the place. The white-washed stone walls arched over to form the curved ceiling, and the way the candles cast shadows over the ribbing and contours made the place look like a white cave or the inside of that whale Martha had imagined herself entering the first time she passed under the jawbone on West Cliff.

The menu offered little choice: pizza with tomato sauce, with mushrooms or with prawns. When the young waitress came, Martha settled for mushrooms.

'What's the wine?' she asked.

'We've got white or red.'

'Yes, but what kind is it?'

The waitress shrugged. 'Medium.'

'What does that mean? Is it dry or sweet?'

'Medium.'

Either she hadn't a clue, or she was clearly taking no chances on offending anyone. Martha sighed. 'All right, I'll have a glass of red.' She hoped it was dry, whatever the quality.

She lit a cigarette and settled to wait. It was chilly in the cellar, despite the warm evening outside, and she put her quilted jacket over her shoulders. She had used it as a headrest during her afternoon on the beach, and when she lifted it, a few trapped grains of sand fell on the tablecloth. She swept them onto the stone floor, wincing at their gritty feel against her fingertips.

She had read until the incoming tide had driven her away from the beach, then she had gone back to the guesthouse for a bath. She had got sweaty sitting in the sun all afternoon with her jeans on and her shirt buttoned up to the neck. After that, feeling restless and edgy, she had gone walking nowhere in particular for a couple of hours, until hunger had driven her in search of somewhere to eat.

While she waited for her pizza, she rummaged in her holdall for the smooth, hard paperweight for the umpteenth time that day. Yes, it was still there. She needed to touch it, her talisman, to bolster her resolve.

At last the waitress returned with a small, thin-crusted pizza and a glass of wine. It was dry: some kind of cheap and ordinary Chianti, but at least drinkable. The pizza was barely edible. The crust was like tough card-board, and about six slices of canned mushroom lay on top of a watery spread of tomato sauce – completely lacking in spicing or herbal ingredients – that dribbled over the edge when she cut into it. Still, it wasn't fish and chips; she had that, at least, to be grateful for.

She ate as much as she could manage, and soon found herself getting full. A young couple came in, looked around the cavern suspiciously, and took a corner table in the shadows. They held hands and made eyes at one another in the candlelight. Martha felt sick. She ordered a cappuccino, wondering how that would turn out, and lit another cigarette. She still had time to kill.

The cappuccino turned out to be half a cup of Nescafé with what tasted like condensed milk, all churned up by a steam machine and dusted with a few grains of chocolate. The lovers talked in whispers, occasionally laughing and stroking one another's bare arms on the tablecloth.

Martha could stand it no longer. She demanded the bill rather snappily as the waitress was dashing off with the couple's order. It was still a good ten minutes before it arrived. Not bothering to leave a tip, Martha took the slip of paper upstairs and paid a sullen young man, who actually did look Italian, at the till.

Outside, it was already getting dark; the narrow channels of water left in the harbour rocked and twisted the strings of red and yellow lights in their oily mirror. It was almost nine o'clock, and the tide was well on its way out.

The man called Jack had left the pub at a quarter to ten the previous evening. Though the whole scene had the appearance of a ritual to Martha, she couldn't be sure he would leave at exactly the same time again, or even if he'd be in the pub. For one thing, the darts game – part of the ritual – might last longer. What was even worse was that he might leave with his friend. Still, Martha planned simply to follow him, if she could, and find out where he lived. Even if he didn't leave alone, he was bound to go home eventually.

It was her intention to lean against the iron railing close to the pub, near the jawbone at the top of West Cliff, and wait for him to come out. She would take note of which way he walked and would follow. She had thought of going inside the Lucky Fisherman again, alone this time, but that would only draw attention to her. He might even talk to her and try to pick her up, then everybody would see them. That was too dangerous to be worth the risk.

If she got there for nine-thirty, she would probably be all right. He would hardly leave before then. More likely later than earlier. That left her time for a quick nip to calm her nerves. She went into the first pub she saw, a bustling tourist place, and ordered a double whisky. She drank it slowly so it wouldn't go straight to her head. The last thing she needed was to get drunk. But the cardboard pizza should be enough to soak up anything that came along in the next hour or so.

At quarter past nine, when she could wait no longer, she set off for the Lucky Fisherman. It was dark by then, and the town's usual illuminations were all on. It took her five minutes to reach her waiting place. Once there, she leaned forward on the railing and looked over first at St Mary's, basking in its sandy light directly opposite, then to her left, out to sea beyond the pincer-like piers, where all was dark. She could see the thin white line of waves breaking on the sand.

She looked at her watch. Nine-thirty-five. It seemed to be taking for ever. Time for a cigarette. No one but the occasional courting couple ambled by. They would pause for a moment, arm in arm, look out to sea by Captain Cook's statue, perhaps kiss, and then walk around the corner by the white hotels along North Terrace. A strong fishy smell drifted up from the harbour. Martha remembered it was Thursday evening. The fishing boats would be coming in tomorrow.

Nine-forty-six. He was late. Must be having trouble

getting that last double twenty or whatever it was he needed. She pictured him carrying his empty glass over to the bar and saying, 'Well, that's my limit for tonight. See you tomorrow, Bobby.' Yes, he *would* be there! He had actually said so, she remembered: 'See you *tomorrow*, Bobby.' And Bobby would say, 'Night, Jack,' as usual. Any moment he would be walking out of that door. Martha was hardly breathing; her chest felt tight with excitement and apprehension. She ground out the cigarette and glanced over at the pub.

At ten o'clock, it happened. The door rattled open and one man – *her* man – walked out in his dark jersey and baggy jeans. She stayed where she was, as if rooted to the spot, her hands frozen to the railing. She must try to look like a casual tourist, she told herself, just admiring the night-time view: St Mary's, the abbey ruin, the lights reflected in the harbour. A slight breeze ruffled her hair and brushed along her cheek like cold fingers.

He was walking in her direction, towards the Cook statue. She turned her head to watch him coming. How it happened, she wasn't sure. Perhaps it was just the sudden movement, or maybe the light from a street lamp had caught her face as she turned. But he saw her. She could have sworn that he smiled and his eyes glittered more than usual. He started walking towards her.

She felt pure terror, as if her very bone marrow had turned to ice. He walked up beside her and rested his hands on the railing too.

'Hello,' he said, in that familiar, hoarse voice. 'Lovely night, isn't it?'

Martha could hardly catch her breath. She was shaking so much that she had to clutch the railings tight to stay on her feet. But she had to go through with it. It was too late to back off now. She turned to face him.

'Hello,' she said, in a voice that she hoped wasn't trembling too much. 'Don't you remember me?'

18

KIRSTEN

The doctor insisted that Kirsten leave the hospital in a wheelchair, though by then she was quite capable of walking unaided. The demand was made even more ridiculous when she reached the top of the front steps and had to get up out of the chair and walk down them.

Her father's Mercedes was parked right outside. With Galen in front, carrying her things, and one parent on each side, Kirsten made her way towards it.

At the car, Galen – who, true to his word, had visited her almost every day that week – shook hands with her father, said goodbye to her mother, who inclined her head regally, and gave Kirsten a peck on the cheek. He had learned, she noticed, not to expect too much from her physically, though she still hadn't told him the full extent of her injuries.

'Are you sure I can't offer you a lift anywhere?' her father asked him.

'No, thank you,' Galen said. 'The station's not much of a walk, and it's out of your way. I'll be fine.'

'Back or front?' her father asked Kirsten.

'Back, please.'

In the spacious rear of the car she could stretch out, her head propped up against the window on a cushion, a blanket over her knees, and watch the world go by.

'Are you sure you want me to go ahead?' Galen asked her through the open window.

Kirsten nodded. 'Be sensible, Galen. There's no point missing the start of term. If you do that, you might as well not bother.'

'And I can't persuade you to come with me?'

'Not yet, no. I told you, don't worry about me. I'll be okay.'

'And you'll join me soon?'

'Yes.'

She had finally managed to convince him to go to Toronto, partly by insisting that she was fine and needed only rest, and partly by promising to join him as soon as she felt well enough. When he agreed, she wasn't sure if it was due to the logic of her arguments or because she had given him an easy way of getting off the hook. He had acted a little stranger each day – distant, embarrassed – and Kirsten had come to believe that perhaps there was something in what Sarah had hinted about men friends turning 'funny' when women became victims of sexual attacks. Also, Hugo and Damon had sent more flowers and messages through Sarah, but they hadn't visited again. Kirsten was beginning to feel rather like a pariah. In a way, it suited her, for at the moment what she wanted above all was to be left alone.

Galen stretched his arm through the window and patted Kirsten's hand. 'Take care,' he said. 'And remember, I want to see a full recovery soon.' Kirsten smiled at him and the car pulled away. She watched him waving as the Mercedes headed down the road, until it turned a corner and she could see him no longer.

Her father cleared his throat. 'I suppose you'd like to drop by the flat first and pick up a few things,' he suggested.

Kirsten didn't, in particular, want to set foot in her

tiny bedsit again, but neither did she want her parents to think she had lost all interest in life. Even if some of her deepest feelings were numb and her instincts were beyond her control, she could still make an effort to behave in the normal, accepted manner. They seemed dispirited enough as it was. Her mother had more or less accused her already of not trying hard enough to 'snap out of it', and her father had become more and more resigned and distant. If she showed no interest at all in her possessions, they would only worry more. So she said yes and offered directions. Appearances were important to her parents.

The car slid smoothly away from the gloomy Victorian hospital and towards the student area of town: rows of tall, old houses in which entire families and servants once used to live. Blackened by two hundred years of industry, and emptied by a succession of changes – the break up of the family unit, the Great War, the Depression, the inability of most people to afford servants – they had fallen into the hands of local businessmen, who transformed the once magnificent rooms, with their high ceilings and fixtures where the chandeliers used to hang, into small flats or bedsits – as many to a building as they could manage – and rented them to students.

Kirsten had an attic room in a cul-de-sac near the park. After spending her first year feeling miserable in a bright, noisy student residence, she had been happy there for the last two years. As the three of them got out of the sleek, silver-grey car, she noticed people along the street looking out through their curtains. It must be quite a spectacle, she supposed, finding a Mercedes parked in such a place, where the cobbles still stuck through the various attempts at tarmac.

Torn newspapers, chip wrappers, empty cigarette packets and cellophane paper littered the pavement and gutters; weeds and unmown grass consumed the garden. In the hallway, which looked as if it hadn't been swept for a month, neat piles of mail lay on a rickety old table.

The time-switch Kirsten pressed revealed a bare bulb on each landing and cobwebs in the high cornices. The walls were painted a colour somewhere between eggshell blue and institutional green – painted, that is to say, some years ago – and the high ceilings were puce – what Sarah called 'puke'. In the light of the unshaded sixty-watt bulbs, the place looked even worse than it was.

As they climbed the stairs, Kirsten was aware of her mother's stiff disapproval. On entry, she seemed to have held her breath and not let it out for fear of having to breathe in again.

Feeling foolish as she did so, Kirsten knocked on her own door. She still had a key, but the room was officially Sarah's now and she couldn't just barge in. She hoped Sarah didn't have a naked man in her bed.

The door opened. Kirsten noted with relief the empty room behind Sarah, who wasn't even wearing one of her calculatedly offensive T-shirts that day. Instead, she wore white trousers and a baggy blue sweatshirt with UCLA printed across the front.

'Kirstie, love!' she yelled. Her fine, porcelain features broke into a smile anyone would have expected to shatter them, and she flung her arms around Kirsten.

Kirsten returned the embrace, then broke away gently. She didn't react as badly as she had to Galen's touch, but she still felt herself drawing back inside, holding in.

'My mother and father.' She stood back and introduced her parents, who hovered in the doorway.

'Cup of tea?' Sarah asked.

'That'd be lovely.' Kirsten looked at her father, who nodded. Her mother shook her head slightly and looked at her watch. 'Not for me, thank you, dear. We really must set off soon if we're to be home this evening.' She directed the comment at her husband.

'Oh, we've time for a cup of tea,' he said, smiling at Sarah and sitting down in the scuffed red armchair with winged arms. It was Kirsten's favourite, the spot where she had sat to do her reading and make notes for essays.

The L-shaped room was just about large enough to hold four people: all it contained were the two matching armchairs in front of the gas fire, a three-quarter mattress on the floor beneath the window, a small clothes cupboard set in the wall, and a desk and bookshelves by the other wall. A portable stereo cassette player stood on one of the shelves beside a rack of tapes. Sarah was playing Bruce Springsteen singing 'Nebraska'. She turned down the volume before she went to put the kettle on in the kitchenette, which was tucked away in the short end of the L and separated from the rest of the room by a thin red curtain.

Kirsten sat on the mattress, which had always had to double as a sofa when she had guests. She gazed over at the poster on the wall above the pillows – a print of Van Gogh's *Sunflowers* – and remembered the first time she and Galen had made love on that very mattress the night after the English Department Christmas dance at the start of their second year. As she thought about it, and about all the other wonderful times they had slept there together, her loins ached with longing and loss. She could still see him standing by the roadside waving. Of course, she would never see him again. It was for his own good.

Her mother made a point of standing by the window with her arms tightly folded. Whether it was the sight of the park – the scene of the crime – at the end of the street that intrigued her, or whether she was just keeping an eye on the Merc, Kirsten didn't know. She could sense her mother's disapproval of the bedsit. Nose in the air, she seemed only a hair's breadth away from running her finger down the wall to see how much dirt came off. If she did that, Kirsten thought, she would run off screaming for the maids in two seconds flat.

Her parents had never visited the room – or even the city – before. The rough and ready atmosphere and basic living conditions must have been just as much of a shock to their tender southern sensibilities as they had been to hers at first. Over two years, though, she had had a chance to get used to it. At her age, too, she was more concerned about parties, books, films, plays and love than she was about living in a spotless mansion. Unlike her mother, Kirsten had never been particularly house-proud. Even her room at home had always been a mess. Surfaces hadn't mattered too much as long as she had been having fun. She washed the dishes regularly, dusted and went to the launderette once a week: that was it. Besides, these houses were so old and decrepit you couldn't do much with them even if you tried. They were only temporary: places to pass through, not to make nests in.

Sarah came back with the cracked teapot and three mugs. Kirsten's father accepted his sugarless tea graciously, and her mother continued to stand like a statue by the window. Her father made small talk with Sarah while Kirsten made a pretence of searching the room for the things she was supposed to want. She picked up the small pile of mail – mostly junk – from the desk and shoved a few clothes and a random selection of books into the old suitcase in the cupboard. Then she sat down to finish her tea, which had cooled by then.

'Is that all you want?' Sarah asked.

'For the moment. I've got plenty of stuff back home – clothes and that.'

'But the books . . . ?'

'Hang on to them for me, will you? I think I need a rest from literature.'

Sarah eyed the shelves, still more than three-quarters full. 'I suppose it's about time I read Shelley and Coleridge,' she said, smiling. 'Though I'd planned on a summer with Thomas Hardy and George Eliot. I don't know about the linguistics and phonetics stuff, though. You know I never could understand all that.'

Kirsten shrugged and took one book down for her. 'That's a good one. The prof who wrote it is supposed to be able to tell what village you come from just by your accent. They say he's usually accurate within ten miles or so. I never got as good as that, but . . .'

'Thanks,' said Sarah. 'I'll give it a try.'

They must all, Kirsten thought, be conscious of her mother looming over them, radiating waves of discomfort. Were the circumstances different, she might have gone into one of her 'Why did you have to leave a clean, decent home?' spiels. Even her father might have reminded her of how he had tried to persuade her to go to a university closer to home instead of moving so far away. But she'd had to fly the coop. She knew she wouldn't have been able to stand living at home while all the other students were free to live their own lives for the first time. How humiliating it would have been to have to run off back to Mummy and Daddy's in time for tea after the Milton lecture. And the further the better, she had thought, while offering convincing arguments about the quality of teaching and the reputations of professors.

'I think we really should go, dear,' her father said finally, looking for somewhere to put down his mug.

Kirsten got up, took it from him and carried it into the kitchen. She was ready, too. She'd had enough of this tension and pretence. If everyone was going to treat her as if she were made of glass for the rest of her life, then she wanted out. She began to get an inkling of what the physically handicapped must feel like: everyone acting so embarrassed, condescending and pitying, and trying so hard not to offend them or refer to their disability in any way. Sex and babies would now be unmentionable subjects back home, she realized, along with all the other dirty words. Taboo. 'Don't mention you-know-whats,' her mother would whisper to visitors at the door, 'or you'll upset poor Kirsten.' She was tired. All she wanted to do was crawl in the back of the car and be chauffeured home quickly and quietly.

Sarah came down the stairs with them and hugged Kirsten again on the doorstep. 'Don't worry,' she said, 'I'll take care of everything. Oh, I forgot, what about your tapes?'

'It's all right, Sarah, you hang on to them. I've got as much music as I want at home.' And it was true. She had a deluxe stereo in her spacious bedroom, the one her father had bought her for her eighteenth birthday. It was too bulky and expensive to cart all the way up to university, so she had made do with the portable system and kept the other at home to enjoy on holidays.

Sarah said she would write soon and come down to visit when she could, and with that they were off. Necks craned behind windows to watch them go. Perhaps, Kirsten thought, it's not so much the posh car as her new celebrity status: 'There's the girl that nearly got herself killed by that maniac,' they would be saying to themselves. How odd the words sounded in her mind: '*Got herself killed.*' As if what happened had been, somehow, her own fault.

Her mother was clearly relieved to be out of the room and back in the more congenial and appropriate environment of the Mercedes. The two of them had, her father told her, been staying in the big hotel near the station all the time she had been in hospital. Poorer or less powerful people, Kirsten knew, would have been able to spare neither the time off work nor afford the luxury. She had always taken her family's wealth and status for granted, as the young do, but now, for the first time, she was conscious of privilege: the private room in the hospital; the family home, a renovated Tudor mansion in Brierley Coombe, near Bath; and the comfortable Mercedes that glided down the M1 towards it.

Through a thin drizzle, she watched the dull South Yorkshire landscape of slag heaps and motionless pit wheels flash by, and soon they were passing turn-offs for Nottingham and Derby. Kirsten's father was a motorway driver as a rule; even if it meant more mileage, he would generally stick to the motorways and drive as fast as he could get away with. But this time, she realized, as he turned off the M1 near Northampton, before it swung south-east towards London, they were taking the scenic route. Perhaps he thought a good dose of the green and pleasant land would prove therapeutic. As if to prove the point, the rain slackened off and the sun burst through before they had even skirted the south Midlands.

Kirsten was comfortable in the back. The Mercedes seemed to float on air without making a sound, and after a few attempts at making conversation, her parents had fallen quiet, too. Her father switched on Radio Three and Kirsten relaxed to the Busoni piano music that was playing. They passed through Banbury and Chipping Norton and soon entered the Cotswolds. By then, it was indeed a perfect day in the English countryside: blue sky, one or two fleecy white clouds drifting over, rounded green hills and quaint villages. Sunlight warmed the weathered limestone cottages, with their flagged roofs and gardens full of roses.

They drove straight through Stow-on-the-Wold, which was jampacked with parked cars and tourists, and finally stopped for a pub lunch at a small sixteenth-century inn near Bourton-on-the-Water. Kirsten's mother seemed at ease there, back in her natural environment of gentility and well-polished brassware. Kirsten picked at a ploughman's lunch. After the intravenous drip and so long on hospital food, she seemed to have lost her appetite.

After lunch, they took a stroll around the town, walked along by the river, and then set off for the last leg of the journey.

Kirsten dozed uneasily as an interminable Mahler symphony played, disturbed even during the clear daylight hours by her dreams of the dark man and the light man cutting at her body, and then, on the long hill that wound down into Bath, she felt the first twinge of fire deep in her loins. She ignored it and looked on the familiar city, its light stone glinting in the sun below. But before they even reached Pulteney Road, the fiery, shooting pains between her legs had her almost doubled up, gritting her teeth in the back of the car.

19

MARTHA

'Remember you?' The man looked puzzled. Then he smiled and jerked his thumb back towards the pub. 'You were in the Fisherman last night with your boyfriend. I remember that.'

'He's not my boyfriend,' Martha said. 'Besides, he's moved on now.'

Martha didn't know whether to feel angry or glad that he didn't remember her. It was an insult, yes, but one that she could use to her advantage. She had stopped shaking now, and her blood was warming a little. All she had to do was keep reminding herself what he was, what he had done, and she would find the courage she needed from her anger and disgust. This was her destiny, after all, her mission; it was the reason she had survived what many had not.

She still found it difficult to look at him, but when she did she noticed, in the dim glow of a street light, that he was not as old as she had first thought: late twenties, perhaps, or early thirties at the most. For some reason, she had expected him to be older. He stood just an inch or so taller than she, with a shaggy thatch of dark hair and the kind of facial growth that looks like a perpetual five o'clock shadow. Just as on the previous evening, he was wearing a navy-blue Guernsey jersey and baggy dark pants made of some heavy material. He had a strong local accent. The voice was right, she was certain. And the face. She had to trust in faith and instinct now; logic alone could never be enough to lead visionaries to their Grails.

'On holiday?' he asked, leaning easily against the railing beside her.

'You could say that.' Martha looked straight ahead as she spoke. Over the water, St Mary's stood squat, as bright as polished sand, in its floodlight. The red and blue and amber lights twisted like oil slicks in the dark harbour below. Footsteps clicked behind her – a woman in high-heeled shoes – and further away, down in the town itself, a group of noisy kids came out of a pub shouting and whooping. Out to sea, something splashed in the water.

'It's just that most people who live here don't really notice its beauty,' the man went on. 'I mean, when it's all around you, the sea and all, you hardly bother to stand and gawp at it.'

'Am I so obvious?'

He laughed. 'I stand and look myself sometimes, especially way out where it's all dark and you just get a tiny speck of light moving across in the distance. I often wonder what it must be like out on the boats like that, in the dark.'

'You're not a fisherman?'

'Me? Good Lord, no! Whatever gave you that idea? I have a small boat and I go out sometimes, but just for myself, and always during the day.'

'I just . . . oh, never mind.'

'As a matter of fact I'm a joiner by trade. Do a lot of work for the theatre, too, in season – chief scenery fixer and bottle washer.'

Martha was confused. She had so much expected her

quarry to be a fisherman. Now she thought about it, though, she didn't know how she had got that idea fixed in her mind in the first place. Perhaps it was the smell, the fishy smell. But anyone who lived by the sea might pick that up easily enough. And he *did* say he went fishing from time to time. No, she told herself, she had to be right. No excuses. Instinct.

'Have you been doing it long?' she asked.

'What – the joinery or the theatre?'

Martha shrugged. 'Both, I suppose.'

'Since I left school. The only thing I was any good at was woodwork, and I've always been interested in the theatre. Not acting, just the practical stuff – the illusions it creates. And you?'

'Have you worked anywhere else, or are you here all the time?'

'I've travelled a fair bit. The provinces. There's not enough work to keep me here all the time, but it's where I live. Home, I suppose.'

'Born and brought up?'

'Aye. Born and bred in Whitby. You didn't answer my question.'

Martha felt a chill in the wind off the sea and put her jacket over her shoulders again. 'What question?'

'I asked about you.'

Martha laughed and pushed back a lock of hair that the breeze had displaced. 'Oh, I'm not very interesting, I'm afraid. I'm from Portsmouth, just a dull typist in a dull office.'

'You'll be used to the sea, then?'

'Pardon?'

'The sea. Portsmouth's a famous naval base, isn't it?'

'Oh yes, the sea. The most I've had to do with it is a

hovercraft trip to the Isle of Wight. And even that made me feel sick.'

He laughed. 'Look, would you like to go for a drink somewhere. I hope you don't think me forward or anything, but . . .'

'Not at all, no.' Martha thought quickly. She couldn't go to a pub with him, that was for certain. So far her only link with him was the lounge of the Lucky Fisherman, and she didn't imagine anyone but Keith had noticed their fleeting eye contact the previous evening. But to go about publicly would be courting disaster.

'Well?'

'I don't really fancy a drink. It's far too lovely an evening to spend sitting in a noisy, smoky bar. Why don't we just walk?'

'Fine with me. Where?'

Martha wanted to avoid the town, where the pubs would soon be disgorging groups of drink-jolly tourists and locals who might just remember seeing the two of them together. If they stuck to quieter, dimly lit streets, nobody would notice them. And she had to get him alone somewhere, somewhere private. No doubt he would have the same thing in mind. He was certainly a cool one. No matter what he pretended, though, she was certain that he must remember her. How could he forget? And how could she forget what he was? She thought of the beach and the caves.

'Let's wander down towards the pier,' she said, 'and take it from there.'

'Okay. By the way, I'm Jack, Jack Grimley.' He stuck out his hand.

'Martha. Martha Browne.' She shook the hand; it

was rough with callouses – from sawing and planing planks of wood, no doubt – and touching it made her shudder.

'Pleased to meet you, Martha.'

They took the steps and cut across Khyber Pass down to Pier Road. It was after ten-thirty now, and all the amusement arcades had closed for the night Only a few pairs of young lovers strolled by the auction sheds, and they were all absorbed in one another.

They walked out on the pier and sniffed the sea air. Martha lit a cigarette and wrapped her jacket a little tighter around her throat against the chill out there. Jack hadn't tried to touch her or make any kind of a pass so far, but she knew it was bound to happen soon. For now, he seemed content to stand quietly as she smoked, watching the distant lights out in the dark sea. She wondered when he would pounce. The pier was too open. It was dark all around them, but the whole thing stood out rather like a long stone stage in the water. It was the kind of place where he might make his first move, though – a fleeting caress or a comforting arm around the shoulders to lull her into a false sense of security.

'Fancy the beach?' she asked, dropping her cigarette onto the pier and stepping on it. 'I like to listen to the waves.'

'Why not?'

He walked beside her back towards Pier Road and down the stone steps to the deserted beach. A thin line of foam broke along the sands, and after that came the sucking, hissing sound of the sea drawing back. The moon, now almost three-quarters full, stood high and shed its sickly light on the water. It seemed to float there like an incandescent jellyfish just below the water's surface.

They walked close to the rock face, where the sand was drier. It was pitch dark down there, apart from the moon. They were hidden from the town by the slightly concave curve of the cliffs.

At last, Jack took hold of her arm gently. This is it, she thought, tensing. She tried to act normally and not freeze as she usually did when a man tried to touch her. She had to distract him for a moment.

'Are you sure you don't remember?' she asked, dipping her free hand into her bag.

'Remember what?'

'Me.' It still seemed the ultimate insult that he pretended not to remember her after all that had happened.

'I looked a bit different,' she said, her hand closing on the paperweight. Warmth and certainty flooded her senses.

He laughed. 'Martha, I'm sure I'd remember if I'd seen you bef—'

'Martha wasn't my name then.'

It wasn't at all as she'd imagined, the way she had made it happen so many times in her mind's eye. He was supposed to just fall down neatly and that was that. But he didn't. When the heavy paperweight smacked into his temple and made a dull crack, he only dropped to his knees, groaned and put his hand up to the wound in disbelief. Blood bubbled between his fingers and glistened in the moonlight. Then he turned and stared at her, his glittering eyes wide open.

For a moment, Martha froze. She just stood there, hesitating, sure that she couldn't go on. She had been through this situation so many times, both in her waking mind and in her dreams, but it wasn't happening the way it was supposed to. Then, out of fear and outrage, she hit out again and heard an even louder crack. This time he pitched forward into the sand. But he wouldn't lay still. His body jerked and convulsed in spasms like a marionette out of control; his stubby fingers clawed at the sand. Martha stood and watched, horrified, as the prone figure danced on the sand. His arms twitched and his whole body seemed to shudder as if it was about to explode and shatter. Then, all of a sudden, it stopped and he lay still at last. The blood around his head looked viscous in the faint white light.

Martha bent forward and put her hands on her knees. She took a few deep breaths and tried to slow her racing heartbeat. She had almost blown it. Reality never happened the way she thought it would. She had left so much of the business to her instinct and imagination that she should have known to allow for things not going exactly as planned. At least it was done now, and he lay at her feet, even if the deed itself had been more horrible and frightening than she had expected. But it wasn't over yet. She couldn't just leave him out here on the beach, and she couldn't stay in the open herself any longer. Glancing around nervously, Martha steeled herself and set to work.

Gasping for breath, she struggled with the heavy body and slowly dragged it into the mouth of the nearest cave. The opening was a rough arch about six feet high, but it narrowed quickly the further in it went. In all, it only extended about fifteen feet into the cliff, curving as it went and ending almost in a point, but that was enough for Martha's purposes. The dark walls glistened with slime, as if the very rock itself were sweating in anticipation.

As soon as she had hauled the body inside the opening, Martha paused and listened. It was after eleven now. The pubs would have closed and some people might fancy a drunken walk on the beach. Moments later, someone giggled by the pier, and then she could hear voices coming closer. Quickly, she braced herself and heaved the body by its ankles back into the cave as far as it would go, just beyond the slight bend in the middle. She almost screamed when she snagged a broken nail on one of his woollen socks and couldn't free it without a struggle.

Finally, she got him as deep in the cave as she could. The effort exhausted her – sweat beaded on her forehead – but at least she was safe now. The slanting moonlight only illuminated the first four or five feet of the interior, and beyond that it was cut off by the top of the arched entrance. Nobody could see them so far back, behind small boulders set in the sand past the kink in the wall.

Cautiously, Martha peered from behind a boulder and saw a young couple framed in the cave's opening. She held her breath. They were about thirty yards away, down by the breaking waves. Even at that distance she could catch fragments of their conversation.

'. . . late. Let's go . . .'

'. . . a minute . . . peaceful . . . give me . . .'

'No! . . . cold . . . Come on!'

Then there was more laughter, and the boy started chasing the girl back towards the steps.

Martha breathed out. It was quiet again. Just to make sure that no other revellers were going to come and spoil her work, she waited, hardly breathing, for about fifteen minutes. When nothing else had happened by then, she pulled the body forward into the patch of moonlight near the cave's entrance to make sure he was dead.

Grimley's body crunched over the dead and dried-out shellfish that gleamed like tiny bones in the moonlight. Strands of dry seaweed crackled under Martha's feet, and the smell of sea-wrack, salt and rotten fish was strong in her nostrils. A small, dark shape scuttled over the sand back in the shadows. She shuddered. Outside there was only the even, quiet rhythm of waves breaking and retreating.

First, Martha washed the paperweight in a small rock pool, dried it off on her shirt and put it back in her bag. She checked her hands and clothing, but could see no blood. She would have to look more closely later, when she got back to her room.

Lastly, she forced herself to look at the body. Blood veiled one side of his face, where his eye bulged from its socket and seemed to stare right at her. His left temple was shattered. In horror, Martha put a finger to it and felt the bone fragments shift under her touch like broken eggshell. The second blow had caught the top of his skull, and she could trace the deep indentation. Again, the bones had splintered, and this time her finger touched something squelchy and matted with hair. She shivered and a cry caught in her throat as she began to heave. Kneeling beside him, she vomited on the sand until she thought she would never stop.

The ancient, rotten sea smell stuck in her nostrils, and the blood and brain matter were smeared all over her fingers. When she could catch her breath again, she washed her hands in the rock pool and knelt there gasping until she had controlled her heartbeat. She couldn't bear being close to the body any longer. Crawling to the mouth of the cave, she listened for a few moments. It was all quiet on the beach, except for the crash and hiss of the waves. Martha slipped out of the cave like a ghost in the moonlight and set off back to the guesthouse.

20

KIRSTEN

'You'll have to expect a bit of pain now and then,' said Dr Craven, writing on her prescription pad with a black felt-tip pen. 'Traumatic injuries often cause extreme pain. But don't worry, it won't last forever. I'll prescribe some analgesic. It should help.' She sat back and handed the slip of paper to Kirsten.

Behind the doctor, a brusque woman in her early forties, with severely cropped grey hair, steady blue eyes and a beak of a nose, Kirsten could see the small Norman church and the village green, with its two superb copper beeches, rose beds, little white fence and benches where the old people sat and gossiped. She could even hear the finches and tits twittering beyond the open window. Brierley Coombe. Home.

The previous evening she had managed to keep the pain from her parents. She had simply claimed tiredness after the journey, then taken four aspirins and a long, hot bath before going to bed. The pain receded, and she had actually slept well for the first time since the attack.

Dr Craven leaned forward and tapped a blue folder. The stethoscope around her neck swung forward and clipped the edge of the desk. 'I've got all your details, Kirsten,' she said, 'and I've been on the telephone to Dr Masterson at the hospital. If anything at all bothers you, please don't hesitate to come and see me. And I'd like you to drop by once a week anyway, just to see how you're doing. All right?'

Kirsten nodded. Dr Masterson? She hadn't even known his name, the man who had probably saved her life. One of her benefactors, anyway. She didn't know the name of the person who had so fortunately been walking his dog on the night of her attack either. But Dr Masterson? She remembered his dark complexion and his deeply lined brow, how he always looked cross but acted shyly and kind. She had even invented stories about him to pass the time. His father must have been an army officer serving in India, she had decided – a captain in the medical corps, most likely – and he had married a high-caste Indian woman. After independence, they had come to England . . .

The ease with which she could make up stories about people on so little evidence always surprised her. It was a skill, or a curse, that she had had since early childhood, when she had filled notebooks with stick drawings and family histories of invented characters. If she could make up lives for others, she thought, then she could probably do the same for herself. That would certainly be preferable to telling the truth to everyone she met. Already, on her way to the doctor's surgery that morning, she had noticed neighbours – people who had known her since childhood – giving her those pitying looks. What was worse was that one of them – Carrie Linton, a stuck-up busybody she'd never liked – had given her a different kind of look: more accusing than pitying.

'Kirsten?'

'What? Oh, sorry, Doctor. I was daydreaming.'

'I said make sure you eat well and get plenty of rest.

The healing process is doing very nicely, or Dr Masterson wouldn't have approved your coming home, but you're still convalescent, and don't forget it.'

'Of course.'

'And if you have any difficulty at all in adjusting to your condition, I can recommend a very good doctor in Bath, a specialist.'

Adjusting? Condition? Good Lord, thought Kirsten, she makes it sound as if I'm pregnant or something.

'I mean psychologically and emotionally,' Dr Craven went on, her eyes fixing on the diagram of the human circulatory system on the wall. 'It might not be an easy road, you know.'

'A psychiatrist?'

Dr Craven tapped her pen on the desk. 'Only if you feel the need. They can help, you know. There's no stigma attached these days, especially . . .'

She's embarrassed, Kirsten thought. Just like all the rest. They don't know what to do with me. 'In cases such as mine?' she offered, finishing the sentence.

'Well, yes.' Dr Craven seemed to miss the irony in Kirsten's voice. The corners of her lips twitched in one of her rare, brief smiles. 'You are rather unique, you know. Few women, if any, have ever survived an attack from such a maniac.'

'I suppose not,' Kirsten said slowly. 'I hadn't really thought of it that way. Like Jack the Ripper, you mean? Did anyone survive him?'

'I'm afraid I don't know. Criminology isn't my forte.' She leaned forward. 'What I'm saying, Kirsten, is that there may be some resultant emotional trauma. I want you to know that help is available. You only have to ask for it.'

'Thank you.'

The doctor sat back in her chair and peered at Kirsten over the top of her half-moon glasses. 'How *do* you feel?' she asked.

'Feel? Not so bad. The pain's eased a little now.'

'No, I mean emotionally. What do you feel?'

'What do I feel? I don't know really. Just blank, numb. I can't remember anything about the attack.'

'Do you keep running over events in your mind?'

'Yes, but I still can't remember. It keeps me awake sometimes. I can't concentrate for it. I can't even sit down and read a book. I used to love reading.'

'The amnesia may only be temporary.'

'I don't know if I *want* to remember.'

'That's understandable, of course. As are all your feelings. You've suffered a tremendous shock, Kirsten. Not just to your body but to your whole being. All your symptoms – emotional numbness, bad dreams, inability to concentrate – they're all perfectly normal given the circumstances. Awful, but normal. In fact, I'd be worried if you *didn't* feel like that. You feel no anger, no rage?'

'No. Should I?'

'It'll come later.'

'I suppose I do feel that I'd like to kill him, the man who did this to me, but it's more of a cold feeling than an angry one, if you can understand what I mean.' She shrugged. 'Still, I don't imagine I'll get the chance, will I? I wouldn't know him from Adam.'

'No. But let's hope the police find him soon.'

'Before he can attack anyone else?'

'Such people don't usually stop at one. And the next victim might not be so lucky.' Dr Craven stood up and held out her hand. 'Don't forget what I said. Take good care of yourself, and I'll see you next week.' Kirsten shook her hand and left.

Outside, the sun was shining in a clear blue sky. The rounded hills that fringed the village seemed to glow bright green with some kind of inner light, as if they formed the backdrop to a painter's vision. Kirsten put her hands in her pockets and ambled along the High Street. Not much there, really: a pub, the village hall (an 1852 construction, the newest building in Brierley Coombe), the shops (converted cottages, most of them) – post office, grocer's, butcher's, chemist's, newsagent's.

The village stood on the edge of the Mendips, between Bath and Wells, and it had its share of thatched roofs and award-winning gardens. Orderly riots of roses, petunias, periwinkles, hollyhocks and nasturtiums assaulted Kirsten's senses as she walked by the trim fences. The place always reminded her of those picture-postcard villages in English murder mysteries – Miss Marple's St Mary Mead, for example – where everyone knew his or her place and nothing ever changed. But no one ever got murdered in Brierley Coombe.

Kirsten took the prescription from her pocket and walked into the chemist's. It was only a small place, more decorative than functional, and one of the few chemist's shops that still kept those huge red, green and blue bottles on a shelf high in the window. The sunlight filtered through them onto Mr Hayes's wrinkled face. He had a good dispensary, Kirsten knew, especially for female ailments.

'Hello, Kirsten,' he said with a smile. 'I noticed you'd come back. Sorry to hear about your trouble.'

'Thank you,' Kirsten said. She hoped he wasn't going to go on and tell her how you couldn't be too careful these days, could you. He was that kind of man. But perhaps something in her voice or expression put him off his stroke. Anyway, he just looked puzzled and went to fill the prescription immediately.

With the painkillers in her pocket, Kirsten headed for the house. Brierley Coombe had been her home ever since the family had moved from Bath itself when she was six. Although the village was equidistant from Bristol and Bath, they had always frequented the latter for shopping and entertainment. Her mother regarded Bristol – big city, once-busy port – as too vulgar, and Kirsten had consequently only been there twice in her life. It hadn't seemed so bad to her, but then neither had the north of England.

Kirsten had no friends left in Brierley Coombe, and the way she felt now, that was a blessing; the last thing she wanted was to have to go around explaining herself to people. Indeed, she had to think hard to remember ever having friends or even seeing any young people there at all. That was another way in which it resembled an Agatha Christie village – there were no children, nor could she remember any. It was absurd, she knew, as she had been a child there herself and played with others then, but there was no village school, and, try as she might, she couldn't bring to mind the voices of children playing on the green. Over the years, they had all drifted apart. They went to prep schools first, of course, then on to public schools as boarders, as she had done, for there were no poor people in Brierley Coombe. After that, it was university – usually Oxford or Cambridge – and a profession in the City. Perhaps when they had inherited their parents' houses and made their fortunes or retired from public office, they would come home to spend their remaining days tending the garden and playing bridge.

The peace and quiet that Kirsten had enjoyed at home during the long summer and Easter holidays had always suited her after the hectic social life up at university. She was a bright and studious girl and managed to get plenty of work done – but she was easily distracted by a good film, a party or the chance of a couple of drinks and a chat with friends. At home, she had usually been able to catch up with her work and read ahead for the next term.

But what would she do with her time now? Her student days were over; her life was utterly changed, if not ruined entirely. She didn't know if she would be able to pick up the pieces, let alone put them back together again. Come to that, she didn't know if there were any pieces left. Perhaps she didn't even care.

She was still thinking about it when she opened the gate and walked down the broad path to the house – more of a mansion than a cottage. Her mother was in the garden doing something nasty to the honeysuckle with her secateurs. Gardening and bridge, they were the strict borders of her mother's existence.

When she saw Kirsten coming, she wiped her brow and put down the clippers, which flashed in the light, and shielded her eyes from the sun as she looked up at her daughter. A difficult smile slowly forced the corners of her lips up, but it didn't reach her eyes. It was going to be a long haul, this recovery, Kirsten thought with a sudden chill of fear. It wasn't going to be easy at all.

21

MARTHA

The seagulls were grotesquely distorted, no longer sleek, white bullet-faced birds. Their feathers were mottled with ash-grey, and their bodies were bloated almost beyond recognition. They could hardly stand. Their wiry legs, above webbed feet as yellow as egg yolk, couldn't support their distended bellies, which were stretched so tight that a pattern of blue veins bossed through the grey and white markings. Their wings creaked and flapped like old, moth-eaten awnings in a storm as they tried to fly.

But mostly it was their faces that were different. They still had seagull eyes – cold, dark holes that knew nothing of mercy or pity – but their beaks were encased in long, gelatinous snouts smeared with blood.

They still sounded like seagulls. Even though they could no longer fly, they waddled on the dark sands and keened like the ghosts of a million tortured souls.

Martha woke sweating in the early dawn. Outside, the gulls were screeching, circling. They must have been at it for a while, she thought as her heartbeat slowed. She must have heard them in her sleep, and her mind had translated the sound into the pictograph of a dream. It was like dreaming of searching for a toilet when you've had a bit too much to drink and your body is trying to wake you up before your bladder bursts.

Just the thought of moisture made Martha thirsty. She

got up and drank a glass of water, then crawled into bed again, the sour taste of vomit still in her mouth. Unable to get back to sleep immediately, she found herself thinking of the gulls as her allies. She could imagine them with their sharp hooked beaks picking and pulling at the body in the cave, snatching an eyeball loose or making an ear bleed. Did they never stop? For them, life seemed nothing more than a long-drawn-out feast: one for which you had to go out and catch your own food and tear it to pieces while it was still alive. Had she become like them?

Martha glanced at her watch: 6.29. That day, she remembered, high tide was chalked in as 0658, so the gulls couldn't have found the body unless it was floating on the water's surface. Already the cold North Sea would have stuck its tongue into the cave and slurped Jack Grimley's corpse into its surging maw.

Shivering with horror at what she had done, Martha turned on her side, pulled the covers up to her chin, and drifted back into an uneasy sleep with the paperweight in her hand and the harsh music of squabbling gulls echoing in her ears.

22

KIRSTEN

They came back again that night, the dreams of slashing and slicing, to invade Kirsten's childhood room. The white knight and the black knight, as she had come to call them, both without faces. This time, they seemed to be trying to teach her something. The black knight handed her a long ivory-handled knife, and she plunged it herself into the soft flesh of her thigh. It sank as if into wax. A little blood bubbled up around the edges of the cut, but nothing much. Slowly, she eased out the blade and watched the edges of torn skin draw together again like lips closing. A pinkish bubble swelled and burst. And all the time she didn't feel a thing. Not a thing. Somehow, she knew the faceless white knight was smiling down at her.

23

MARTHA

The dead fish stared up at Martha with glazed, oily eyes. Pinkish-red blood stained their gills and mouths, and sunlight glinted on their silvery scales and pale bellies. The fishy smell was strong in the air, overpowering even the sea's fresh ozone. Holidaymakers paused as they walked along St Ann's Staith and took photographs of the fish sales. The people involved, no doubt used to being camera-fodder for tourists, didn't even spare them a glance.

The auction sheds that Friday morning were hives of activity. Earlier, while Martha had still been sleeping, the boats had come in, and the fishermen had unpacked their catches into iced boxes ready for the sales. Crab pots were stacked and nets lay spread by the sheds. As Martha watched, a man hosed fish scales from the stone quay. Gulls gathered in a raucous cloud, and occasionally one swooped down after a dropped fish.

Of course, Martha realized, they only *sold* the fish here; they didn't clean them and gut them. That must be done elsewhere – in canning factories, perhaps, where the loaded lorries were headed. How little she really knew about the business.

It didn't matter now, though, did it? Odd that he had turned out not to be a fisherman, after all. But you can't be right about everything. Even so, as she walked by and watched the sales, she scanned the groups of fishermen by the railings and the auctioneers and buyers in the open sheds. It was what she had planned to do, and she was doing it anyway, even though there was no longer any point.

Martha felt strangely dazed and light-headed as she walked down the staith towards the bridge. She hadn't slept well after the gulls had woken her, and the thought of what she had done haunted her. At breakfast time she'd been very hungry and had even eaten the fried bread she usually left.

The old couple at the window table were still there, he grinning and even, now, winking, while his wife glared with her beady eyes. But all the others were gone, or had changed into someone else. Martha was finding it hard to keep track. The guests were all starting to look the same: serious young honeymooners; tired but optimistic couples with mischievous toddlers; old people with grey hair and morning coughs. She felt the same way she had on the only occasion she had tried marijuana. She could see more, sense more, each line on the face, the flecks of colour in the eyes, but ultimately it all added up to the same. The more individual the people became to her, the more they became alike.

She crossed the bridge, bought a newspaper, and turned up Church Street. It was becoming a routine. Still, this morning she needed waking up even more than usual: there were important decisions to be made. In the Monk's Haven, she sipped strong black coffee and smoked a cigarette while she flexed her brain on the crossword. Then she flipped through the headlines to see if there was anything interesting going on in the world. There wasn't.

Only for a short while, when she had finished with the paper and still had some coffee and cigarette left, did she allow herself to think of the previous evening. It had been awful, a million times worse than anything she had imagined. She could still feel the loose fragments of bone shifting under her fingers, and that soft, pulpy mass, like a wet sponge, at the top of his head. She didn't feel sorry – he had deserved everything he got – but she was appalled and amazed at herself for really going through with it. After leaving the body in the cave, she had run down to the sea and rinsed her hands and her paper-weight again before going back to the guesthouse. She hadn't seen a soul on the way. The door opened smooth-ly on its oiled hinges and the carpet muffled her ascent to her room. Once safe, she had brushed her teeth three times, but still hadn't been able to get rid of the bitter taste of vomit. Even now, after the breakfast, coffee and cigarettes, she felt herself gagging as she recalled Grimley's body jerking on the sand and those long minutes in the dank, stinking cave: the blood, the staring eye.

The tide would have carried the body out to sea by now. She wanted it to be found soon, wanted to be there to enjoy all the fuss. It wasn't because she was conceit-ed or proud or anything, but because the discovery was all part of the same event. To go now would be like leaving a book unfinished. And Martha *always* finished the books she started, even if she didn't like them. Surely, when they found out the dead man's identity, they would go to his home and find something to con-nect him with the atrocities he had committed? A man like that can't avoid leaving some kind of evidence behind. And Martha wanted to be around when the full story hit the newspapers. Even if there was a little risk involved, she wanted to stay to hear the gossip and whispers in the pubs and along the staith – to *know* that she was the one who had rid the world of such a monster.

She knew nothing of the tides and currents, but hoped the body would wash up soon somewhere nearby. It would be too much to expect it to land back on Whitby Sands, but it might drift only a short way up the coast to Redcar, Saltburn, Runswick Bay or Staithes, or even further down to Robin Hood's Bay, Scarborough, Flamborough Head or Bridlington. Wherever it turned up, she hoped it wouldn't take long.

She finished her coffee and stubbed out her cigarette. It was eleven o'clock already. Now that she had fulfilled the main part of her purpose here, time was beginning to hang heavy; all she could do was wait, a much more passive activity than searching and planning.

To kill time until lunch, she found herself again mounting the 199 steps to St Mary's and the abbey ruins. There were even more people about this time: children racing one another to the top, counting out loud as they did so – 'Eighty-four, eighty-five, eighty-six . . .' – old folk in elastic stockings, wheezing as they went, dogs with their tongues hanging out running back and forth as if they didn't know up from down.

Martha climbed steadily, counting under her breath. Again, it came to 199, though legend said it was hard to get the same figure twice. At the top stood Caedmon's Cross, a thin twenty-foot upright length of stone, taper-ing towards the top, where a small cross was mounted.

The length of it was carved with medieval figures – David, Hilda and Caedmon himself – like some sort of stone totem pole, and at the bottom was the inscription, 'To the glory of God and in memory of Caedmon the father of English sacred song fell asleep hard by 680.' Martha knew it wasn't that old, though; it had been carved and erected in 1898, not in the real Caedmon's time. But it still had power. She particularly loved the understated simplicity of 'fell asleep hard by'. When she had to die, that was the way she would like to go. Again, she thought of Jack Grimley and shivered as if someone had just walked across her grave.

Getting her breath back after the long climb – it came less easily since she had started smoking – she paused in the graveyard and looked at the town spread out beyond and below the cross. She could easily pick out the dark, monolithic tower of St Hilda's at the top of her street, and the stately row of white four-storey hotels at the cliff-side end of East Terrace. She could see the whale's jawbone, too, that entry to another world. The rough, sandy gravestones, with their burnt-looking knobbly tops, stood in the foreground; the trick of perspective made them look even bigger than the houses over the harbour.

Martha turned and wandered into the church again. A recorded lecture was in progress in the vestry. It sounded tinny from constant playing. She found herself drifting almost unconsciously towards the front of the church, where, below the tall, ornate pulpit she slipped into a box marked FOR STRANGERS ONLY. It was the same one she'd been in before, and again she felt that sense of luxurious isolation and well-being. Even the sounds of the tourists in the church, with their whispered comments and clicking cameras, were barely audible now. In the hush, she ran her fingertips over the green baize and knelt on a red patterned cushion. There, cut off from the rest of the world, she offered up a prayer of a kind.

24

KIRSTEN

Kirsten lay in bed late the next morning. Outside her window the birds sang and twittered in the trees and the village went about its business. Not that there was much of that. Occasionally, she could hear the whirr of bicycle wheels passing by, and once in a while the thrum of a delivery van's engine.

She put the empty coffee cup back on the tray – break-fast in bed, her mother's idea – and went to open the curtains. Sunlight burst through, catching the cloud of dust motes that swirled in the air. It's all dead skin, Kirsten thought, wondering where on earth she'd heard that. Probably one of those educational television pro-grammes, science for the masses. She opened the window and warm air rushed to greet her, carrying the heavy scent of honeysuckle. A fat bee droned around the open-ing, then seemed to decide there was nothing for him in there and meandered down to the garden instead.

Kirsten's room reflected just about every stage of her transition from child to worldly student of language and literature. Even her teddy bear sat on the dressing table, propped against the wall. Stretching, she wandered around touching things, her feet sinking deep into the wall-to-wall carpet. The walls and ceiling were painted a kind of sea-green, or was it blue? It really depended on the light, Kirsten decided. Those greeny-blue colours often looked much the same to her: turquoise, cerulean, azure, ultramarine. But today, with the light shimmering on it as on ripples in the ocean, it was definitely the colour of the Mediterranean she remembered from family visits to the Riviera. The walls seemed to swirl and eddy like the water in a Hockney swimming-pool painting. When Kirsten stood in the middle of the room, she felt as if she were floating in a cave of water, or frozen at its centre like a flower in a glass paperweight.

It was two rooms, really. The bed itself, with a three-quarter-size mattress far too soft for Kirsten's taste, was set in a little recess up a stair from the large main room, just below the small window. Also tucked away in there were the dresser and wall cupboards for her clothes. Down the step was the spacious study-cum-sitting room. Her desk stood at a right angle to the picture window, so that she could simply turn her head and look out at the round, green Mendips as she worked. There, she had written essays during her summer vacations and made notes as she read ahead for the following term.

Above the desk, her father had fixed a few book-shelves to the wall on brackets. Apart from some old childhood favourites, like *Black Beauty*, *The Secret Garden*, *Grimm's Fairy Tales* and a few Enid Blytons – *Famous Five*, *Secret Seven* – most of the books were to do with her university courses. They were either for subjects she had studied over the past three years, brought home to save space in her bedsit, or books she had bought second-hand, usually in Bath, for courses she had intended to take in the future. Like the ones on medieval history and literature – including Bede's *An Ecclesiastical History of the English Nation*, Julian of Norwich's *Revelations of Divine Love*, and the anonymous *The Cloud of Unknowing*. But Kirsten had never taken that course. Instead, she had chosen at the last moment special tutorials on Coleridge with a visiting world expert in the field, an American academic who had turned out to be a crashing bore far more interested in trying to look up the front-row women's skirts than in the wisdom of *Biographia Literaria*.

By the side of the shelves was a corkboard, still spiked with old postcards from friends visiting Kenya, Nepal or Finland, photos of her with Sarah and Galen, and poems she had clipped from the TLS. There were no posters of pop stars in the room. She had taken them all down last year, thinking herself far too mature for such things. The only work of art that enhanced her wall was a superb Monet print, which looked wonderfully alive in the sunlight that rippled over it.

She also had an armchair with a footrest, for reading in, and the expensive stereo system. Her records were mostly a mixture of popular classics – Beethoven's Ninth, Tchaikovsky's *Pathétique* (which she had bought after seeing Ken Russell's *The Music Lovers* at the University Film Society) and the soundtrack of *Amadeus* – and a few dated pop albums: Rolling Stones, Wham, U2, David Bowie, Kate Bush, Tom Waits. She wasn't interested in any of these now, and had a hard time choosing the music she wanted to listen to. Finally, she settled for the *Pathétique*, and dressed as the music swelled and surged from its slow and quiet beginning.

But she couldn't stand it. As soon as the lush romantic theme came in, she snatched the needle from the turntable, scratching the record's surface as she did so. The burning pain in her loins had receded, but she had a headache that made music difficult to bear. She was sure it was caused by that dark mass lodged in her mind.

If she closed her eyes, she could even see it, a globe blacker than the rest of the darkness behind her eyes: a black hole, perhaps, that sucked everything in and turned it inside out; or the beginning of an emotional or spiritual cancer about to spread through her whole being.

Kirsten sat down cross-legged on the carpet, holding her head in her hands. With the music gone, she could hear the birds again. Someone called a greeting out in the lane. She could even hear her mother pottering around downstairs.

It was after ten o'clock and such a beautiful day outside that she felt she ought to go for a walk. Any other day, she would have been up before breakfast and down to the woods at the back of the house for a leisurely stroll under the light-dappled leaves. Not today, though. After ten and she still had no idea what to do with herself.

She tried to look ahead into the future, but it was all darkness. Before that night in the park, she had never really given it a thought. Somehow, she had always believed, the future would take care of itself and would be just as privileged, as bright and exciting as the past. But now she had no idea what to do with her life. Whenever she thought of such things her head began to ache even more, as if the bubble were growing inside it and pushing at the inside of her skull. She couldn't concentrate well enough to read a book. She couldn't bear to listen to music. What the hell was she supposed to do? She put her fists to her temples and tensed up. The headache was pounding inside her. She wanted to scream. She wanted to crack open her skull and claw her brain out with her fingernails.

But the rage and the pain ebbed away. Slowly, she got to her feet and walked up the step to the bedroom. There, she took her clothes off again, dry-swallowed three prescription analgesics and crawled back into bed.

25

MARTHA

Saturday brought Martha two important pieces of news: one that she had been expecting, and another that changed everything.

The day started as usual with a wink from the old man and a glare from his wife at breakfast. Martha wasn't very hungry, so she skipped the cereal and just picked at her bacon and eggs. She was wondering whether to move out that day and find somewhere else in another part of the town. It seemed a good idea. People were getting far too used to her here, and there might come a time when awkward questions would be asked.

After breakfast, she went back up to her room and packed her gear in the holdall. She had one last smoke there, leaning on the window sill and looking left and right, from the close and overbearing St Hilda's to the distant St Mary's. It was the first overcast day in the entire week. A chill wind had blown in off the North Sea, bringing the scent of rain with it. Already a light drizzle was falling, like a thin mist enveloping the town. Visibility was poor, and St Mary's looked like the blurred grey ghost of a church on top of its hill.

After checking the room once more to make sure she had forgotten nothing, Martha padded downstairs and found the proprietor helping his wife carry the dirty dishes through to the kitchen.

'I'd like to settle up now, if that's all right,' she said.

'Fine.' He wiped his hands on the grubby white apron he was wearing. 'I'll make out the bill.'

Martha waited in the hallway. The usual flyers about Whitby's scenic attractions, restaurants and entertainments lay on the polished wood table by the registration book. On the wall above was a mirror. Martha examined herself. What she had done hadn't changed her appearance. She looked no different from when she had arrived: same too-thin lips, tilted nose and almond eyes, the same untidy cap of light brown hair. All she needed was pointed ears, she thought, and she might be able to pass for a Vulcan.

'Here you are.' The man eyed her with amusement as he handed over the bill. Martha checked the total and pulled the correct amount from her purse.

'Cash?' He seemed surprised.

'That's right.' She didn't want to use cheques or credit cards; they could be too easily traced. She had cashed her father's cheque and emptied her bank account before she set off for Whitby, so she had quite a bit of money – not all of it so obviously bulging out of her purse, but hidden away in the holdall's 'secret' pockets.

'I suppose you'll need a receipt?'

For a second she was puzzled. Why would she want a receipt?

'For tax purposes,' he went on.

'Oh. Yes, please.'

'Hang on.'

Tax purposes? Of course! She was supposed to be a writer here to do research. She could deduct her expenses from her income tax. She was slipping, forgetting the details.

The man returned and handed her a slip of paper. 'I hope the book's a success,' he said. 'Certainly plenty of atmosphere in Whitby. I don't read romances myself, but the wife does. We'll look out for it.'

'Yes, please do,' Martha said. She wanted to tell him it was an academic, historical work, but somehow that just didn't seem important now. It was all lies anyway: romance or history, what did it matter? 'Thank you very much,' she said, and walked out of the door.

It really was cool outside. She had been intending to carry the quilted jacket over her arm, but she put it on instead as she set off on her usual morning trek to the Monk's Haven. She wasn't sure what to do with the rest of the day. Maybe go up to St Mary's again and shut herself in the box pew. She hadn't felt as safe and secure in years as she had the previous day up there. And then she would have to find another B&B to stay at.

The rain smelled of dead fish and seaweed. Browsers on Silver Street and Flowergate wore plastic macs or carried brollies, and fathers held onto their children's hands. Martha thought that was odd. When the sun shone, everyone seemed more relaxed and the children ran free, swinging their buckets and spades, dancing along the pavement and bumping into people. But as soon as it rained, pedestrians drew in and held on tight to one another. It was probably some primordial fear, she decided, a throwback to primitive instinct. They weren't aware they were doing it. After all, man was just another species of animal, despite all his inflated ideas about his place in the great chain of being. People had no idea at all why they behaved the way they did. Most of the time they were merely victims of forces beyond their control and comprehension, just as she had been.

You could only depend on reason and organization to a certain degree, Martha had discovered, and beyond that point lived monsters. Sometimes you had to cross the boundary and live with the monsters for a while. Sometimes you had no choice.

At her usual newsagent's on the corner just past the bridge, she bought a local paper and the *Independent* and headed for warmth, coffee and a cigarette.

First, she picked up the local paper and found what she was looking for on the front page. It wasn't much, just a small paragraph tucked away near the bottom, but it was the seed from which a bigger story would soon grow. BODY WASHED UP NEAR SANDSEND, the small-caps headline ran. Sandsend was only about four miles away. That was better than she'd hoped for. She thought it would have been carried further than four miles, and such an event might not seem so important in a large town like Scarborough. She read on:

> The body of man was discovered by a young couple on an isolated stretch of beach near Sandsend last night. So far, police say, the man has not been identified. Chief Superintendent Charles Kallen has asked anyone with information about a missing person to come forward and contact the police immediately. Time of death is estimated at no earlier than Thursday, and the body appears to have been drifting in the sea since then. Police had no comment to make about the cause of death.

They didn't know very much. Or if they did, they weren't saying. Martha would have thought it was obvious how the man had met his death. But the sea did strange things, she reminded herself. The police would probably think that his head injuries had been caused by rocks. The forensic people were clever, though, and they would soon discover at a post-mortem examination what had really happened.

A little disappointed at the thinness of the story, Martha ordered another black coffee and lit her third cigarette of the day. Should she stay in town until the real news broke? she wondered. This story just seemed so flat and anti-climactic. She should hang on at least until he was identified. On the other hand, that news would make the national dailies, which she could read anywhere. No, it was best to stay. Stick close to the action. She had gone so far that it would be futile to pull out now.

Next she turned to the *Independent*. She didn't expect to read anything about the discovery of Grimley's body there, but she looked just the same. At the bottom of the second page, tucked away like a mad relation in a cellar, was a short paragraph that caught her eye. It appeared under the simple heading, ANOTHER BODY FOUND. Perhaps that was it. Martha folded the paper and read on.

Police last night say they found the body of a nine-teen-year-old female on a stretch of waste ground near the University of Sheffield. Evidence suggests that the girl, a student at the university, was killed shortly after dark on Friday evening. Detective Superintendent Elswick, in charge of the field investigation, told reporters that evidence indicates the unnamed woman is the sixth victim of the killer who has come to be called the 'Student Slasher'. All his victims have been female students at northern universities. Police refused to reveal the exact nature of the girl's injuries. The killer has been operating in the north for over a year now, and there has been much criticism of the police's handling of the investigation. When asked why the killer hadn't been caught yet, Superintendent Elswick declined to comment.

Martha felt herself grow cold. The conversations going on around her turned to a meaningless background hum. All she could hear clearly was the litany of names running through her mind: Margaret Snell, Kathleen Shannon, Jane Pitcombe, Kim Waterford, Jill Sarsden. And now another, name unknown. Hands shaking, she lit another cigarette from the stub of her old one and read the article again. It said exactly the same, word for word. The 'Student Slasher' had struck again. She had been mistaken in Grimley. She had killed the wrong man.

Choking back the vomit, she crushed out her cigarette, rushed to the tiny toilet and locked the door behind her. After bringing up her breakfast, she splashed icy water on her face and leaned against the sink breathing fast and deep. She still felt dizzy. Everything was spinning around her as if she was standing on a high balcony suffering from vertigo. Her skin felt cold and clammy; her mouth tasted dry and sour. She took a deep breath and held it. Another. Another. Her pulse began to steady.

The wrong man, she thought, sitting down on the toilet and holding her head in her hands. And she had been so damn *sure*. The hoarse voice, the accent, the calloused hands, the low, dark fringe, the glittering eyes – it had all been right. So where did she go wrong? She couldn't have been thinking clearly at all. It had already occurred to her that her original theory – that he was a fisherman – must have been wrong, but she had gone ahead anyway. Her search had been based on slender enough evidence from the start. Anyone else would have said that she was looking for a needle in a haystack and, what's more, that she had no idea *which* haystack it was supposed to be in. But Martha had trusted her instincts. She had been sure that she would find him and that she would know him when she did. Well, so much for her bloody instincts.

Looking back, she could see that she should have known, that her perception had been flawed. He was too young, for a start, and though the voice was close, certainly in accent, it was pitched lower and had less of a rasp. The eyes and hands were the same, but there had been no deeply etched lines on his face.

How could she have let herself get carried away? This made her a murderer, pure and simple. There was no excuse. She remembered with a shudder his body twitching on the sand in the moonlight, the shattered bone and the sticky brain matter beneath her fingertips and the stifling sea-wrack smell of the cave. She had killed an innocent man. A man who would probably have forced himself on her eventually anyway, true – but an *innocent* man. And now she had to live with it.

She got up, drank some water from the tap and washed her face. She looked pale, but not enough that people would really notice. Taking another deep breath, she unbolted the door and walked back to her table. She seemed steady enough on her feet. She hoped nobody in the cafe had seen the way she had panicked. Still, they would have no idea why. Her coffee had cooled down, but the cigarette, improperly stubbed out, still smouldered in the ashtray. The story in the folded paper stared up at her. She turned it over and looked out of the window. Holidaymakers drifted by like shades in limbo. 'I had not thought death had undone so many,' she found herself thinking, but she couldn't remember where the words came from.

Should she call the hunt off, then, go back home to the shell of a life she had made for herself? No. Even now, at such a low point, she knew she must not do that. If she did, then it all came to nothing. Grimley would have died for nothing. Only if she fulfilled her purpose, set out to do what she had to, would any of it mean anything. She was still convinced she had got the right place: she would find her man in Whitby, or somewhere very close by. He was still here.

She grieved for Jack Grimley, would do anything to undo what she had done. But, she reminded herself, this was a war of a kind, and in war there are no innocent bystanders. Grimley might have been a good person, but he was still a man. To Martha, all men were potentially the same as the one she sought. Grimley, given the chance, would have led her into one of those caves and tried to rip her clothes off and . . . It didn't bear thinking about. Men were all the same, all violators and murderers of women. No doubt the real 'Student Slasher' was an ordinary, well-respected citizen on the outside. Maybe he even had a wife and children. But Martha didn't care about that. She just wanted to kill him.

Why did he travel inland so often? Was it just because that was where the universities were, or was it something to do with his work? She could no longer bank on his being a fisherman, after all, so maybe he was a travelling salesman based in Whitby. This was the kind of thing she had to do now – think again, plan again, act again. She couldn't let herself get dragged down by one mistake, no matter how horrifying it was. She had simply been too eager, too sure of herself, too impatient. She would have to focus more clearly on the task ahead, bring her intellect into harmony with her instinct. So start by *thinking*, she told herself. He travels inland frequently. Why? There, at least, was something concrete, a place to start.

'Anything else, love?'

'What?'

It was the waitress clearing away the empty table next to hers. 'Another cup of coffee?'

'Yes, all right.' Her last one had gone cold, anyway, Martha remembered.

'You stay there and I'll bring it over, love. You're looking a bit peaky. Had a shock?'

Martha shook her head. 'Thank you. No, no. Nothing serious.' She would have to watch herself, she realized. It wouldn't do at all if she went around town making a spectacle of herself. People would remember her.

When the waitress had brought the coffee, Martha returned to her thoughts. She knew that Superintendent Elswick and his minions would be wasting their time trying to figure out the killer's motives and come up with a psychological profile. It hadn't got them very far yet, had it? But she didn't give a damn about the man's unhappy childhood or the time he'd been forced to kiss his dead grandmother. Maybe his mother had abandoned him and gone to university. Perhaps that was why he always attacked young female students. Perhaps he had a daughter who had been corrupted as a student. Or maybe he just thought university campuses were dens of iniquity, full of sluts and sex-crazed bitches, the kind of place he was most likely to find loose women – and liberated women, careless or foolish enough to walk home alone in the dark. Again, she didn't care. When she found him she wasn't going to psychoanalyse him. She was going to kill him. Simple as that.

The rush of thoughts lifted Martha's spirits. It proved that her mind was working clearly again and that she could harden herself against experience, as she had to. When she looked back on what she had done the other night, keeping the grotesque images at bay, she saw that there was good in it, too. It hadn't really been a wasted effort at all. If she looked at it from a positive viewpoint, she could see killing Grimley as a kind of dress rehearsal for the real thing. A horrible thought, perhaps, but at least now she knew she could go through with it. Grimley's murder had also been an initiation of a kind, a baptism in blood. She had killed once; therefore, she could kill again. Only next time, she thought, fingering the paperweight in her holdall, she would be certain to get it right.

26

KIRSTEN

Kirsten remembered how she used to love the gossamer light in the woods, green and silver filaments dancing in the leaves, and the way it shot through gaps in the foliage here and there and lit up clumps of bluebells or tiny forget-me-nots by the brook, making them seem like still-life paintings rather than living, growing plants.

Today, though, she felt no elation as she trudged along the winding path under the high trees. After two days of hiding in her room, she had made the effort to go out – more for her parents' sake than for her own. Her father was beginning to look even more haggard than ever, and her mother was getting more impatient by the minute. They were almost at their wits' end with her, she knew. They wanted to tell her to put the unpleasantness behind her, stop moping and get on with her life. Only pity prevented them. They still felt sorry for her, and it was a sorrow they couldn't give voice to. So she had come to the woods to get them off her back. If she pretended all was well, they wouldn't know any different.

And it had worked. As soon as she had come downstairs the previous evening, they had cheered up, offered her a drink and sat companionably watching television with her. That morning, her father had returned to work, albeit reluctantly, and her mother had said she was going to Wells to do some shopping, as Bath was getting far too shabby and touristy of late.

But nature did nothing for Kirsten. As she walked, she remembered a passage from Coleridge's ode 'Dejection':

A grief without a pang, void, dark, and drear,
A stifled, drowsy, unimpassioned grief.
Which finds no natural outlet, no relief.
In word, or sigh, or tear.

Looking at the flowers in the light, she felt for Coleridge when he wrote, 'I see, not feel, how beautiful they are! . . . I may not hope from outward forms to win / The passion and the life, whose fountains are within.' Too true, Kirsten thought. The light that danced among the leaves could give her nothing, and her inner fountains had all dried up, had all been sucked through the dark star in her mind and turned to blood.

There was no point going on. About halfway along her usual route, she turned around and headed back home. Her room was the best place to be, and the house would be quiet with everyone out. Maybe in a few weeks the emptiness and the pain would go away and she would find herself back to normal. Already, though, she was finding it hard to remember what normal was.

Two black and white cows watched her with their big mournful eyes as she crossed the narrow stretch of grass between the woods and the back gate of the house. Her head still ached, and the depression suddenly gripped her more tightly than before.

Back in the house, she wandered aimlessly from room to room for a while, thought of making a sandwich, then decided she wasn't hungry. Getting drunk seemed like a good idea at first, but she had an even better one.

First she took a plastic bag from the cupboard under the stairs, then went up to the bathroom and opened the cabinet. Inside were the usual things: aspirin, antihistamine, antacid tablets, cold capsules, cough medicine and some old prescription antibiotics. Leaving only the cough mixture, she emptied the rest into the bag.

Next she crept into her parents' room. They kept their various pills in the top drawer of the bedside dresser. She took out her mother's tranquillizers and Mogadons and her father's blood-pressure tablets and poured them all into the plastic bag too.

In her own room, she opened her shoulder bag and found the prescription analgesic the doctor had given her for her pain. It was the same bag she'd been carrying the night of the attack, and she realized that she had never really wondered what had happened to it before. The police must have been through it, then had probably returned it to her room at the hospital while she was still unconscious. Emptying it on her bed, she found half a month's supply of birth-control pills still left. Smiling at the irony, she added them to her bagful and carried the lot back downstairs.

The living room was a huge split-level affair. At the front was a bay window that looked out on the lawn, the honeysuckle, the rose beds and the High Street beyond the white fence; at the back, French windows opened out onto the large garden, with its central copper beech, more flower beds and a croquet lawn. Beyond that was the woods. Kirsten opened the windows to let the sun slant in and sat on the carpet in its rays. She had taken a bottle of her father's best whisky from the cocktail cabinet – Glen-where-am-I, he always called it – and set it down beside her.

She picked up the plastic bag and poured the collection of pills onto the carpet in front of her. They were all the colours of the rainbow, and more besides: blue, green, red, white, yellow, pink, orange. Then she picked a few up, trying to get a nice selection of colours in her palm, swallowed them, and washed them down with a belt of Scotch straight from the bottle.

It was idyllic, sitting cross-legged there in the honeyed sunlight as the bees droned from flower to flower outside the French windows. Kirsten hadn't eaten all day, and she soon began to feel light-headed – light except for the dark cloud, which was far more dense than possible for something so small. At least it was small today. Sometimes it swelled up like a balloon, but today it was a nasty black marble. If she held it in her hand, she thought, it would probably burst right through her flesh with its weight.

A red one, a blue one, a yellow one, and a gulp of fiery whisky. So it went on; the level in the bottle dropped and the pile of pills on the tan carpet diminished handful by handful. Soon, Kirsten's head was swimming. Specks of light danced behind her closed eyes. When she opened them and looked out onto the sunlit garden again, she could have sworn it was snowing out there.

27

MARTHA

After Martha got off the bus at the station near Valley Bridge Road in Scarborough at about one o'clock in the afternoon, the first thing she did was grab a ham and cheese sandwich and a half-pint of lager and lime in the nearest pub, a quiet, run-down place with sticky tables.

She felt much calmer than she had earlier in the day. The news had hit her so hard she had almost given up, but in the end it had only strengthened her resolve. She couldn't go back without finishing her business on the coast. But now she knew that her precious instinct wasn't infallible, she would have to be much more certain the next time. How she could find proof beyond what she remembered of his appearance and voice, she didn't know. Perhaps she would have to lure him on and confront him. When Grimley had said he didn't remember her, he had been telling the truth. The real killer most likely *would* remember her, and if she could get him to admit to that, then she would be sure. She didn't want to leave a string of bodies behind her before she got the right one. She shivered at the thought of turning into the kind of monster she was out to destroy.

She stubbed out her cigarette and got up to leave. Things weren't as simple as they had been a couple of days ago. Now there was a chance that the police would soon identify Grimley and start looking into his death. Martha couldn't let herself get caught. She had already moved out of the Abbey Terrace room, but there were a few other things she could do to preserve her freedom before returning to Whitby.

She walked past the train station, then turned right down Westborough, where there seemed to be plenty of activity. The street guide she'd bought in Whitby gave her some sense of direction as she explored the side streets, but it didn't mark the main shopping areas. From what she could see, however, she was close to what she needed. The weather was just as grey as it had been earlier in Whitby, though the drizzle had stopped and it was warm enough now for her to take off her quilted jacket and carry it over her arm.

What she needed first was a big department store. Marks & Spencer would do fine, she thought, noticing the frontage: the clothes there were well made and reasonably stylish, but not too expensive. After wandering around the ladies' wear floor and flicking through the racks, she chose a plain, pleated black skirt, which hung well below her knees, and some black patterned tights to go with it. For the top, she bought a cream cotton blouse which buttoned up to the throat. She also picked out a navy-blue cardigan in case it got cool again.

In the shoe department, she chose a pair of no-nonsense pumps – sensible shoes, her mother would have called them – durable enough and easy to walk in. As soon as she had made her purchases, she went outside to a public toilet and changed, storing her old gear – jeans, T-shirt, sneakers and quilted jacket – in the holdall. No point throwing the stuff away, she thought. Nobody was likely to want to search her bag, and she could certainly wear the clothes again. She studied herself in the mirror and approved of the result. Nice girl, secretary perhaps, or receptionist. It was just the right inconspicuous, anonymous effect she was after. To improve the new look, she could also start wearing her glasses instead of contact lenses.

The sun had bored a few ragged holes through the cloud covering, and families were heading down Eastborough towards the South Beach. The children no longer hung onto their parents' hands, but dawdled and squabbled, swinging bright plastic buckets and spades. The occasional courting couple ambled by, hand in hand, in no hurry to be anywhere as long as they were with each other.

Martha found a Boots and made a beeline for the make-up counter. There she bought the basics: lipstick, eye-shadow, mascara, foundation, blusher – all in perfectly ordinary, conservative colours. In a cafe toilet across the street, she stood next to another woman who was also doing her face. The woman smiled and made small talk about the weather and the way men always complained about how long a woman spent in the toilet.

'And do you know,' she went on, squinting as she applied thick mascara, 'I don't even think they notice the difference when we come back. What do they think we're doing in here all that time? Do they think our bladders take longer to empty or something?' She chuckled, then sighed. 'Is it worth it? I ask myself.' She put on a coating of glossy red lipstick and patted her lips with a Kleenex to remove the excess. Then she sucked and pursed them a few times, just to make sure.

Martha looked at her and noticed the red stain on her front teeth. It made her think of vampires. 'I don't know,' she replied. 'I suppose it depends on what you want.'

This was too philosophical for the woman. She

crumpled the smeared tissue and dropped it in the bin, then frowned, sighed again, patted her hair and left.

Martha did the best she could. She had never been very good with cosmetics, never used them much except for dances and parties. The object this time, though, was not so much to turn herself into an irresistible beauty, but simply to look different from the young woman who had left Whitby that morning. This turned out to be surprisingly easy. The eyeshadow and mascara accentuated her eyes, but helped to disguise their shape. Blusher highlighted her cheekbones, and the shadows it cast below altered the planes of her face. The lipstick thickened and lengthened her lips just enough to make her mouth look larger and fuller. All in all, she thought, admiring the result, it was a success. Already she looked like a different person, and she hadn't even finished yet. She decided against wearing her glasses for the time being. Why go too far?

In the next department store, she headed for the small wig section. She didn't want anything showy, like platinum blonde or jet black, but something perhaps just a little darker than her natural colour. It had to be longer, though, and it had to look real.

'Can I help you, madam?' an assistant asked.

'Just browsing.' Martha didn't want anyone helping her on and off with wigs and making up her mind for her. That was the kind of thing a shopgirl might remember. Luckily, another customer came along, an older woman with tufts of hair missing, as if she'd been undergoing chemotherapy for cancer, and the assistant sidled up to her. The two of them began an involved discussion on exactly what was required, and the assistant led the woman over to a chair in front of a mirror.

Martha had never bought a wig before; she had never even tried one on. Gingerly, she picked up a long ash-blonde one just to see what it looked like on her. The effect was astonishing. The make-up alone had done a good job, but the addition of the wig changed her looks completely: it turned her into an entirely new person with a different history and personality. Martha stood and stared at herself, making up a story about the young woman she saw there: born in King's Lynn, Norfolk, educated at an exclusive girl's boarding school; sexy, independent, the owner of a chain of boutiques, perhaps, and often abroad on buying trips. Suddenly, afraid that people might be watching her, she snapped out of the game and got back to business.

After trying on a number of other hairpieces when she was sure nobody was paying her much attention, Martha finally found one that suited her. It was chestnut-coloured, but not unrealistically shiny, and curled under just above her shoulders. A short fringe fell over her forehead, too, and somehow this made her eyes look even more different. She carried the wig over to the near-est till, paid and took it away with her.

She took the escalator to the women's toilets on the fourth floor. When she pushed the door open, a frail-looking woman with a scrawny body and a large head jumped up from where she'd been sitting on the edge of a sink and quickly stuck her hand behind her back. Martha noticed that she was wearing a sales assistant's uniform – blue suit and white blouse, with a brass name-tag on the jacket identifying her as Sylvia Wield – and she looked as guilty as a schoolkid caught smoking behind the cycle sheds. When she saw it was only a customer, she relaxed and put her free hand to her chest.

'You gave me the fright of my life,' she said. 'I thought it was the supervisor. Do you know, we're not even allowed to smoke in our own lounge these days? That's why I have to sneak in here whenever I want a fag. It's usually quiet up here in furnishing.'

Martha smiled in understanding, then she went and sat in a cubicle until the saleswoman had gone. The shock of the meeting had made her own heart beat faster, too. When all was quiet again, she put on the wig and, looking around the door on her way out to make sure she wasn't noticed, she slipped down the nearest staircase back into the street.

She knew she should get back to Whitby soon and check into a different bed and breakfast place, but while she was in Scarborough, she couldn't resist a walk down to the harbour, just in case.

There wasn't much activity there. The lobster pots were stacked on the quay, and only one or two locals stood around, painting their boats or fiddling with the engines. The smell of fish was even stronger there than it was in Whitby. Mixed with the stink of diesel oil, it made her feel nauseated. As soon as she became aware of a young lad leaning nearby against the wall and giving her the eye, she decided she was wasting her time and headed for the bus station.

On the journey back to Whitby, she read *Jude the Obscure*, which she had bought at the same little bookshop on Church Street after finishing *Emma*. Within half an hour or so, it was time to get off again. This time, instead of climbing up to West Cliff, she turned into the area behind the station, another part of the town noted for its holiday accommodation. On a terrace of tall, dark guesthouses facing the railway tracks, all with VACANCY signs in their windows, she chose the middle one.

Moments after she had pushed the doorbell, a stout young woman with rubbery features came rushing from somewhere out the back and opened the door. Her hands were wet, and she looked tired and flustered, as if she was trying to juggle ten domestic chores at once, but she managed a smile when Martha said she'd like a room. She was probably only in her twenties, Martha thought, but hard work, children and worry had aged her.

'Single, love?' Her voice had a sing-song, whining quality.

'Yes, please. An attic will do, if you've got one.' Martha liked being high up in rooms with beams and slanting ceilings.

'Sorry, love,' the woman said, drying her hands on her pinafore. 'The only single we've got is a small room at the back.'

'I'll take a look,' Martha said.

It was on the second floor, a depressing little room with white stucco-effect wallpaper, looking out on backyards full of dustbins and prowling cats.

'It's quiet,' the woman said. 'Being at the back, like, you can't hardly hear the trains. Not that there are many these days.'

She seemed anxious to please. Martha reckoned that she and her husband probably hadn't been in the place long and were finding it difficult to make ends meet. The woman had clearly made an effort to make the hall and rooms appear cheerful, but the house itself was drab and old; it gave the impression of being damp and chilly even though it wasn't, and its proximity to the railway tracks must surely put people off. Martha didn't mind, though.

It was hidden, anonymous. Even if it didn't boast a view of St Mary's, it would make a cosy retreat. And she liked this woman, with her tired eyes and wash-reddened hands, felt sorry for her. In a way, Martha saw herself as perhaps a champion of women like this one – not just the obviously abused, attacked and assaulted, but the weary, the downtrodden and the dispirited.

'How much is it?' she asked.

'Eight pounds fifty, love. And we don't do evening meals. I'm sorry.'

'That's all right. I'm usually out then, anyway.' Martha thought it over quickly: it was cheap, obscure, and the woman hadn't asked her any awkward questions about what she was doing in Whitby all alone. There would be a husband around, no doubt, but he'd probably have a day job and, with luck, she wouldn't see much of him. Even the husband at the other place had stayed out of the way except when she had arrived and left. 'I'll take it,' she said, dropping her holdall on the pale green bedspread.

The woman looked relieved. 'Good. If you'll just come down and register, I'll give you the keys.'

Martha followed her back down, noticing as she went how the stairs creaked here and there. That could be a problem if she had to sneak in late like before. But if she did a bit of discreet checking on her way up and down in the first day or so, she could find out exactly which stairs to avoid.

The hall was much shabbier than the one in Abbey Terrace. There was no mirror, and even the advertising flyers looked dusty and curled at the edges.

'I'm Mrs Cummings, by the way,' said the woman, giving Martha a card to fill in. 'Sorry if I seem to be rushing you, but my husband's usually out on the boats so I've got to run the place more or less by myself.'

'Boats? Is he a fisherman?'

'Well, sort of. He takes groups of tourists out for morning and afternoon fishing trips. It's not as if they catch enough to sell or anything, some of them just want a ride out in a boat. But he makes a decent living in season. Still, it means he's up before dawn and often not back till after teatime. Depends on the tides, like, and how many want to go out. There's good days and bad. We get by.'

It would have been too ironic to be true, Martha thought, if she had actually found herself staying in the same house as the man she wanted. But at least he might know where the fishermen hung out and what other local industries had close links to fishing. She could only question him casually, like an interested tourist, but it might be worth a try.

'Breakfast is eight to eight-thirty,' Mrs Cummings said. 'I have to get it all over and done with quickly so I can get the kids off to school. And here are the keys.' She handed Martha two keys on a ring. 'The big one's for the front door. We always lock up at about half past ten but you can come in when you want, and the Yale's for your room. There's a small lounge on the ground floor – it's marked – with a kettle and a telly. Only black and white, I'm afraid. But there's teabags and a jar of Nescafé. You can brew up there any time you like.'

'Thank you,' Martha said with a smile. 'I'm sure everything will be fine.'

Mrs Cummings took the card Martha had given her. 'Going out now, are you?'

'Yes, I thought I'd just have a little walk before dinner.'

'Good idea. Well, see you later . . . er . . . ' She looked
at the card. 'Susan, is it?'

'Yes, that's right. Bye for now.' And Susan Bridehead
walked out into the late Whitby afternoon.

28

KIRSTEN

'Yes, I *am* sure that Kirsten doesn't need her stomach pumped,' Dr Craven repeated patiently. 'You saw for yourself, she brought up the tablets before they had time to work their way into her bloodstream. At worst she'll feel a little sick and dizzy for a while – which is no more than she deserves – and she'll probably have a heck of a headache.'

They stood in Kirsten's room, where she lay tucked up in bed. Her mother was flapping about and wringing her hands like a character in a Victorian melodrama.

'You're upset, understandably,' the doctor went on. 'Perhaps it would be best if you were to take a tranquillizer and lie down for a while yourself.'

'Yes.' Kirsten's mother nodded, then she frowned. 'Oh, but I can't.' She looked at her daughter. 'She took them all.'

It wasn't meant as an accusation, Kirsten knew, but she was made to feel once again that she had done nothing but make a nuisance of herself since she got back home: first she had refused to go out, then she had been sick all over the living-room carpet, and now she was depriving her mother of the oblivion the poor woman so desperately needed in order to cope with the nasty twists of fate that had disrupted her life of late.

Luckily, Dr Craven reached for her bag and came to the rescue.

'Samples,' she said, tossing over the small foil and cellophane package. Inside were four yellow pills, each in its own compartment. 'And I'll give you another prescription to replace the ones you lost. Kirsten needs rest now.'

She scribbled on her pad, ripped off the sheet and passed it over. The brusqueness of her tone and gesture got through even to Kirsten's mother, who normally seemed impervious to hints that her company wasn't required.

'Yes . . . yes . . .' Clutching the package and the prescription, she drifted towards the door. 'Yes . . . I'll just go and get a glass of water and have a lie-down . . .'

When she had finally gone, the doctor sighed and sat on the edge of the bed beside Kirsten. 'She means well, you know,' she said.

Kirsten nodded. 'I know.'

Dr Craven let the silence stretch for a while before she said, in a tone far gentler than Kirsten would have believed possible for her, 'But it *was* a silly thing to do, wasn't it?'

Kirsten didn't answer. She wasn't sure.

'Look,' Dr Craven went on, 'I can't pretend to know what you feel like after what happened. I can't even imagine what you went through, what you're still going through, but I can tell you this: suicide isn't the answer. Why did you do it?'

'I don't know,' Kirsten said. 'It just seemed like a good idea at the time. I'm not being facetious. I didn't know what else to do.'

Dr Craven looked puzzled. 'What do you mean?'

'I didn't enjoy being outside. I wasn't really hungry. I didn't fancy reading a book or watching television. I was just at a loose end. Then I thought I'd get drunk, then . . . I've not been sleeping well.'

'There *are* other options, Kirsten. That's what you've got to remember. I don't suppose I should be all that surprised you tried something foolish. As I said, I can't imagine how you feel, but I know it must be terrible. What you have to do now is understand that there's no quick and easy way back to health. Your body is taking care of itself well enough, but your emotions, your feelings are damaged too, perhaps even more than we realize. Rest will help, of course, and time, but you won't be able to go on hiding for ever. There'll come a time when you have to make the effort to start living again, to get out and about, meet people, get involved in life. I know it probably sounds terrifying just at the moment, but you must make that your goal. If you let your fears dominate you, then you've lost. You mustn't give in, you have to fight it. Do you understand what I'm trying to tell you?'

'I think so,' Kirsten said. 'I . . . I just don't know if I can. I don't know how.'

'Sermon over.' Dr Craven's lips twitched in a smile again. 'Now back to practicalities. Nobody can make you, but I strongly suggest that you see a specialist in Bath, someone who knows about the kinds of things you're feeling. I can recommend just the right person.'

'A psychiatrist, like you mentioned before?'

'Yes. I feel it's even more important now. I'll set up an appointment for you, but what I want to know, Kirsten, is will you go?'

Kirsten turned her head aside and looked through the small window at the sky and tree tops. At least it had stopped snowing, she thought. That had been the last thing she had registered before coming over faint and retching on the carpet: how odd that it was snowing in August. It hadn't been snowing at all, of course; it had just been her vision going haywire.

She turned back to Dr Craven. 'All right,' she said, 'I'll go. I don't suppose I've got anything to lose.'

'You've got quite a lot to gain, young lady,' the doctor said, patting her hand. 'Good. I'll fix up an appointment and let you know. Now are you sure you're feeling all right physically? No ill effects?'

'No, I'm fine. Just a bit woozy. Mostly I feel silly.'

'And so you jolly well should.' Back to her normal self, the doctor stood up and walked to the bedroom door. Just before she left, she turned and said, 'You can stay in bed till tomorrow morning, that's quite reasonable for someone who's done what you just did, but after that I want to see you up and about. Understood?'

Kirsten nodded. Left alone, she pulled the sheets up to her chin and stared at the long, faint crack in the ceiling. Her head was still throbbing and her stomach felt sore, but apart from that, everything seemed in working order, considering the mixture of pills and the amount of alcohol she had taken. As Dr Craven had said, none of the tablets had had time to do any damage, and she was suffering more from the effects of the Scotch, which was all the stomach wall had had time to absorb.

She would go to the specialist in Bath, she decided. Though she had little faith in psychiatrists, having studied and dismissed both Freud and Jung in a first-year general studies course, she felt desperate enough to try anything. If only he could get that dark cloud out of her mind and give her something – anything – to replace the terrible cold emptiness that she felt about everything. It wasn't fear that kept her indoors, in her bed, it was just apathy. There was nothing she wanted to do, nothing at all. She felt foolish and despised, and that was about it. With a bit of luck, perhaps the specialist really could help. Maybe he could give her something to live for.

29

SUSAN

During the night, the seagulls by the lower harbour were just as noisy as the ones on West Cliff, but breakfast at Mrs Cummings's establishment was an altogether less elaborate affair. For a start, there was no cereal, just a small glass of rather watery orange juice for each person. Nor was there a choice between tea or coffee, only tea. The main course consisted of one fried egg with the white still runny, two thin rashers of bacon and a slice of fried bread; there were no grilled tomatoes, mushrooms or slices of black pudding. There was, of course, plenty of cold toast and marmalade.

And the whole meal seemed to be taking place at fast forward. Sue was a little late coming down, as she had her face to fix and her wig to secure. No sooner had she sat down than the plate appeared in front of her. The tea had already been mashing for some time, and it tasted so bitter by then that she had to resort to sugar. She never had time to get around to the orange juice.

The only other guests in evidence were a bedraggled-looking bachelor in a grey sleeveless V-neck pullover, who hadn't either shaved or combed his hair, and two bored teenage girls with multicoloured spikes of hair and warpaint make-up. Sue finished quickly, went up to her room to smoke a cigarette and pick up her bag, then wandered out.

It was another grey day outside, but the thin light was

piercingly bright. Weather like this always puzzled Sue. There was no sun in sight, no blue sky, no dazzle on the water, but she found that she had to screw up her eyes to stop them from watering. She considered buying sunglasses and perhaps a wide-brimmed hat, but decided against it. Enough was enough; there was no point in going overboard and ending up *looking* like someone in disguise.

First she bought cigarettes and newspapers at the closest newsagent's, then she found a different cafe on Church Street in which to enjoy her morning coffee. She had read in crime novels about people changing their appearance but still getting caught because they were stupid enough to stick to the same inflexible routines.

When she looked at the local newspaper, she noticed that it was a Saturday late edition she hadn't seen. Of course! Today was Sunday; there would be no local papers, only the nationals. In the stop-press section at the bottom of the left-hand column on page one, she saw an update on the Grimley story:

> Police are not satisfied that the body washed up on Sandsend beach last night, now identified as that of Mr Jack Grimley, died of natural causes. Detective Inspector Cromer has informed our reporter that a post-mortem has been ordered. Mr Grimley was last seen alive when he left a Whitby pub, the Lucky Fisherman, at about 9.45 p.m. Thursday evening. Anyone with further information is asked to get in touch with the local police as soon as possible. Mr Grimley, 30, was a self-employed joiner and part-time property assistant at Whitby Theatre. He lived alone.

Sue chewed on her lip as she read. Slowly but surely, they were stumbling towards the truth, and the police always knew more than they told the newspapers. She felt a vacuum in the pit of her stomach, as if she were suspended over a bottomless chasm. But she told herself she mustn't panic. There might not be as much time left as she had hoped for, especially if she were racing against the police investigation, but she must stay calm.

She lit a cigarette and turned to the *Sunday Times*. This was hardly the place to look for salacious, sensational and scandalous news, but surely they would at least report the latest developments in the Student Slasher case. And so they did. Police simply confirmed that the Friday evening murder was the work of the same man who had killed five other girls in the same way over the past year. They refused to discuss details of the crime, but this time they gave a name. Susan added it to the other five she knew by heart, another spirit to guide her: Margaret Snell, Kathleen Shannon, Jane Pitcombe, Kim Waterford, Jill Sarsden and now the sixth, Brenda Fawley.

Sue idled over the rest of the paper, hardly paying attention, and by mid-morning she had come up with a plan for the day. It was time to start checking out the nearby fishing villages. First, she headed back across the bridge and picked up a timetable at the bus station. It took her a while to figure out the schedule, but in the end she discovered that there were no buses going up the coast on Sundays. The service ran between Loftus and Middlesbrough, further north, and that was it.

She thought of renting a car, though she knew that might also be difficult on a Sunday. Even if she could get one, she realized, it might cause all kinds of problems with identification – licence, insurance, means of payment – and that was exactly the kind of trail she didn't want to leave behind her.

There was no train line, so it had to be a bus, then, or nothing. Turning to the Scarborough–Whitby service, she found that there were buses to Robin Hood's Bay. They ran regularly at twenty-five past the hour and took less than half an hour. Coming back would be simple, too. She could catch a bus at Robin Hood's Bay Shelter, which would be up on the main road, at 5.19 or 6.19 in the evening, or even later, right up to 11.19 p.m.. Robin Hood's Bay it would have to be.

Sue wasn't sure what she would find there, but the place had to be checked out. She was certain that her quarry came from Whitby and that he had something to do with fishing, but it was quite possible that he lived in town and worked in one of the smaller places nearby, or vice versa, for that matter.

Besides, she also felt the need to get away from Whitby for a while. She knew the town too well now and was becoming tired of tramping its streets day in, day out. The place was beginning to feel oppressive; it was closing in on her.

Breakfast at the Cummingses' had been a depressing and suffocating affair, too – the obvious poverty; the noise of children; the lack of cleanliness (the teacups were stained, and there had been one or two spots of dried egg that hadn't been washed off her plate properly); and the sense of hurry and bustle that even now was causing her heartburn. Yes, another day trip out of Whitby would be a very good idea.

Checking her timetable again, she found that she had missed the 10.25. Never mind, she thought, finishing her

Kenco coffee, she was in no hurry. There were the papers to read, crosswords to do, plenty to keep her occupied. She could even go up to St Mary's and spend a while in her favourite box if she wanted.

30

KIRSTEN

'Come in, Kirsten. Sit down. Make yourself comfortable.'

Dr Henderson's office was on the second floor of an old house, and the window, which was open about six inches, looked out over the River Avon towards the massive abbey. The last of the great medieval churches to be built in England, it was still very much in use.

Instead of a couch, Kirsten found a padded swivel chair opposite the doctor, who sat at the other side of her untidy desk with her back to the window. Filing cabinets stood to Kirsten's right, and glass-enclosed bookcases to her left, many of them filled with journals. From one shelf, a yellowed skull stared out. It seemed to be grinning at her. Behind her was the door, and beside that, an old hat stand.

Dr Henderson leaned back in her chair and clasped her hands on her lap. Of course it had to be a woman, Kirsten realized; they wouldn't have sent her to a male psychiatrist after what happened. But she hadn't expected such a young woman. Dr Henderson looked hardly older than Kirsten herself, though she must surely have been at least thirty. She had short, black hair, neatly trimmed so as not to be a nuisance, which complemented the angles of her face and emphasized her high cheekbones. She had dark blue eyes, kind but glinting with an edge of mischievous humour. Her voice was soft, husky and deep, with just a trace of a Geordie accent, and her lips were turned up slightly at the corners, as if always on the verge of a smile. A smattering of freckles covered her small nose and the tight skin over her cheekbones.

Kirsten made herself comfortable in the swivel chair, and after glancing around nervously at the office she turned to face the doctor, who smiled.

'Well, Kirsten, how do you feel?'

'All right, I suppose.'

Dr Henderson opened a file on her desk and pretended to read. Kirsten could tell she knew the contents already and was just doing it for effect. 'Dr Craven has passed on the full medical details, but they're not what interest me. Why don't you tell me what happened in your own words?' Then she leaned back and clasped her hands again. The springs in her chair creaked as she moved.

Kirsten felt her mouth turn dry. 'What do you mean? What details?'

Dr Henderson shrugged. 'Perhaps you could start with the attack itself.'

'I was just walking home and somebody grabbed me, then everything went black. That's all.'

'Hmm.' The doctor started playing with a rubber band, stretching it between her fingers like the silence she was stretching in the room. Kirsten shifted in her seat. Outside on the River Avon a young couple rowed by. Kirsten could hear them laugh as their oars splashed water.

'Well?' Kirsten said, when she could bear the tension no longer.

Dr Henderson widened her eyes. 'Well what?'

'I've told you what happened. What do you think? What advice have you got for me?'

'Now hold on a minute, Kirsten.' Dr Henderson put the rubber band down and spoke softly. 'That's not what I'm here for. If anybody has given you to believe that you're coming to me for some kind of magic formula and – hey presto! – everything's back to normal again, then they've seriously misled you.'

'What *are* you here for then?'

'The best way to look at the situation is that you are here, and that's what's important. You're here because you've got problems you can't deal with alone. I'm here to help you, of course I am, but you're the one who'll have to do all the work. Your description of what happened, for example – a bit thin, wasn't it?'

'I can't help it, can I? I mean, I can only tell you what I remember.'

'How do you feel about it?'

'How do you think I feel?'

'You tell me. Your description sounded curiously flat and unemotional.'

Kirsten shrugged. 'Well, I suppose that's how I feel.'

'How are you getting along with your parents?'

'I don't see what that's got to do with anything.'

'Have you told them about your feelings?'

'I told you, I don't see what that's got to do with anything. Of course I haven't told them. Do you think I . . . ?'

'What?'

'Nothing.'

'Kirsten, have you ever been able to talk to your parents about your feelings?'

'Of course I have.'

'When?'

'What do you mean?'

'Give me an example of something you've discussed with them.'

'I . . . I . . . well, I can't think of anything offhand. You're making me flustered.'

'All right.' Dr Henderson sat up straight. 'Let's take it easy then, shall we?' And she smiled again. Kirsten found herself relaxing almost against her wishes. The doctor took out a packet of ten Embassy Regal from her desk drawer. 'Mind if I smoke?'

Kirsten shook her head. She was shocked to find a real doctor smoking – especially, for some reason, a young female doctor – but she didn't mind. Dr Henderson turned in her chair and opened the window a little further.

'Can I have one?' Kirsten asked.

'Of course.' The doctor pushed the packet towards her. 'I didn't know you smoked.'

Kirsten almost said, 'I don't,' but she managed to stop herself. 'Sometimes,' she said, then lit up. Though the first few drags hurt a bit, she didn't make a fool of herself and start coughing and spluttering and crying. She had smoked once or twice before, just to see what it was like. The smoke made her feel a little dizzy and sick at first, but her system seemed to adapt quickly.

'And my first name's Laura,' the doctor said. 'I want us to be friends.' She poured two cups of coffee from a Thermos on the desk and pushed one towards Kirsten. 'Milk? Sugar?'

Kirsten shook her head.

'Black, then. So, I take it you haven't really been able to talk to anyone about what happened to you?'

'No. I can't remember, you see, I really can't. It's like

there's a heavy black cloud inside my head where it's all stored, and I can't see inside it.'

'I don't mean the event itself so much as your feelings about it now,' Laura said.

'I don't think I feel anything.'

'Why did you take all those pills? Was it because of this cloud?'

'Partly, I suppose. But it's mostly because I don't feel I'm really living. I mean, I don't enjoy things like before. Reading . . . company . . . and I don't sleep well. I have bad dreams, over and over again. I thought it might just be better if I . . .'

'I see.' Dr Henderson made a note in the file. 'How important are sex and children in your life, Kirsten?'

Kirsten swallowed, shocked by the sudden change of direction. Her mouth turned dry again and the bitter coffee made it worse. She turned away. 'Never thought about them. I don't suppose one does till . . . till . . .'

'Till they're gone?'

'Yes.'

'Had you ever considered having children?'

Kirsten shook her head. 'One day. I imagined I'd have some one day. But not for a long time.'

'What about sex? Were you sleeping with your boyfriend regularly?'

In spite of herself, Kirsten blushed as she told Dr Henderson about Galen and about how she was now trying to cut him out of her life. The doctor listened, then made more notes in her file.

'As far as I understand it,' she said, 'Dr Masterson told you that sexual intercourse would be painful, if not impossible. Am I right?'

Kirsten nodded.

'But that's not all there is to sex, is it?'

'What do you mean?'

'What I mean,' said the doctor, 'is that perhaps you should start thinking about the pleasurable things you *can* do, rather than the ones you can't. I'm not going to embarrass you by explaining them, but there are manuals available. What I'm saying is that you have to accept the loss of your full sexuality, yes, but that you mustn't think that means the end of your entire sensual and erotic life. It's important to know that you can still have those feelings and can still satisfy them in some ways – you can still touch and you can still feel.'

Kirsten stared down at the floor. She hadn't thought about this, had tried not to think about sex at all since leaving the hospital, and she didn't know what to say. It was probably best to let it go by for the time being.

'Just think about what I've said, anyway,' the doctor said. 'It might be a long haul, Kirsten, but if you stick with it we'll get you there. And if at any time you feel the need to talk to someone, please call me. Any time. Do you understand?'

Kirsten nodded.

'What about dreams? You said you've been having bad dreams about what happened?'

Kirsten told her about the black and white figures slashing and slicing at her in the recurring dream.

'Are you talking about nightmares?' Laura asked. 'Do you wake up screaming?'

'No, nothing like that.'

'How do you react, then?'

'I don't really. It's all very ordinary. A bit frightening, I suppose, but there's no pain. It's like I'm detached from it all, just watching.'

'Why do you think you keep having that dream?'

'I don't know. I suppose it's some version of what happened. But I didn't see anything, so it can't be real.'

'Why are there two figures, a black one and a white one?'

'They're both doing the same thing.'

'Yes, but why two?'

'I don't know. Like I said, it can't be anything to do with what happened. I didn't see anything.'

The doctor stubbed out her cigarette and drank some more coffee. 'The mind's a curious thing,' she said. 'It remembers things that happen even when you're asleep or unconscious. Obviously, if your eyes are closed you can't see, but you can hear and smell, for example. Some of those things that happen come up in dreams. What the imagination does is translate them into pictures, based on what the sensations were and what you feel about them. I'm not a Freudian, but I do think dreams can tell us a lot. These two figures cutting you, who do you think they are?'

'I suppose one of them – the black one – must be the man, the one who . . . you know. Or maybe they both are.'

'White and black?'

'Yes. But if what you say is true, and I remember things even when I'm unconscious, then maybe the white one's the doctor. They operated on me for a long time, cutting in the same way I suppose. White and black. One for good, one for evil.' She felt pleased with herself, as if she had finally cracked a particularly obscure code, but Laura didn't seem impressed. 'Perhaps,' she said. 'Now what's in this cloud, do you think?'

'I don't know. Everything.'

'Everything?'

'What happened that night.'

'Do you believe that you were conscious for part of the time? That you saw the man and struggled, and that you've repressed the memory?'

'I don't know for certain, but I must have, mustn't I? Otherwise why would I feel there's something in me I can't get at?'

'Do you want to get at it?'

Kirsten crossed her arms and drew in on herself. 'I don't know.'

'It might be necessary. If you're to make any progress.'

'I don't know.'

The doctor made some more notes in the file, then closed it and put it in an overflowing tray – whether it was 'In', 'Out' or 'Pending', Kirsten couldn't tell. She suspected that Laura Henderson had no such efficient system for dealing with paperwork.

'Well,' said Laura, 'I don't suppose it matters for the moment. You'll come again?'

'I have a choice?'

'Yes. You must come of your own free will.'

'All right.'

'Good.' Laura stood up and Kirsten noticed how slim and healthy her figure looked, even under the loose white coat. It made her feel unattractive herself. In hospital, her skin had acquired that yellowish-grey pallor that sick people get, and the stodgy food had done her figure no good at all. Later, when she had lost her appetite, she had lost weight again, and now her skin felt wrinkly and loose. Her face was spotty too, as it hadn't been since she was fourteen, and even her hair seemed to hang lifeless and dry.

They walked over to the door, which Laura opened for her. 'And Kirsten,' she said finally, 'remember this: it's all right to feel things, even bad things. It's all right to feel hatred and anger towards whoever did this to you. In fact, if you want to get better, you must. The feelings are there, in you, and you have to admit them to yourself.'

Kirsten nodded and left. She felt, even as she walked out and crossed Pulteney Bridge to Grand Parade, that the doctor's words had planted the seeds of a recovery in her. As she watched the daring canoeists go through their paces in the wild water down by the city weir, she reminded herself of the doctor's last words: 'It's all right to hate him, it's all right to hate him.' And she did. Something inside her began hardening into a cold enduring hatred for the man who had shattered her future and crippled her sex. Below, the canoeists manoeuvred deftly, tracing crazy patterns on the water. Kirsten joined the crowd and watched them for a while longer. For some reason, they reminded her of Yeats's lines: 'Like a long-legged fly upon the stream / His mind moves upon silence.' It was an image she found strangely comforting.

31

SUSAN

Monday morning found Sue riding up the coast towards Staithes on the 10.53 bus. Her plan was to have lunch there, look around, then walk the three miles or so along the Cleveland Way to Runswick Bay for tea. From there she could get a bus back to Whitby at 6.25 in the evening.

Robin Hood's Bay, though quaint enough with its hotchpotch of pastel cottages almost sitting on top of one another, had proved disappointing. Not only had Sue seen no evidence of fishing there, she had felt very strongly that this was not the place she should be wasting her time in.

That evening, she had ventured into the lounge alone to watch TV and make a cup of instant coffee, and Mr Cummings had joined her for a while. He was a pleasant, ruddy-faced young man, more than willing to talk about fishing in the Whitby area. It turned out that there were more jobs connected with the industry than Sue had imagined – canning, freezing, processing, shipping – and some of them might be worth looking into. But Staithes was a strong fishing community, so she couldn't afford to overlook it.

The coast road to Staithes cut across a landscape of rolling farmland that ended abruptly in sheer cliffs at the North Sea. To the west lay a patchwork quilt of hedged fields. Some were brown after harvest, some still pale gold with uncut wheat and barley, while others were plain green pastures where black and white cows grazed. The bus passed a far-off village, a cluster of light stone houses with red pantile roofs, almost hidden by a clump of trees in a hollow. The weather had turned sunny again, and the colours of the landscape were saturated with light, like a colour transparency. On the seaward side, in a field next to a local rubbish dump, hundreds of white gulls squatted fat and replete after feeding. The sight disgusted Sue and made the bile rise in her throat. She looked beyond them to the clear blue sea, where the sun glinted silver on distant ships.

The bus stopped in the modern part of the village up on the main road, and Sue had to walk about a mile down to the village itself. The street, by Roxby Beck, was so steep that cars weren't allowed down it. Below her, the houses, a mixture of different stones, colours and styles, seemed to tumble over one another down to the sea. On the way, she stopped at a newsagent's and bought a local paper and a *Daily Mirror*.

The village at the foot of the hill was penned in on both sides by high headlands, huge skulls of grass-topped rock, where the horizontal strata of light sandstones and reddish-brown clays had been bared by the wind and rain over the centuries. The only view from the promenade was of the cliffs looming on each side, or out to the sea itself. There was nobody about; the place was deathly quiet. Even the gulls seemed to be swooping in silence, and the air was thick with the smell of rotten fish.

First, Sue wandered into the Cod and Lobster, a white-washed pub right on the seafront above the thick stone wall. She ordered a lager and lime and, surprised to find they didn't do meals, sat down for a cigarette and a read. There weren't many people in: a man in a Yorkshire Dales T-shirt scratched the neck of his red setter, two lads in navy jerseys, baggy jeans and wellingtons chatted up the young barmaid, and that was it. In fact, she hadn't seen many tourists at all, even on her way down the hill. Staithes seemed to be much more of an isolated, working village than Robin Hood's Bay. It seemed to be the kind of place where she might have more luck in finding the man she wanted.

As she smoked, Sue examined the photographs on the walls. Some of them showed a terrible storm that had hit Staithes in 1953 and damaged the pub badly. Others showed groups of local fishermen, and Sue studied them keenly. She knew she could rely on her visual memory least of all in her quest, but she *had* glimpsed him briefly in the moonlight and remembered the thick black eyebrows meeting in the middle, the Ancient Mariner eyes and the thatch of dark hair. No one in the photographs resembled him, so she turned to her newspapers.

There was nothing more on the Sandsend body in the local paper. Obviously, the police were stuck and the reporters couldn't justify repeating the same story day after day. It didn't mean that the investigation had come to a dead end, though, she realized. The police would still be working on it, questioning people, digging around for evidence. The very idea that they might be drawing closer gave her butterflies in her stomach.

She had bought the *Mirror* because she thought it might have more news about the Student Slasher. She found a whole page recapping his exploits, with the familiar blurred photos of the victims' faces taken from old students' union cards or passports (not Sue's, of course, for she had never been officially identified as his first victim). There they were: Kathleen Shannon with her long, wavy hair; Jane Pitcombe with her large, far-apart eyes; Margaret Snell with her lopsided smile . . . and the three others. Apart from veiled hints about what he did to the nubile young bodies (suggesting, between the lines, that some of them asked for it), and a number of editorial calls for the police to get a move on and catch him ('This could happen to *your* daughter, too!'), there was no real information at all. Sue stared at the six faces. She had never met any of the women, but she felt closer to them than she did to anyone else. Sometimes late at night, she had even fancied she heard them whispering in her ear. They helped her, guided her when she felt weak and lost, and for them, if not for herself, she had to carry on to the end.

Feeling hungry, she stubbed out her cigarette and finished her drink. Outside, a little further around the harbour from the Cod and Lobster, was a cafe attached to a private hotel. She walked in and found the small room crowded with full tables and only one waitress try-ing to deal with all the orders. Though she was obviously rushed off her feet by a recent influx of six or seven customers, the woman managed everything as quickly as she could, and with a smile. From the glimpses Sue got when the kitchen door swung open, there was only one cook, too. The menu offered little choice. The special of the day was cod and chips. Sue ordered it.

Smoking was not allowed in the cafe, so she passed the twenty minutes or so she had to wait for lunch doing the crosswords and reading about the sexual exploits of famous TV personalities and pop stars in the *Mirror*.

When the meal finally came, it was good. Sue realized that she had spent too much energy avoiding fish and chips in Whitby – because it seemed that that was the only food available – as she actually enjoyed it, at least in moderation.

As she ate, she remembered the local chippie near the university, where she and her friends had often stopped on their way home from the pub and eaten out of newspaper as they walked. If only her mother could have seen her; she'd have had a fit. But the north seemed so full of fish and chip shops, what could you do? Though she had never thought about it at the time, she guessed now that much of the fish came from places like Whitby and Scarborough, and even the smaller villages like Staithes. It came? Well, obviously it was delivered. It didn't fly there by itself. A whole fleet of vans must be constantly rushing back and forth from the coast to service inland towns and cities. Sue paused with her fork in the air as the simplicity of it all came to her: the final piece of the puzzle. Of course! How could she be so stupid? Now she knew exactly what to do next.

When she had finished eating, she pushed the empty plate aside and lit a cigarette. One or two fellow diners gave her nasty looks, but no one actually walked over and asked her to stop. The waitress also ignored her. She had much more on her mind than telling a patron to stop smoking. Eventually Sue got the bill, paid it, and walked out into the sea air. Its rotten-fish smell now seemed mingled with the odours of seaweed and ozone, and just a trace of diesel fuel from the boats.

There was no point remaining in Staithes any longer, she thought as she walked along the harbour wall. She had always been certain, in her heart of hearts, that

Whitby was the place where she would find him. Now even logic backed up her instinct.

Still, it was pleasant enough walking in the sun and watching the placid blue sea. The place seemed less oppressive now that she had decided to leave it soon. She could at least wait until she had digested her lunch. The only discomfort she felt was a hot and itchy scalp under her wig.

She sat down on the sea wall and let her legs dangle over the edge. Stretching her arms out behind her and resting her palms on the warm tarmac, she leaned back and let the sun warm her closed eyelids. One more cigarette, she decided, then back up the long hill to the bus stop. Shifting position, she checked her timetable and found out that there was a bus at 2.18. It was twenty past one now, so she had just missed the one before. Plenty of time.

As she sat watching a distant tanker move across the horizon, she became aware of someone staring at her. The hackles at the back of her neck, under the wig, stood on end. At first, she brushed off the feeling as ridiculous. Hadn't she just decided that she would find her man in Whitby? He couldn't be here. Then, for a moment, she panicked. What if it was the police? What if they had somehow got on to her? Or were they just following her, watching? She could bear it no longer. Turning her head slowly and casually towards the rail in front of the Cod and Lobster, where she thought the watcher was standing, she picked out the tall, tanned figure.

It was Keith McLaren, the Australian she'd met at the Abbey Terrace guest house. And he recognized her. Even as she looked, he waved, smiled and started to walk towards her.

32

KIRSTEN

August gave way to September and the nights turned cooler. As the weeks passed, Kirsten began to look forward to her sessions with Laura Henderson. They smoked and sipped terrible coffee together in that cosy room overlooking the River Avon. The immediate sights beyond the window became as familiar to Kirsten as if she had looked out on them all her life: Robert Adam's Pulteney Bridge, with its row of shops along each side, all built of Cotswold stone; the huge square late-Gothic tower of the Abbey; the Guildhall and municipal buildings. Often she stared over Laura's shoulders during the long silences or stood at the window as Laura sought out an article in a journal. Some evenings, when their sessions ran late, Laura would take a bottle of Scotch from her filing cabinet and pour them each a drink.

They talked more about Kirsten's childhood, her parents, her feelings about sex. Laura said that Kirsten was making progress. And so she was. She still didn't like going out or meeting people, but she began to enjoy the simple things again: mostly solo pursuits like a walk in the woods, music, the occasional novel. She even found that she could concentrate and sleep well again. Though she no longer flirted with suicide, she hung on to her cold hatred, and the dark cloud still throbbed inside her mind. Sometimes it made her head ache. She and Laura didn't talk about the attack. It would come,

Kirsten knew, but only when Laura thought she was ready.

At home, her mother continued to fuss and fret, and she often seemed to regard her daughter with a combination of embarrassment and pity. But Kirsten grew used to it. The two of them kept out of each other's way as much as possible. It wasn't difficult. With her garden, her croquet, her bridge parties and her myriad social engagements, Kirsten's mother managed to keep busy.

Hugo and Damon sent get-well cards, and Galen phoned several times during August. At first, Kirsten instructed her mother to tell him she was out. Soon, however, she realized that wasn't fair. She spoke to him and tried to respond to his concern without encouraging him too much. One Friday, he paid a visit and tried again to persuade Kirsten to go with him to Toronto. They walked in the woods and she let him take her hand, though her flesh felt dead to his touch. It wasn't too late, he said, they had both been accepted and term didn't begin for a few weeks yet. Gently, she put him off, told him she would join him later, and sent him away partially appeased. Finally, at the beginning of September, he went to Canada and sent her a postcard as soon as he got to Toronto. She had never told him what was really wrong with her; nor had she mentioned the suicide attempt.

If anyone sustained Kirsten outside Laura Henderson's office, it was Sarah, who phoned almost every week and wrote long, entertaining letters in between. Always outrageous, funny and compassionate, she made Kirsten laugh again. When she asked if she might visit over Christmas, when her own parents would be touring Australia, Kirsten jumped at the chance. Her father saw that it was a good idea, too, but her mother, perhaps recalling her only meeting with Sarah in the dingy northern bedsit, was reluctant at first. Christmas was a family time, she said. She didn't want strangers around. Her husband argued that it wasn't a very big family anyway. Kirsten's grandparents, two uncles and aunts usually came for Christmas dinner, then her parents visited friends in the village for drinks on Boxing Day. Surely, he argued, it would be good for Kirsten to have a friend of her own age around. Finally, her mother gave in and it was settled. Sarah was due to arrive on 22 December, and Kirsten would pick her up at the station after her late-afternoon session with Dr Henderson. She would have her mother's Audi, as usual.

One day in early October, when the elegant old city looked grey and a cold wind drove the rain through its Georgian crescents, circles and squares, Kirsten forsook her usual walk by the Avon and drove straight home from Laura's office. When she arrived, she noticed a strange car parked in the drive and her mother peeking out from behind the lace curtains – something she didn't usually do – and her heart began to beat faster. Something was wrong. Was it her father? she wondered as she hurried to the door. Her ordeal had taken a terrible toll on him, and though he did seem stronger and happier of late, the bags still hung dark under his eyes and he had lost his boyish enthusiasm for things. Was his heart weak? Had he had an attack?

Her mother opened the door before Kirsten even had time to fit her key into the lock. 'Someone to see you,' she said in a whisper.

'What is it?' Kirsten asked. 'Is father all right?'

Her mother frowned. 'Of course he is, dear. Whatever gave you that idea?'

Kirsten hung up her coat and dashed into the split-level living room. The two men sat close to the French windows, near the spot on the carpet, now dry-cleaned back to perfection, where Kirsten had had her Scotch and pills picnic. One of the men she recognized, or thought she should, but the memory was vague: spiky grey hair, red complexion, dark mole between left nostril and upper lip. She'd seen him before. And then it came to her: the policeman, Superintendent . . .

'Elswick, Miss,' he said, as if reading her mind. 'Detective Superintendent Elswick. We have met before.'

Kirsten nodded. 'Yes, yes of course.'

'And this is Detective Inspector Gregory.'

Inspector Gregory stretched out his hand, which was attached to an astonishingly long arm, and Kirsten moved forward to shake it. Then he disappeared back into the chair – her father's favourite armchair, she noticed. Gregory was probably in his mid-thirties, and his dark hair was a bit too long for a policeman. He was dressed scruffily, too, with brown corduroy trousers, threadbare from being washed too many times, a tan suede jacket, and no tie. Kirsten thought he seemed a bit shifty. She didn't like the way he looked at her. Superintendent Elswick wore a navy-blue suit, a white shirt and a black and amber striped tie. It was the same one he wore last time, she remembered. Probably from an old school or regiment; he looked like an ex-military type.

'How are you, Kirsten?' Elswick asked.

Kirsten sat down on the sofa before answering. Her mother hovered over them and asked if anyone would like more tea.

'I haven't had any yet,' Kirsten said. 'Yes. I'd like some, please.'

The two policeman said they wouldn't be averse to another cup, and Kirsten's mother walked off promising to make a fresh pot.

Kirsten looked at Elswick. 'How am I? I suppose I'm doing fine.'

'Good. I'm very glad. It was a nasty business.'

'Yes.'

They sat in tense silence until Kirsten's mother returned with the tea tray. Having deposited it on the mahogany coffee table before the stone hearth, she disappeared again, saying, 'I'll leave you to it, then.'

After her sessions with Dr Henderson, Kirsten was used to silence. At first it had disconcerted her, made her fidgety and edgy, but now they sometimes sat for as much as two minutes – which is a *very* long time for two people to be silent together – while Kirsten meditated on something Laura had said, or tried to frame a reply to a particularly probing and painful question. Elswick and Gregory were easy meat. There was something they wanted, obviously, so all she had to do was wait until they got to the point.

Gregory played 'mother', clearly an unsuitable role for him, and spilled as much tea in the saucer as he got in the cups. Elswick frowned at him, and added milk and sugar. Then, when they were settled again, Gregory crossed his long legs and took out a black notebook. He did his best to pretend he was part of the chair he was sitting in.

'Kirsten,' said Superintendent Elswick, 'I should imagine you've guessed that I wouldn't come all this way unless it was important.'

Kirsten nodded. 'Have you caught him?' For a moment she panicked and thought the attacker might actually be someone she knew, someone from the party. She didn't know if she would be able to handle that.

'No,' said Elswick, 'no, we haven't. That's just the point.'

It was obviously very difficult for him to talk to her, Kirsten realized, but she didn't know how to make it any easier.

Finally, he managed to blurt it out, 'I'm afraid there's been another attack.'

'Like mine?'

'Yes.'

'In the park?'

'No, it took place on some waste ground near a polytechnic not far away. Huddersfield, in fact. I thought you might have read about it in the papers.'

'I haven't been reading the papers lately.'

'I see. Anyway, this time the victim wasn't quite as lucky as you. She died.'

'What's her name?'

Elswick looked puzzled. 'Margaret Snell,' he answered.

Kirsten repeated the name to herself. 'How old was she?' she asked.

'Nineteen.'

'What did she look like?'

Elswick tipped the tea from his saucer into his cup before answering. 'She was a pretty girl,' he said finally, 'and a bright one too. She had long blonde hair and a big crooked smile. She was studying hotel management.'

Kirsten sat in silence.

'The reason we're here,' Elswick continued, 'is to see

if you've remembered anything else about what happened. Anything at all that might help us catch this man.'

'Before he does it again?'

Elswick nodded gravely.

'Does that mean there's some kind of maniac, some kind of ripper, running loose up there?'

Elswick took a deep breath. 'We try to avoid alarmist terms like that,' he said. 'It was a vicious attack, much the same as the one on you. From our point of view, we're pretty sure it was the same man, so it looks like we've got a serial killer, yes. But the newspapers don't know that. They don't know anything about the similarity between your injuries and those of the dead girl, and we're certainly not going to tell them. We're doing our best to prevent anyone linking you to the business.'

'Why?' Kirsten asked, suddenly apprehensive.

'All the bad publicity. It would upset your parents, make your life a misery. You've no idea how persistent those damn reporters can be when they get on the scent of a juicy story. They'd be up here from London like a shot.'

Kirsten could tell he was lying. He wouldn't look her in the eye. 'It's because you think he might come after me, isn't it?' she said. 'You're worried that if he knows you connect him to two victims and he knows one is still alive, then he'll want to finish me off in case I know something, aren't you?'

'It's not as simple as that, Kirsten.' Elswick shifted in his chair. 'When you were in hospital—'

'He's already tried?'

'Yes. You must have noticed that we had a man on the door all the time. As soon as news of your survival hit the papers, the attacker came back. Apparently he must have entered the hospital dressed as an orderly. He can't have been all that bright, otherwise he'd have known we'd be guarding you. Anyway, when he turned the corner, he spotted the constable and ducked quickly back the way he came. Our man was good. He saw from the corner of his eye that someone was behaving suspiciously, but he had orders not to leave his post. A more head-strong bobby might have done just that. But if he'd gone chasing after the intruder, looking for the glory of an arrest, then he could easily have got lost in the maze of corridors and chummy could've nipped back in and . . .'

'Finished me off?'

'Yes. Instead, the constable stayed put and called in on his radio, but by the time we got there our man was long gone. We didn't even get a description.'

'And he never tried again?'

'No. Not as far as we know.'

'Does he know where I live?'

'I don't think so. How could he? The press details were sketchy. The local police have been warned to keep a lookout for any strangers in the area, but I don't think you've got anything to worry about.'

Kirsten thought of all her walks in the woods, all the times she had lingered in the streets of Bath after sessions with Dr Henderson. She felt a sudden chill. 'Why didn't you tell me all this before?' she asked.

'We didn't want to alarm you.'

'Thanks a lot.'

Elswick leaned forward and rested his palms on his knees. 'Believe me, Kirsten, you've been perfectly safe. I can understand how you feel, but look at it this way. Whoever attacks you is worried when he hears you've survived, so he rushes over to the hospital with some half-baked scheme of trying to silence you. He fails. Time goes by, he no doubt loses track of you when you come down here, and lo and behold, it's already three months ago and nothing's happened to him. He's still free as a bird. So obviously, from his point of view, you can't know anything, you're not a threat.'

'Until he strikes again?'

'I still don't think you're in any danger. We'll keep an eye on you, don't worry, but it's more for form's sake than anything else.'

Kirsten felt a little relieved. There was some truth in what Elswick had said. If anything was going to happen, it would have happened long before now. And she wasn't about to start walking around in fear of her life; it wasn't worth that much. Though she no longer felt suicidal, she did feel reckless sometimes and often drove the car too fast or walked alone after dark in streets she shouldn't visit. Even genteel Bath had its seedy characters and sleazy areas. So she wasn't going to give in to fear. She had determined not to spend the rest of her life jumping at every sound and running from every shadow. If he found her, so be it; may the best person win. More than anything, she was angry at the police for being so useless and for joining the growing list of people who didn't want to 'alarm' her by telling her the truth.

'Why does he do it?' she asked. 'Mutilate women like that. Why does he hate us so much?'

Elswick shook his head. 'If we knew the answer to that we might have an easier job stopping him. Usually it's a him, and that's about all we can be sure of. Who can say what sets them off? We have people in to do profiles and doctors write books, but who knows really?

Often it's prostitutes they go after, but this time it seems to be female students, if we're reading the pattern correctly. No doubt there's a million unresolved conflicts from his childhood on, that have turned him into what he is. Perhaps he was sexually abused. But plenty of other people suffer from cruel parents and don't turn into killers. We don't know what the trigger is that makes the odd one different.' He shrugged. 'I suppose it comes down to fear, really. People like him are terrified by women, whatever the reason, and the only thing they can do about it, because of the kind of people they are, is strike out and despoil and kill.'

'How do you know it's the same person?' Kirsten asked. 'You said something earlier about the similarity of injuries.'

Elswick looked at her grimly. 'Do you really want to know?' he asked.

Kirsten wasn't sure, but she certainly didn't intend to give in. 'Considering that so much else has been kept from me, I think I have a right, don't you?'

Elswick sat back and studied her face for a moment. 'All right,' he said. 'The wounds were the same, the areas he used his knife on were the same; there was also bruising about the face consistent with punching and slapping. And that strange cross he cut, with the long vertical and short horizontal just below the breasts, that was found on her body, too. Do you want me to go on?'

Kirsten nodded.

'When he was with you, he was disturbed. The dog, we assume. Up to that point your injuries are identical with those of the other victim.'

'What killed her, then?'

'She was strangled.' Elswick pinched his nose, then scratched the mole lightly. 'Oh, she'd no doubt have died of loss of blood or internal bleeding, but just to make sure, the bastard strangled her. And according to our forensic experts, he did this *after* he had inflicted the other injuries.'

'Are you saying that she was conscious while he did all . . . what he did to me?'

Elswick shook his head. 'We don't know. It would have been difficult for him if she'd been able to struggle. The blows to the face and head were probably enough to cause loss of consciousness, and it seems that they were the first injuries. He grabbed her from behind, threw her down onto the ground, straddled her, pinning her arms down with his knees, and then began beating her about the face. Perhaps it wasn't until she was unconscious that he went on to the more serious business. And this time he wasn't disturbed.'

Kirsten felt sick. She could feel the blood drain from her cheeks. She struggled to control herself. She wasn't going to be sick. She wasn't going to let Elswick say, 'I told you so.' She wouldn't appear as the weak woman in front of these men who were intimate with every aspect of her brutalization. To cover up her discomfort, she poured another cup of tea. Inspector Gregory shook his head quickly when offered some. He was so still and silent he seemed really to have become part of the chair.

'What we were wondering,' Elswick went on slowly, 'was whether you'd remembered anything else, no matter how insignificant or unimportant it might seem to you.'

Kirsten shook her head. 'No, I haven't. I've tried, of course, but after what I told you, it's all still a blank.'

'You see,' Elswick persisted, 'what we think is that the victim must have still been conscious, at least at the time he threw her onto her back. And if that's so, then it might have been the same with you. You might have got a glimpse of his face. Maybe he was wearing a mask or a stocking, but even that could help us. Or maybe he said something. Anything.'

'I'm sorry,' Kirsten said, 'really I am. But I just can't remember. You might be right. Maybe I did see his face, maybe he did talk to me. But I *can't remember*. Do you think I don't want to? Of course I'd like to help you, but I can't. After that rough hand closed over my mouth, I can't remember a thing.' She felt tears in her eyes and fought to hold them back.

'There was a moon that night,' Elswick said.

'Yes. I was looking for it when . . . before. But I couldn't see it.'

'It was there, behind you, just over the tops of the trees. We've checked.'

'Why?'

'Light. Because if you were conscious when he pushed you down to the ground, there would have been just enough light to make out at least something about his appearance. It was a clear night – a bit hazy maybe – and there was a full moon.'

'But I can't have been conscious,' Kirsten said. 'I don't remember.'

'Never mind, then.' Elswick glanced over at Inspector Gregory, who slipped his notebook back in the inside pocket of his tan jacket, and both men swung forward in their chairs, preparing to leave. 'I'm sorry to have brought such bad news and stirred up painful memories,' Elswick went on, getting to his feet. His knees cracked and he put his hand to the small of his back as if it hurt. 'Getting old. I hear you've been seeing a doctor, Kirsten.'

'There's not much you don't know, is there?' Kirsten said. 'As a matter of fact, yes, I have. Her name's Laura Henderson and she's a psychiatrist.'

Elswick smiled indulgently. 'Yes, we know.'

'Don't tell me – you checked her out?'

'It's standard procedure in cases like this.' Elswick followed her out of the room down to the hall. 'Doing you any good?'

'Yes, I think she is. She says my loss of memory might be anterograde amnesia, caused by the trauma.'

'Hmm, yes, we'd heard. And it's consistent with the facts. All you remember is the hand, and you've blotted out all the violence, all the pain. According to our medical experts, the memory may or may not come back.'

'You've certainly done your homework, haven't you, Superintendent?'

Elswick seemed embarrassed again. He changed moods remarkably quickly for a policeman, Kirsten thought. One minute he was all confident and superior, the next he was avuncular, and then he got all tongue-tied. This time she decided to help him.

'What is it you want?' she asked. 'Do you want to talk to her? Do you want access to her records of our sessions? They won't tell you anything, you know.'

'Er, no, no, that won't be necessary,' Elswick said as Kirsten handed them their coats from the hall cupboard. She sensed from his hesitation that he might already have had such access or could easily get it if he wanted, and she felt a surge of anger towards Laura.

'What I was wondering was,' he went on, scratching

his mole again – Kirsten felt like telling him to get it seen to before it turned cancerous – 'was, well, with the doctor's permission, of course, I was wondering if you'd consider trying hypnosis?'

33

SUSAN

'It was partly the way you smoke your cigarette,' Keith said. 'Everybody's different. You hold it straight out between your first two fingers like a real lady, or like you're just pretending to smoke.' He grinned. 'But why the change in appearance? You look so *feminine*. I mean, not that you didn't before, it's just . . .' He slowed to a halt.

Sue smiled and flicked her cigarette end onto the sand. 'You know what they say: a change is as good as a rest.' Why the hell did he have to turn up? she asked herself. And what am I supposed to do about him?

'Did you need a rest?'

'No, I needed a change.'

They both laughed.

'But seriously, Martha,' he persisted, 'it's almost as if you're trying to avoid someone. You aren't, are you?'

'It's nothing but a skirt and a blouse. You're acting as if I'm dressed like Richard III or something.'

'There *is* the wig.'

Sue touched the false hair. 'I was sick of having it short. I couldn't wait.'

'And the make-up.'

'Can't a girl put a bit of lipstick on any more?'

Keith smiled. 'I'm still not convinced. I think you're a spy. I just don't know whose side you're on.'

He seemed happy to meet up with her again, despite

the sour note they had parted on, but she could tell he was suspicious by the way he studied her. He had recognized her without much difficulty, that was clear enough. Maybe it was because he fancied her, and when you fancy someone you notice little things like how they hold their cigarettes and the way they walk. She was sure that strangers, people she had passed in the street or sat near in a pub, wouldn't connect her with the short-haired, tomboyish Martha Browne. But Keith could be a problem.

'What are you doing up here?' he asked.

'Just taking a break for the day. And you? I'd have thought you'd be in Edinburgh by now.'

'Oh no, I'm moving very slowly. First Sandsend, then Runswick Bay, now Staithes.' Sue noticed again how pronounced his Australian accent was: Staithes came out as Stythes. 'I'm in no hurry,' he went on. 'I might never see these places again. And the weather's been so bloody good. Another first in England from what I've heard. You still in Whitby?'

'Yes.'

'Still in the same bed and breakfast?'

'Yes.'

'Still get black pudding for breakfast?'

'Most days.'

Sue's mind was working fast. She didn't want to be noticed with him in public, for a start, and they could hardly get more public than here on the sea wall. Luckily, though, there was hardly anyone around at the moment. One or two people sat on the beach, but they were facing the sea, and two blonde children, dressed identically in white shorts and blue and red striped T-shirts, stood eating ice-cream cones near the Cod and

Lobster. Everyone else was either in the pub, at the shops, or waiting for lunch in the restaurant. The steep hill down to the village probably put a lot of older visitors off, too, Sue thought. No matter how warm it was, people so much liked to sit in their cars right beside the sea, but they couldn't do that here. Though it was easy enough getting down to the beach, the walk back up the hill was no doubt too great a price for many to pay for a day at the seaside.

So far, no one had so much as glanced at them. The first thing to do was get Keith away somewhere off the beaten track, then she would be able to think clearly. She didn't like the idea that was forming, forcing itself on her, but she hadn't thought of another way out yet.

'What are your plans?' he asked.

'Well,' Sue said, 'I was intending to walk along the coast to Runswick Bay, then catch the bus back to Whitby. What do you think? Is it too far?'

'No, it's not far at all. I've done it myself. Nothing to it. Tell you what, if you've no objection, I'll come with you. There's an even better walk in my guidebook, though. You walk along the cliffs to Port Mulgrave, then cut back inland through some woods and circle around to the main road. That'll take you to your bus stop, and me back to Staithes. How about it?'

'All right. Are you sure you don't have anything else you want to do?'

'I told you, I'm on holiday. No plans, no newspapers, no television. A vacation from the world.'

Sue remembered the bit about not reading newspapers from their last meeting. It made her feel a little safer – especially as he had made no mention of Jack Grimley's death – but there were still too many ways that someone like Keith could come across a local news story: a photo of Grimley and a request for information in some pub or cafe up the coast, for example; or from the newspaper used to wrap his fish and chips one evening. Perhaps someone might be watching a local news programme on the TV in the lounge of his guesthouse just as he walked in to make a cup of tea. And he would remember, that was the problem. He recognized her, even in disguise, so he would surely recognize Jack Grimley, the man he had caught her staring at in the Lucky Fisherman. Then he might remember how he had thought she knew Grimley. The more she worried about what Keith knew, the more she realized she didn't feel safe at all. Why hadn't he gone straight up to Scotland, or taken the plane back to Oz?

Keith took her silence for hesitation. 'Look, Martha,' he said, scratching his earlobe and looking out to sea. 'I know I was out of order, like, before when . . . you know . . . and I'm sorry. I want you to know I'm not on the make. I just think it'd be nice to go for a walk with you. I won't try anything. Honest.'

Sue got to her feet and brushed the sand from the back of her long skirt. She was forming a plan and a little inducement would go a long way. 'It's all right,' she said. 'I didn't mean to seem so brusque with you before. It's not that I'm a nun or anything. It was just too soon. I mean, I hardly knew you.' She smiled at him.

Keith looked surprised. 'Yes, well . . . er . . . shall we be off?'

'Haven't you got your gear?'

'Gear? Good Lord, you don't need gear for a simple walk like this.' He looked her up and down. 'You could even do it dressed like that, though I wouldn't recommend it. No, all I've got is my Ordnance Survey guide.' He patted the back pocket of his jeans.

'No, I mean your stuff, your rucksack and all that.'

'It's back at the B&B. I was only having a little stroll around the village. No, what you see is what you get.' He spread his arms and stood before her, tall, slim, thin-faced and tanned. His curly, black hair still looked glossy, as if he had just stepped out of the shower, and his eyes reflected a bluer ocean than the one that stretched before them.

'What did you mean about me not being dressed right?' Sue asked.

'I was only joking really. It's not a hard walk. It's just that skirts tend to snag on thorns and things, and those pumps will take a hell of a beating.'

'Wait here a minute.'

Sue hurried into the public toilet, made sure that no one was around and went into a cubicle to change. First she took off her wig, scratching her head in relief when she had done so, then she put on her jeans, a dark-blue checked shirt and her trainers. Carefully, she rolled up the wig, long skirt, white blouse and cardigan and placed them in the holdall. Sometimes, she thought, it was a nuisance having to carry the damn thing everywhere with her, but it was light enough, and she could adjust the strap and carry it over her shoulder if she wanted.

She put the quilted jacket on top of everything in case it got chilly high up on the cliffs. Finally, she combed her hair in the cracked and grimy mirror above the sink and examined her make-up. It wasn't bad. She hadn't put too much on that morning as she had intended to be out of Whitby for the day anyway, and now there was no point in standing here and washing it all off. Someone might come. Quickly, she gave her lips a dab with a Kleenex, then dashed back outside to join Keith.

'Lead on,' she said, bowing and standing aside for him.

Keith laughed. 'Are you *sure* you're not a spy or an actor or something?'

'Not at all.' Sue gave him what she intended to be an enigmatic smile, and they set off.

They wound their way up by the Mission Church of St Peter the Fisherman, then followed the signs for the Cleveland Way past some farm buildings, over a couple of stiles and right up the hill to the cliff edge. The village lay spread out below them. Even though it was a clear, warm day, smoke drifted lazily from some of the chimneys. Up on the cliff top, there was a cool breeze from the sea. Pausing for breath, Sue put on the quilted jacket she'd been carrying in her holdall.

'What have you got in that thing?' Keith asked. 'Your life's work?'

'Something like that.'

The unfenced path ran close to the edge of the cliff, and the drop was sheer. After Keith had stopped to point out Boulby cliffs further up the coast, they started walking in single file. The pathway was rough, though mostly level, and they soon got into a comfortable rhythm. Keith was talking most of the time, half turning his head to look at her. He talked about how he was loving England but still felt homesick, and about a body that had been washed up on the beach at Sandsend while he was staying there. No, he hadn't got a good look at it. By the time he had noticed that something was happening quite a crowd had gathered and the police had arrived.

Sue realized now that she would have to kill him. He was just too much of a liability to let go free. She didn't know how the police were progressing on the Grimley investigation, but she was sure that, without Keith, they couldn't link her to the dead man. Keith might not have seen the body, but there was a chance he might find out who it was and, if questioned, remember that strange girl who had acted as if she recognized the man . . . the girl who kept changing her appearance.

But she didn't know if she could do it. Keith had done her no harm; he had only tried to kiss her. But he could give her away before she'd finished, and she couldn't afford to let that happen – not after everything else. Grimley had been a mistake in the first place, and one that almost sent her screaming back home. Now Keith. All she had wanted to do was find the man who had hurt her and murdered the other girls and kill him, put a stop to his carnage once and for all, but she was so deep in blood already and she hadn't even found him yet. How much further would she have to go?

With an effort, she pulled her mind back from this negative track. It wasn't as if she had any choice in the matter, she told herself. Somehow, from somewhere, she would have to dredge up the courage. He was a man, after all, wasn't he? When it came down to it, they were all the same underneath. Hadn't he tried to force himself on her, and wouldn't he do the same again? She shuddered at the thought.

It would be easy to do it up here. Just a gentle push over the edge, or quick kick at the ankles to make him stumble and fall. An accident. But it was too open, and she could see two other walkers approaching from the opposite direction. As it was, they turned out to be serious hikers with binoculars, boots and rucksacks, far more interested in distant seabirds than in fellow human beings, but there must be no witnesses and no probing, time-consuming inquest. As the men passed, Sue looked the other way. So far she was sure that nobody would remember seeing her with Keith, but there was no point in being careless.

Gulls swooped low, flashing white in the sun, and curious insects buzzed around Sue's head. Before long, she could see the crumbling jetty of Port Mulgrave way below, and they began their descent into the tiny village. Keith wanted to stop for a cup of tea and a sandwich at the Boat House Tea Room, but Sue urged him on, saying she was still full from lunch. She was nervous now she had made her decision, and that made her cautious. When she took his hand, he gave in quite easily and they set off up the road to Hinderwell.

Soon they were on a rough track approaching a caravan site, then they turned right, crossed some more fields, and walked down a steep hill to a footbridge over a beck. It was a dramatic change of landscape, from coast to inland valley. They walked through brambles and blackberry bushes, and Sue could see what Keith had meant about snagging her skirt on the thorns. Even in jeans she had to walk carefully. The smell was different here, too. Rotten fish and seaweed were distant memories, replaced by crushed berries and wild garlic in the honeyed air droning with insects.

Beyond the brambles, they entered the woods. The path was bounded on both sides by dense thickets and tall trees. They passed an elderly couple, who smiled and said hello, then after a few minutes walking in the quiet woods, Sue suggested that maybe it was time for a rest.

'But there's nowhere to rest here,' Keith said. 'Just the path.'

'There's the woods, isn't there?' Sue broke free and ran off through the undergrowth. 'Come on, it's nice in here!' she called back. 'Cool and dark. I'm sure we'll find somewhere to sit down.' Keith ran after her.

When they'd gone far enough that they couldn't be seen from the path, Sue pointed to a concave patch of ground between two trees. 'There. Perfect.' She sat and leaned back against a tree trunk. Filtered green light streamed down through the leaves and birds called to one another from their high nests, passing on warnings that intruders had come. Keith lowered himself down beside Sue, so close that their arms touched.

It wasn't long before his hands started wandering, as she had expected, just touching her hair and throat at first. The tension inside her was almost unbearable, but she tried not to stiffen up. Then he kissed her. She let him. She took off her quilted jacket to make a pillow against the rough bark and he started fiddling with the buttons on her shirt. She let him. One button, two buttons, three buttons . . . she had one arm around him and the other groping in her holdall. Her mouth was dry and it still tasted of greasy cod. Four buttons. Now her bra was exposed and he bent forward and kissed the dark cleavage. She sighed. His fingers quickened and soon unbuttoned the shirt right down to her waist. Without bothering to take it off, he pulled the bra up over her breasts. She let him. Her free hand stroked the nape of his neck and tears ran down her flushed cheeks.

Suddenly, he froze.

'My God, Martha! What happened? What on earth happened?'

He pulled back and stared in horror at the puckered zigzags across the skin of her breasts. They looked like an old hag's dugs, as Sue well knew. Her hand closed on the paperweight.

'Nothing,' she said softly. 'Nothing for you to worry about. Why, does it turn you off?'

'Well, no,' he said awkwardly. 'I didn't mean that. I just . . .'

'Go on then, Keith. Go ahead. Kiss them if you like.'

She put her free hand on the back of his head and drew him towards her. As she felt him resist, she pushed harder. She could feel his oily black hair under her fingers and the strength in the knotted muscles at the back of his neck as he shoved against her hand. Tears of anger burned in her eyes. His lips brushed the dead skin where the severed nerve ends had never knit back together. He strained back, but she kept pushing him down. When his mouth reached the place where her right nipple used to be, she brought the paperweight down on the side of his head.

He didn't jerk and twitch like Jack Grimley, and for that she was grateful. She didn't know if she would have been able to stand that without going mad. He just slumped forward into her arms. She rolled him off and he fell onto his back at her feet. Blood bubbled over his ear through his glossy hair onto the earth. She wasn't going to make the mistake of touching the wound this time. Her heart was beating wildly, but at least she didn't feel sick. Perhaps, like everything else, murder got easier with practice.

Sue raised the paperweight again, but the sound of rustling in the undergrowth stopped her. Heart thudding, she looked up straight into the eyes of a large panting collie. The dog just stared at her with its tongue hanging out and its head cocked to one side, as if it wondered what the hell was going on. Sue felt more naked under its gaze than she had under Keith's, and she quickly pulled down her bra and began to button up her shirt. The dog just stood there, watching her with that pained and puzzled expression in its eyes.

Then she heard a faint cry in the distance. The dog's ears pricked up and with a final, despairing glance at her, it turned and ran off through the thicket towards two distant figures standing on the path. This place was too dangerous; she had to get out before someone else came. First, she took Keith's Ordnance Survey guide from his back pocket. She would need that to find her way back to the main road. Then she felt for his pulse. She didn't really know where to look, except from programmes she'd seen on television, but she couldn't feel anything on his wrist. Quickly, she hit him once more, just to make certain. Surely one of the blows must have fractured his skull, she thought. She wiped the paperweight carefully on his shirt, wrapped it in paper handkerchiefs and put it back deep in her holdall.

Next she piled all the loose brush and dead leaves she could find over Keith's body. He looked so innocent lying there, such a babe in the woods. Then she remembered the pressure of his muscles as he had pushed himself away from her, rejected her, and that split second of balance when their strength had been equal and she had killed him. She patted her hair and brushed the leaf mould and twigs from her jeans, then hurried back towards the path. Looking behind her, she couldn't see anything of Keith, just a small mound that looked like an old tree stump. She followed the map about three-quarters of a mile to the main road without passing another soul. Not that it mattered anyway. If anyone did recollect her, it would be Martha Browne they remembered. The police might find Keith soon, and they would make enquiries and track down the bus driver too. But it would be Martha Browne he remembered. And as soon as she got to the toilets near Whitby bus station, Martha Browne would disappear for ever and Sue Bridehead would return.

At the bus stop, she caught her breath, then sat on the warm brick wall at the bottom of someone's garden, where she watched the ants and smoked a cigarette as she waited for the 4.18 back to Whitby.

34

KIRSTEN

'You realize it might take several sessions,' said Laura Henderson, brushing some ash off her white coat, 'and even then there's no guarantee?'

Kirsten nodded. 'But you can do it?'

'Yes, I can do it. About ten per cent of people aren't susceptible to hypnosis, but I don't think we'll have much trouble with you. You're bright, and you've got plenty of imagination. What did Superintendent Elswick say?'

Kirsten shrugged. 'Nothing much. Just asked me if I'd give it a try.'

Laura leaned forward. 'Look, Kirsten,' she said. 'I don't know what's on your mind, but I sense some hostility. I want to remind you that what goes on between us in this office is confidential. I don't want you thinking that I'm somehow just an extension of the police. Naturally, they're keeping tabs on you, and when they found out you were seeing me they made enquiries. I want you to know, though, that I haven't told them anything at all about our sessions, and nor would I, without your permission.'

'I believe you,' Kirsten said. 'Besides, there's been nothing to tell, has there?'

'Hypnosis might change that. Do you still trust me?'

'Yes.'

'And even if we do come up with something, even if the man told you his name for some reason, and you remember it, none of what we discover will be of any legal use.'

'I know that. Superintendent Elswick just said that I might remember something that would help them catch him.'

'Right,' Laura said, relaxing again. 'I just don't want you to expect too much, that's all – either from the hypnotherapy or from the police.'

'Don't worry, I won't. Are you going to get your watch out and swing it in front of my eyes?'

'Have you ever been hypnotized before?'

'Never.'

Laura grinned. 'Well, I'm sorry, but I don't carry a pocket watch. I'm not going to make hand passes at you, either. And my eyes won't suddenly start to glow bright red. You do need something to fix your attention on, true, but I think this'll do fine.' She picked up the heavy glass paperweight from on top of a pile of correspondence. Inside, caught in the glass globe, was what looked like a dark green tangle of seaweed and fronds. 'Do you want to start now?'

Kirsten nodded. Laura got up and closed the blinds on the grey afternoon so that the only light left shone from a shaded desk lamp. Then she took off her white coat and hung it on the stand.

'First of all,' she said, 'I want you to relax. Loosen your belt if it's too tight. It's important to feel as comfortable as possible physically. Okay?'

Kirsten shifted in her chair and tried to relax all her muscles the way she had done in yoga classes at university.

'Now I want you to look at that globe, concentrate, stare into it. Stay relaxed and just listen to me.'

And she started to talk, general stuff about feeling at ease, heavy, sleepy. Kirsten stared into the globe and saw a whole underwater world. The way the light caught the glass, the green fronds seemed to be swaying to and fro very slowly, as if they really were seaweed at the bottom of the sea, weighed down by so much pressure.

When Laura said, 'Your eyelids are heavy,' they were. Kirsten closed her eyes and felt suspended between waking and sleep. She could hear a distant buzzing in her ears, like bees in the garden one childhood summer. The soft voice went on, taking her deeper. Finally, they went back to that night last June. 'You're leaving the party, Kirsten, you're walking out into the street . . .'

And she was. Again it was that muggy night, so vivid that she really felt as if she was there. She entered the park, aware of the soft tarmac path yielding under her trainers, the amber street lights on the main road, the sound of an occasional car passing by. And she could almost recapture the feelings, too, that sense of an ending, the sadness of everyone going his or her own way after what seemed so long together. A dog barked. Kirsten looked up. The stars were fat and blurred, almost butter-coloured, but she couldn't find the moon.

She was at the centre of the park now, and she could see haloed street lights on the bordering roads. She felt a sudden impulse to sit on the lion. The grass swished under her feet as she walked over and touched the warm stone of the mane. Then she mounted it and felt silly but happy, like a little girl again. She thought of cockatoos, monkeys, insects and snakes, then she threw her head back to look for the moon again, and felt herself choking.

Laura's voice cut through the panic, steady and calm,

but Kirsten was still struggling for breath as she tried to drag herself out of the trance. She could feel the calloused hands with their stubby fingers over her mouth, and she was being turned around, pulled off the lion's back onto the warm grass. The world went dark and she couldn't breathe. The cloud in her mind hardened and gleamed like jet, blotting everything out. She felt her back pushed hard against the grass, a great weight on her chest, then she burst up to the surface, gasping for air, and Laura reached forward to hold her hand.

'You're all right,' Laura said. 'It's over. Take a deep breath . . . another . . . That's right.'

Kirsten glanced around her, terrified, and found she was back in the familiar office with its glass-enclosed bookcases, filing cabinets, grinning skull and old hat stand.

'Will you open the blinds?' she asked, putting a hand to her throat and rubbing, 'I feel like I'm at the bottom of the sea.' She was still gulping for breath.

Laura pulled the blinds up, and Kirsten walked over to look out hungrily on the twilit city. She could see the river below, a slate mirror, and the people walking home from work. It was just after five o'clock and the street lights had come on all over the city. She stood there taking in the ordinariness of the scene and breathed deeply for a couple of minutes. Then she sat down opposite Laura again.

'I could do with a drink,' she said.

'Of course.' Laura fetched the Scotch from the cabinet, poured them each a shot, and offered her a cigarette. 'Are you all right now?'

'Better, yes. It was just so . . . so *vivid*. I felt as if I was really living through it all again. I didn't expect it to be as real as that.'

'You're a very imaginative woman, Kirsten. It's bound to be that way for you. Did you learn anything?'

Kirsten shook her head. 'No, it all went black when he turned me around and dragged me to the ground.'

'He did that?'

'Yes, of course he did.'

Laura tapped a column of ash into the tin ashtray. 'That's not what you said before.'

'What do you mean?'

'Don't you remember? Before, you could only remember up to the point of the hand coming from behind. You said nothing about being dragged down.'

Kirsten frowned. 'But that's what must have happened, isn't it?'

'Yes, but this time you actually relived it.'

It was true. Kirsten had remembered the sensation of falling, or of being pushed, onto her back on the ground, and the soft warmth of the grass as it tickled the nape of her neck . . . then the darkness, the weight. 'I didn't see anything, though,' she said.

'Perhaps not. I told you this might take several sessions. The point is that you've made progress. You remembered something you didn't remember before, something you'd buried. It might not be much, and it might not tell you anything, but at least it proves that you can do it, you *can* remember.'

'There's something else, too,' Kirsten said, reaching for her Scotch. 'It's true that I didn't see anything new this time, but you're right, I did get further than I've been before. It's not just images, visual memories, but there are feelings, too, that come back, aren't there?'

'What kind of feelings do you mean? Fear? Pain?'

'Yes, but not just that. Intuitions, inklings . . . it's hard to describe.'

'Try.'

'Well, what I felt was that I *did* see his face. I don't mean now, today, but when it happened. I know I saw him, but I'm still blocking the memory. And there was something else as well. I don't know what it was, but there was definitely something else about him. It was almost there, like a name on the tip of your tongue, but I resisted. I couldn't breathe, and it was so dark I just had to come out.'

'Do you want to carry on?' Laura asked, offering the bottle again. 'You don't have to. Nobody can make you. You know how painful it can be.'

Kirsten tossed back the last of her Scotch and held her glass out. The experience had terrified her, true, but it had also given her something she hadn't felt before: a resolve, a sense of purpose. Her cold hatred had crystallized into a desire to see her attacker. It was all connected, in some strange way, with the dark cloud that weighed down her mind.

When she finally spoke, her eyes were shining and her voice sounded strong and sure. 'Yes,' she said. 'Yes, I do want to carry on, whatever happens. I want to know who did this to me. I want to see his face.'

35

SUSAN

The newspapers had nothing much to report the next morning. Sue sat in her new cafe on Church Street, drinking coffee to get rid of the taste of Mrs Cummings's tea. She knew she would be better off not drinking the vile brew in the first place, but she needed something hot and bitter to wake her up. It was drizzling outside, and the cafe was full of miserable tourists keeping an eye on the weather, spinning out a pot of tea and a slice of gateau until the rain stopped and they could venture out again.

Sue hadn't slept well. She had already been awake when the seagulls started at a quarter to four. Even under the blankets and the bedspread, she had been trembling with delayed shock at what she had done to Keith McLaren. She could still see his stunned, innocent face, the blood pouring over his tanned cheek. She told herself he was just like the rest, like all men, but she still couldn't help hating herself for what she had been forced to do.

When she came to analyse her actions, it was mostly the way she had deliberately set up the situation that disgusted her. Because she didn't see herself as a cold-blooded killer, she had lured Keith into the woods and forced him to put her in a position from which she could strike out in self-righteous anger. In a way, it had been as cold-blooded as any execution; she had just needed to get herself excited enough to kill, and to that end she had seduced Keith, seduced him to death. There was a perverse logic in that somewhere that made even Sue twist her lower lip in the semblance of a smile the next morning, but the night had been dreadful, full of self-loathing, recrimination, loss of nerve. Even the talisman and the litany of victims had offered scant comfort in the small hours.

She had also worried. As it happens when you lie awake during those dreadful hours of the not quite morning with something on your mind, one fear leads directly to another. The disturbed mind seems to toss up terrors with the prolific abandon of a tempestuous ocean. By killing Keith, she had more than doubled her chances of getting caught before she finished what she had set out to do. With two murders to investigate, the police would surely spot the similarities and start stepping up their search. Somebody might have seen her with Keith in Staithes, Port Mulgrave or Hinderwell, and then someone else might remember seeing her with Grimley outside the Lucky Fisherman. Her only hope was that Keith's body would remain undiscovered in the woods until she had finished her task, and that was what she prayed for as she tossed and turned and finally slipped into an uneasy sleep, lulled by the cacophonous requiem of the gulls.

The coffee and cigarette helped her wake up. There was nothing in the nationals about the Student Slasher, but according to the local paper, the police were now certain that Jack Grimley had been murdered. Detective Inspector Cromer said that they were looking into his past for anyone who might have a grudge against him, and they still wanted to know if anyone had seen him after he left the Lucky Fisherman on the night of his death. Clearly no one had come forward so far. Sue remembered that night. She was sure nobody had noticed them, and once they had gone down to the beach and the cave, no one had even known they were there.

Sue's hands shook a little as she combed the rest of the paper for news of Keith's body. Thank God, there was nothing; they clearly hadn't found him yet. But she would still have to move quickly. With the police stepping up their search and Keith's body lying out in the woods for anyone to find, time was no longer on her side.

She knew what she had to do next, but it was still too early in the day. A short distance inland, on the eastern edge of town by the River Esk, stood a factory complex. There, much of the locally caught fish was cleaned, filleted and otherwise processed for resale. Some of it was frozen. The factory employed about a hundred and fifty workers, an even mix of men and women. If the person she was looking for was not a fisherman but was still connected with the industry, that had to be the place to look. She was thinking much more clearly now after the mistake with Jack Grimley.

Even though she knew where to look, she still wasn't sure how to go about it. She could hardly hang about outside the factory gates, check everyone's appearance and ask all likely suspects to say a few words. But what else could she do but watch? She had thought of applying for a job there to get her foot in the door, but that would raise questions of identification, references and National Insurance stamps. She couldn't afford that. Another alternative was to find out if the workers had a favourite pub. Whatever she decided, she would have to start with hanging around the place at five o'clock, when the workers left for the day. Then she could take it from there.

Much as she wanted to, she *couldn't* rush things. The plan left so much time on her hands, and time was a gift to the enemy. Also, today was not the kind of day for sitting on the beach reading, and her room at Mrs Cummings's was far too depressing to spend a whole day in. She had the perennial problem of the English person at the seaside: what to do on a rainy day. She could always look for a cinema that showed afternoon matinees, she thought, or spend her time and money on the one-armed bandits in an amusement arcade. Then there were the Museum and Art Gallery, and Captain Cook's house. There would also be bingo, of course, last resort for the truly desperate.

But Sue knew she wouldn't be able to concentrate on things like that. She had to be actively engaged in her search or her fears would get the better of her. At least she could walk up to the factory and reconnoitre; that would be a positive step. It was in a part of the town that she had never seen before, and she needed to know its layout, its dark corners, its entrances and exits. She also had to find a suitable spot to watch from. There was a chance that she might even need binoculars, though they would look a bit too suspicious if she had to use them in the open.

But first, she realized, there was something else she must do: something she had decided on during her restless, guilty, paranoid hours awake in the night. She needed something to replace her holdall. It wasn't especially conspicuous, just a khaki bag with side pockets and an adjustable strap, but she had been carrying it all the time she had been staying in Whitby, whether as Martha Browne or as Sue Bridehead. It was exactly the kind of mistake that could get her caught. Far better, she thought, to buy something else, fill the holdall full of stones and dump it in the sea along with all her Martha Browne gear – jeans, checked shirt, quilted jacket, the lot. It would be a shame to throw away such good-quality clothing, but it would be dangerous not to. Apart from those few moments on the front at Staithes, it was only as Martha Browne that she could be linked with Keith McLaren and Jack Grimley, so Martha Browne would have to disappear completely.

She paid her bill, then crossed the bridge and walked up to one of the department stores on Flowergate. There she bought a smaller, dark grey shoulder bag – she wouldn't have as much bulky clothing to carry around – a lightweight navy-blue raincoat, and a transparent plastic rainhood. In the toilet, she transferred all the things she would need – paperweight, money, make-up, underwear, book – into the new shoulder bag, and put the old one in the empty plastic bag bearing the store's logo. Anyone who noticed her would think she was simply carrying her shopping. That would do for the moment, but sometime soon she would have to go for a walk along the cliffs and get rid of the holdall permanently.

She walked back over the swing bridge, and instead of turning left onto the touristy part of Church Street, she went right and continued about half a mile along, past New Bridge, which carried the A171 to Scarborough and beyond over the River Esk. To her right, rain pitted the grey surface of the river, and on her left she came to one of those functional, residential parts of town that every holiday resort tucks away from public view. Consulting her map, she turned sharp left, perpendicular to the river, and walked a hundred and fifty yards or so up a lane at the southern edge of a council estate. Finally, she turned right and found herself in the short cul-de-sac that ended at the large mesh gates of the fish-processing plant.

It was the kind of street that would look drab and uninviting whatever the weather. Terraced houses stood on both sides, set back from the road by small gardens complete with privet hedges and wooden gates with peeling paint. The houses were pre-war, judging by the crust of grime and the white patches of saltpetre that had formed on the grey-brown brick. On the road surface, the ancient tarmac had worn away in spots, like bald patches, to reveal the outline of old cobbles beneath. To Sue's left, a short section of the terrace had been converted into a row of shops: grocer, butcher, newsagent-tobacconist, video rental; and on the right, about twenty yards from the factory gates, stood a tiny cafe.

Certainly from the outside there was nothing attractive about the place. The white sign over the grimy plate-glass window was streaked reddish-brown with rusty water that had spilled over from the eaves, and the R and the F of ROSE'S CAFE had faded to no more than mere outlines. Hanging in the window itself was a bleak, handwritten card offering TEA, COFFEE and SAND-WICHES. The location was ideal, though. From a table by the window, Sue would just about be able to see through the film of dirt, and she would have a fine view of the workers filing out of the gates down the street. As far as she could tell, there was no other direction they could take.

She walked all the way up to the gates themselves.

They stood open, and there was no guardhouse or sentry post. Obviously, national defence wasn't at stake, and a fish-processing plant had little to worry about from terrorists or criminal gangs. A dirt path ran a hundred yards or so through a weed- and cinder-covered stretch of waste ground to the factory itself, a long two-storey prefab concrete building with a new red-brick extension stuck on the front for clerical staff. Inside the glass doors was what looked like a reception area, and the windows in the extension revealed offices lit by fluorescent light. Apart from the front, the only other side of the factory that Sue could see was the one closest to the river, and it was made up entirely of numbered loading bays. Several white vans were parked in the area and drivers in blue overalls stood around talking and smoking.

As Sue stood by the gates memorizing the layout, a loud siren sounded inside the building and a few seconds later people started to hurry out towards her. She looked at her watch: twelve o'clock, lunch hour. Quickly, she turned back and slipped into the cafe. A bell pinged as she entered, and a wrinkled beanpole of a woman in curlers and a greasy smock glanced up at her from behind the counter, where she had been buttering slices of thin white bread for sandwiches.

'You must have nipped out early, love,' the woman said cheerfully. 'Usually takes them all of thirty seconds to get here after the buzzer goes. Them as comes, that is. Now the Brown Cow up the road does pub lunches, there's plenty 'as deserted poor Rose's. Don't hold with lunchtime drinking, myself. What'll you have then? A nice cup of tea?'

Was there any other kind? Sue wondered. 'Yes, thanks, that'll do fine,' she said.

The woman frowned at her. 'Just a cup of tea? You need a bit more than that, lass. Put some meat on your bones. How about one of these lovely potted-meat sandwiches? Or are you one of them as brings her own lunch?' Her glance had turned suspicious now.

Sue felt flustered. It was all going wrong. She was supposed to slip into the place unobtrusively and order from a bored waitress who would pay her no attention. Instead, she had gone and made herself conspicuous just because she had run for cover when the siren went and everyone had started hurrying towards her. She was too jumpy, not very good at this kind of thing.

'I'm on a diet,' she offered weakly.

'Huh!' the woman snorted. 'I don't know about young 'uns today, I really don't. No wonder you've all got this annexa nirvana or whatever they calls it. Cup of tea it is, then, but don't blame me if you start having them there dizzy spells.' She poured the black steaming liquid from a battered old aluminium pot. 'Milk and sugar?'

Sue looked at the dark liquid. 'Yes, please,' she said.

'New there, are you?' the woman asked, pushing the cup and saucer along the red Formica counter.

'Yes,' said Sue. 'Only started today.'

'Been taking time off for shopping already, too, I see,' the woman said, looking down at Sue's carrier bag. 'Don't see why you'd want to shop in that place when there's a Marks and Sparks handy.' She looked at the bag again. 'Pricey that lot are. They charge for the name, you know. It's all made in Hong Kong anyroads.'

Would she never stop? Sue wondered, blushing and thinking frantically about what to say in reply. As it happened, she didn't have to. The woman went on to ask an even more difficult question: 'Who d'you work for, old Villiers?'

'Yes,' said Sue, without thinking at all.

The woman smiled knowingly. 'Well take my advice, love, and watch out for him. Wandering hands, he's got, and as many of 'em as an octopus, so I've heard.' She put a finger to the side of her nose. The door pinged loudly behind them. 'Hey up, here they come!' she said, turning away from Sue at last. 'Right, who's first? Come on, don't all shout at once!'

Sue managed to weave her way through the small crowd and take the table by the window. She hoped that old Villiers and his friends were among the people who had deserted Rose's for the Brown Cow. If they were management, it was very unlikely that they spent their lunch hour eating potted-meat sandwiches and drinking tannic tea in a poky cafe.

Still, it was a bloody disaster. Sue had thought she could come to this place every day at about five o'clock for as long as it took without arousing much attention. After that, providing the weather improved and the police didn't catch up with her, if she needed to stay any longer she could buy some cheap binoculars and watch from the clump of trees just above the factory site. But now she had been spotted and, what's more, she had lied. If the woman found out that Sue didn't work at the factory, she would become suspicious. After all, Rose's Cafe was hardly a tourist attraction. She would have to spy from the woods now, whatever the weather. The only bright spot on the horizon was the Brown Cow. If workers went there at lunchtime, perhaps some also returned in the evening after work. It was easier to be unobtrusive in a large busy pub than in a small cafe like Rose's.

Annoyed with herself and with the weather, Sue lit a cigarette and examined the faces of the other people in the cafe, making the best of what time she had. Calm down, she told herself. It won't take that long to find him if he's here. It can't.

36

KIRSTEN

'What else did you remember?' Sarah asked, leaning forward over the table and cupping her chin in her hands.

'That's just it,' Kirsten said. 'Nothing. It's so frustrating. I've had two more sessions since then and got nowhere. Every time I pull back at the same point.'

It was seven o'clock in the evening. Kirsten had parked the car off Dorchester Street and met Sarah at the station about an hour earlier. They had walked up to the city centre in the lightly falling snow and now sat in a pub on Cheap Street near the Abbey. The place was busy with the after-work crowd and Christmas shoppers taking a break. Kirsten and Sarah had just managed to squeeze in at a small table.

'Are you going to carry on?' Sarah asked.

Kirsten nodded. 'I've got another session in the morning.'

'So you *do* want to know?'

'Yes.'

'You know there's been another one, don't you, just before the end of term? That makes two now – three including you.'

'Kathleen Shannon,' Kirsten said. 'Aged twenty-two. She was a music student. I only wish . . .'

'What?'

'Nothing.'

'Come on, Kirstie. It's me, Sarah, remember?'

Kirsten smiled. 'You'll probably think I'm mad. I feel so empty sometimes and then I get so angry. I keep thinking of those two others. And there's this block, like a huge black lump or a thick cloud in my mind, and the whole memory's locked in there. I don't think it will go away, Sarah, even if the police do get him. What if they find him and they can't prove he did it? What if he gets off with probation or something? He might even slip away from them.'

'Well, that's their problem, isn't it? You know I'm not the police's greatest fan, but I suppose they know their job when it comes to things like this. After all, it's respectable middle-class girls getting killed, not prostitutes.'

'Maybe. But I just wish *I* knew who it was. I wish I could find him myself.'

Sarah stared at her and narrowed her eyes. 'And what would you do?'

Kirsten paused and drew a circle on the wet table with her finger. 'I think I'd kill him.'

'Vigilante justice?'

'Why not?'

'Have you ever thought that it might turn out the other way round, that he'd be the one killing you?'

'Yes,' Kirsten said quietly. 'I've thought of that.'

'Don't tell me you're feeling suicidal?'

'No, that's gone. Dr Henderson, Laura, helped a lot. They all say I'm making wonderful progress, and I suppose I am really, but . . .'

'But what?'

Kirsten fumbled for a cigarette. Sarah raised her eyebrows, but said nothing. The couple beside them left and two young men took their place. Someone put a U2 song on the jukebox and Kirsten had to speak louder to make herself heard. 'They don't know what it feels like to be me, do they? Living half a life, in limbo. I don't feel that I'll get out of it until I've met him again and I know he's dead.'

'That's ridiculous,' said Sarah. 'Besides, you wouldn't know where to look for him any more than the police do.'

'No, I wouldn't. Not yet, anyway.' She took a long deep drag on the cigarette and blew the smoke out slowly. 'Shall we have another drink? Then you can tell me all about the others and how Harridan's doing.'

Sarah nodded and Kirsten made her way to the bar. She didn't have to wait long to get served. The crowd had thinned out a bit now, as many of the after-work drinkers had gone home and the evening regulars hadn't arrived yet. The two lads at the next table were still there, though, talking enthusiastically about girls. Kirsten ignored the way they looked at her as she walked back, and sat down again.

'What about Galen?' Sarah asked.

'I got a Christmas card from him. He seems to be doing all right.'

'Are you two . . .?'

Kirsten shook her head. 'It's not his fault, really. He tried – God, how he tried – but I put him off. I don't think I could handle a relationship with a man right now.' She remembered that she had never told Sarah the full extent of her injuries and wondered whether she should do so. Not now, she decided, but perhaps sometime over the next few days. Sarah had stuck by her; she deserved to know. Kirsten also remembered the small pile of unopened letters, most of them from Galen, that she had put away in her drawer.

As they chatted about old friends, the bookshop and the bedsit, Kirsten noticed the two lads looking at her again and talking to one another. During a lull in the conversation, the old Kinks song on the jukebox ended and she overheard them.

One said something about her looking stuck up and needing a really good fuck. The other laughed and said something she could only catch the end of: '. . . enough cock to pave the road from here to Land's End – ends up!' And they burst into laughter.

Kirsten whirled round and flung the rest of her lager at them. As they recoiled in shock, their knees knocked the table and their glasses tipped over, rolled onto the stone floor and smashed. Beer spilled all over the place. In a flash, the landlord rushed over. 'Hey! I don't want no trouble.' Before they knew what had happened, Kirsten and Sarah found themselves back out in Cheap Street. They had no idea where the two boys had got to.

Kirsten leaned against a lamppost to catch her breath, and Sarah stood beside her, laughing. 'Well, you really showed them, didn't you? And I thought getting chucked out of pubs was my speciality.'

'Did you hear what they said?'

'Yeah, some of it. Come on, love, let's walk a bit. Their kind's not worth bothering about. Besides, it's not as far from here to Land's End as it is from up north.'

'I suppose that does water down the insult a bit,' Kirsten said. 'Lancashire, I'd say, from the way they talked. Probably Manchester.'

Sarah raised her eyebrows. 'I'm impressed. I've already forgotten most of what I learned last year, but you still remember that linguistics stuff.'

Kirsten managed a smile. 'I suppose it's like riding a

bike. You never forget. Anyway, we should be going home soon. I said we wouldn't be late.'

The snow was still falling. Now the flakes were bigger and fatter, and an inch or two had settled on the roads and pavements, where it was soon churned up into grey slush by cars and pedestrians. They walked past the floodlit Abbey and turned right onto Pierrepont Street. Beyond Parade Gardens, the river reflected the strings of red and green Christmas lights, and snowflakes drifted down to melt on the water's surface. There were still plenty of shoppers about with huge carrier bags full of presents.

'Nice,' said Sarah, when she saw the Audi.

Kirsten took a scraper from the boot and wiped the snow from the windscreen, then she negotiated the one-way system onto Wells Road. Soon they had left the city behind and turned off the main road onto the narrow country lanes. Here the snow lay undisturbed before the car's wheels, a pristine white carpet glittering in the headlights. Thick flakes fell and stuck to the window, melting before the wipers could brush them away.

Almost without realizing it, Kirsten found herself pressing her foot down on the accelerator. She knew these winding roads like the back of her hand. They were all so narrow that drivers had to pull into the frequent passing places if they met someone coming in the oppo-site direction, and the hedgerows were so tall that no one could see what was around the next corner. Kirsten felt the car going faster and faster, the snow rushing at the windscreen like a blizzard. She started to slip a little on the corners. The needle edged higher and adrenalin surged in her veins. She couldn't stop herself even if she wanted to.

After a while, she became aware of a distant voice and felt a hand shaking her. It was Sarah yelling for her to slow down. She looked terrified. All of a sudden, Kirsten felt herself snap back, and eased her foot off the accelerator. She felt drained. Sarah was still ranting on about getting them killed and asking her if she was crazy. Finally, Kirsten just had to stop. She pulled into the first passing place she came across, put on the brakes and turned off the engine. Her hands were shaking on the wheel.

'Are you trying to get us both killed?' Sarah yelled.

Kirsten couldn't speak.

'Well, it's all right with me if you want to kill yourself,' Sarah went on angrily, 'but just leave me out of it, all right? I'd rather bloody well walk, even though I don't know where the hell I am.' And she reached for the door handle.

Kirsten leaned over to stop her. 'Don't,' she said urgently. 'I'm sorry, Sarah, I . . . I don't know . . .'

Sarah paused and turned back, concern showing in her fine, pale features. 'You all right?'

Kirsten's hands still gripped the wheel so tightly that her knuckles shone as white as the snow. She shook her head. She could feel the intense silence and darkness outside the car. Without lights, the snow only showed up as a faint pearly sheen on the road and hedges. The Mendip Hills were lost somewhere in the night. Inside, their breath misted the windows.

'Kirstie?' Sarah asked again. 'Are you all right, love?'

Kirsten let go of the wheel and threw herself towards Sarah with a strength and desperation that almost sent them both flying out of the door.

'No,' she cried. 'No, I'm not all right at all.'

She hung on tight and felt Sarah's arms close around her, holding her and muttering soft words. For the first time since it happened, she began to really cry. The warm salt tears didn't just trickle down her cheeks, they welled up in her eyes and poured over onto Sarah's shoulder as Kirsten clung on and sobbed.

37

SUSAN

After two days without success, Sue almost gave up. There seemed to be too many obstacles in her way, and she was making too many mistakes. For a start, the conversation with the woman in Rose's Cafe worried her, then she overheard two workers talking and learned that the factory operated on a shift system. Only the office workers came teeming out of the mesh gates at five o'clock. Most of the people on the shop floor worked one of the shifts: noon to eight, eight to four, and four to noon. Finding him now seemed like an impossible task. She could hardly turn up there at four in the morning and stand gawking as the workers filed out.

Even the weather continued to work against her. It rained on and off, and the temperature dropped low enough that she had to wear her cardigan under the raincoat. She was quite prepared to spend some of her fast-dwindling money on binoculars and go up to the woods, even though the ground would be wet, but fortunately it didn't come to that. A couple of pieces of good luck kept her going.

The first evening at five, she approached the gates again, and when she passed the cafe she noticed a different woman behind the counter. This one was younger, with long, stringy blonde hair. There were a few people sitting in the place already, so Sue entered, head bowed like someone just seeking refuge from the rain, bought a cup of tea without having to answer any questions, and took the window seat. Perhaps the woman she had met there before only worked lunchtimes? She wouldn't need to spend so much of her money on binoculars and end up catching pneumonia in the damp woods after all.

The problem of the shifts remained, and Sue didn't know how to get around that one. She certainly couldn't afford binoculars with infrared lenses, so the four a.m. changeover was beyond her. That left noon and eight at night, both of which she could cover from the Brown Cow.

Cheered by the turn in her fortunes, Sue left Rose's Cafe just after five-thirty on the first day, treated herself to cannelloni and salad in a rather expensive restaurant on New Quay Road near the station – a place that didn't specialize in fish and chips – and then went back over the Esk at a quarter to eight to find the Brown Cow. Instead of turning right at the cul-de-sac that led to the factory, she continued up the lane past the edge of the council estate and found the pub about a hundred yards further on. It was an undistinguished modern red-brick place with a Tetley's sign hanging outside.

The doors opened into a large lounge, completely lacking in character: dull beige wallpaper and a stained brown carpet, sticky and worn in patches. The tables were made of some kind of tough black plastic, and the moulded seats were uncomfortable. It was a functional place. Clearly the only people who went there were those who lived on the nearby estate. Factory workers might drop by at lunchtime, Sue thought glumly, but they weren't likely to make an evening of it there when the shift ended at eight o'clock.

However depressing the Brown Cow seemed to Sue, though, it was certainly busy enough. Well over three-quarters of the tables were occupied, and everyone seemed to be having a good time. The obligatory jukebox had a tendency towards ancient Engelbert Humperdinck and Tom Jones songs, and the row of one-armed bandits and video games winked seductively by the far wall like a line of tarts in a brothel. Plump women smoked and gossiped while plump men smoked and shoved coins into the machines.

In her raincoat and hood, Sue thought she looked drab and anonymous enough not to attract too much attention in her dim corner. As it turned out, though, she didn't have to stay long. When no crowd of workers had turned up by twenty-five past eight, she felt her suspicions confirmed and left. Like most seaside cafes, Rose's had closed at six o'clock, just about the time when people were ready for dinner, so there was nowhere else to watch from.

Lunchtime on the second day seemed more promising. Not only did several of the office workers call in at the Brown Cow, but quite a few of the factory men came in for a pie and a pint at the end of their shift. Sue still didn't see the man she wanted, and she began to wonder how much longer she could go on. Though Keith's body hadn't been found yet and nothing new had appeared in the papers, she was beginning to worry that the police might be getting close. Her money wouldn't last for ever, either, and she hardly dared contemplate the consequences if she was wrong about her quarry's origins. She had put so much energy into the search, gambled so much of herself on the outcome, that failure didn't bear thinking about.

Especially now that two innocent people lay dead because of her.

She went to Rose's Cafe again that evening around five and turned up at the Brown Cow at eight. Still nothing. By the third day she was thoroughly discouraged and depressed by the endless shuttling between two such awful environments. The world she now seemed to inhabit, though no more than a mile or so from the beach, the whale's jawbone, Captain Cook's statue, St Mary's and the twee shops of Church Street, was so drab and anonymous that it could have been almost anywhere in any English city.

It was also a world of shadows. She was getting jumpy, thinking people were following her and watching her. It was silly, she told herself. She was the one doing the watching. But she couldn't get the feeling out of her mind. She hardly slept at night, and not only because of the gulls. She started to think that her days in the sun on West Cliff had been a dream; now she had passed through the whale's jawbone into its dark, dank, dripping belly and there was no way out. Then, on the third day, she saw him.

38

KIRSTEN

The green fronds began to sway and Kirsten felt the weight of the ocean on her eyelids. Laura's voice murmured in the distance, urging her deeper, pressing her on, and then she heard the buzzing in her ears and she was walking out into the street one muggy June night aeons ago . . .

She could feel the tarmac path, softened by the day's heat, yield like a pile carpet under her feet and hear the swishing of her jeans as she walked. A car droned in the distance. A dog barked. Kirsten looked up. The stars were fat and blurred, almost butter-coloured in the haze, but she couldn't find the moon. It must be behind those high trees, she thought as she hurried on.

She stood at the centre of the park, where she could see the glow of the haloed street lights beyond the trees, and felt an urge to sit on the lion. She walked across the narrow patch of grass and mounted it. Images of cockatoos, monkeys, insects and snakes ran through her mind. She laughed and tossed her head back to look for the moon again behind the trees, then she felt the rough hand over her mouth and nose.

Her chest was tight and she knew she was kicking and struggling for air as someone manoeuvred her off the lion onto her back. Long grass tickled the nape of her neck.

And suddenly there was a moon. It was shining

through a gap between the trees on the spot where she had been dragged. And it lit up his face. It was dim and ghostly in the pale light, but a face nonetheless: deeply lined, with a short, black fringe low on the broad forehead and dark eyebrows that met in the middle. And his eyes. Even in the poor light she could see how they glittered and how they were far beyond reason.

For a moment, the image seemed to freeze and two time frames superimposed. She lay pinned to the ground, looking up into his face, but at the same time she seemed to be facing him directly through a haze. The vision disappeared almost as soon as it had formed. Again she lay on the ground fighting for breath as he shoved a coarse oily rag in her mouth. She was gagging, suffocating, she couldn't go on . . . The next thing she heard was Laura's voice slowly drawing her up from the depths.

Kirsten opened her eyes and took several deep breaths. Laura poured her a cup of coffee. As usual after the hypnotherapy sessions, Kirsten was grateful for the big window and its view of the city. She felt she had been lost in a deep airless vault and needed some air in her lungs, to see horizons again. Laura always waited a while before speaking, but this time Kirsten broke the silence.

'Did you get it all down?'

Laura nodded. She looked pale. 'You went further than you've ever been before.'

'I know. This time it was different. I couldn't stop myself going on even if I'd wanted to. Until he put that awful smelly rag . . . I couldn't breathe. I was choking.' She put her hand to her throat as if she still felt the pain.

'Your voice wasn't always easy to catch,' Laura said.

'You spoke very quickly, and sometimes you mumbled. Could we go over some of the details?'

Kirsten nodded, and Laura took notes as they analysed the session. When it was over, Kirsten wandered out into the grey day and stood watching the Avon churn down by the city weir. She felt curiously detached from the bustling city life around her. She knew that she could have gone on reliving the experience if it hadn't been for the choking sensation. That had felt too real to suffer through. But she did remember something else now, something she hadn't been quite able to grasp at the time. Hands in pockets, she sauntered towards High Street to meet Sarah for lunch.

The pub was warm and noisy. Conversations swirled around Kirsten like the buzzing of insects. She felt as if she was floating. It was a pleasant sensation, though; it had been a long time since she had felt grateful for the atmosphere of a crowded pub. Sarah was sitting close to the side door, a half of lager in front of her and a paperback in her hand. Kirsten waved to her, stopped at the bar for drinks and went over. Sarah shifted some parcels from the chair next to her and put them on the floor. Kirsten sat down.

'Christmas presents,' Sarah said.

Kirsten sipped her double Scotch and reached for her cigarettes.

'Are you all right?' Sarah asked. 'You look a bit pale.'

'I'm fine,' Kirsten said. 'I just had a bit of a shock, that's all. I feel dazed.'

'What was it? The hypnosis?'

Kirsten nodded. 'I remembered, Sarah. I remembered what he looked like.' Her voice sounded shaky and far away to her.

Sarah put her hand on Kirsten's arm. 'You don't have to talk about it—'

'No, it's all right. I don't mind. At least not with you anyway . . . a friend. Laura's a doctor. She's being paid to help me, however nice she is. I mean, I like her and I'm very grateful to her, but . . .'

'It doesn't go any deeper?'

'No. When it's not me in the office, it's someone else, isn't it? And she's probably just the same with them. It's nothing special; it's impersonal, like the police.' And she told Sarah about finally seeing her attacker.

'How old do you think he was?' Sarah asked.

'I never really thought. About forty, forty-five, I suppose. Pretty old. It's just that he had this lined face, you know, rough-hewn, lines from the edges of the nose and the mouth.' She drew them with her fingers on her own face, then she shuddered. 'It was awful, Sarah. It was like going through the whole thing again, but I couldn't stop myself. I didn't want to.'

'What happened next?'

'Laura brought me out of it.'

'Have you told the police what he looked like?'

Kirsten sipped some Scotch and glanced towards the bar. Things were coming into clearer focus now; her feet were touching the ground.

'Not yet. Laura's going to phone them and send a report.'

'Are you sure you're telling me everything?' Sarah asked.

'Why?'

'You sound vague, and you've got that shifty look on your face. I've known you long enough to tell when you're holding something back. What is it?'

Kirsten paused and swirled her drink in her glass before answering. 'There was something else . . . just an impression. I can't really be sure.'

'What was it?'

'When he put the gag in my mouth, I was too busy struggling, trying to catch my breath, to really notice at the time.'

'Notice what?'

'The smell. There was a smell of fish. You know, like at the seaside.'

'Fish?'

Kirsten nodded. 'It probably doesn't mean anything.'

'What did the doctor say?'

'Nothing.'

'What do you mean?'

'I didn't remember it until I'd left her office, when I was coming here to meet you.'

'Why don't you phone her?'

Kirsten shrugged. 'Like I said, it's probably not important.'

'But that's not for you to decide.'

Kirsten toyed with her cigarette in the large blue ashtray, shaping the end in one of its grooves. She felt herself starting to drift again like the smoke that curled and twisted in front of her. 'I don't know,' she said. 'It just seems that I keep feeding them bits of my memory, you know, things I've had sweated out of me, and nothing happens. They're so impersonal, just a big bureaucratic machine. I mean, two more girls have been killed since my . . . *two*. I can't explain myself, Sarah, not yet, but it's me and him. I feel I've got it in me to find him. It's as if he's inside me and I'm the only one who can flush him out.'

'And then what?'

'I don't know.'

'Jesus Christ! Kirstie. If you ask me you're turning a bit batty. It must be all that solitude and country air.' She put her hand on Kirsten's arm again. 'You really should tell the police everything you can remember. Like you said, he's killed two women already, and there's bound to be more. People like him don't stop till they're caught, you know.'

'Do you think I don't know that,' said Kirsten, pulling her arm away angrily. 'Do you think I don't feel for those women? I have to live what they died.'

'Come again?'

'It doesn't matter. I'm sorry if I seem so touchy about it. I can't explain. I'm not even sure what I mean myself.'

Kirsten sipped some more Scotch and looked around the pub again. The people looked indistinct; their conversations were just meaningless sounds. Sarah changed the subject to shopping.

As she half-listened and let herself be lulled by the buzz of talk around her, Kirsten came to a decision. People didn't understand her, it seemed. Not even Sarah. People didn't understand how *personal* it was. Not just for her, but for Margaret Snell and Kathleen Shannon too. Doctors, police . . . what did they know? In future, she would have to be careful just how much she told them.

When she tasted that foul rag he had stuffed in her mouth and smelled his rough stubby fingers, she recognized the saltwater taste as well as the fishy odour. The rag tasted as if it had been dipped in the sea. Wasn't there, then, a good chance that he had come from a coastal town?

And there was something else. Not only had she

remembered the smell, but when he had thrown her to the ground and put the rag in her mouth as she stared up at him in the moonlight, his mouth had been moving. He had been talking to her. She couldn't hear any sounds or words, but she knew he had spoken, and if she could bring that back, there was no knowing what it might tell her about him. It might even lead her to him.

39

SUSAN

As Susan approached the Brown Cow at lunchtime on the third day, she saw two white factory vans parked in front, and before she had even got near the entrance, two men came out of the pub and walked over to them. It was impossible to be sure from such a distance, but one of them matched the image in her memory: low, dark fringe, the thick eyebrows meeting in the middle. She had to get closer to see if he had deep lines on his face and, most of all, she needed to hear his voice.

When they started their vans and pulled out, she followed on foot. At least she could see which way they turned as they drove down the lane. If they went left, they would be on their way to the factory, and if they carried on down to the main road, they would be off making a delivery somewhere. She was in luck. They turned left.

Sue hurried after them. She didn't know what she was going to do, but there was no point in hanging around the Brown Cow any longer. When she reached the turning, the vans had already pulled up outside the loading bays a hundred yards beyond the mesh gates, and the drivers were nowhere in sight. She walked along the street as far as the row of shops. She couldn't just wander through the factory gates and go looking for the man;

nor could she sit in the cafe where the inquisitive woman would be on duty. What could she do?

Before she had time to come up with a plan, she noticed the man walk out of the glass doors of the office building. He seemed to be slipping a small envelope of some kind into his pocket. A pay packet, perhaps? Whatever it was, he looked as though he had finished for the day. If he was a driver, the odds were that he had just returned from an overnight run, padded his time sheet with an hour or so at the Brown Cow, and was now on his way home.

He was walking towards her, only about forty yards away now on the dirt track that led out of the factory. She had nowhere to hide. She couldn't just stand there in the street until he came level with her. What if he recognized her? She had changed a lot since their last meeting, lost a lot of weight, though her wig was about the same length as her hair had been then. Surely he couldn't have got a much clearer impression of her looks than she had of his? But she couldn't stand rooted to the spot.

There was only one thing to do. She rushed forward and ducked into the newsagent's. She needed her morning papers anyway, as she had been so absorbed in her new routine that she hadn't even spent her usual hour in the Church Street cafe. She hadn't looked for news of Keith, and she was still feeling nervous about the Grimley investigation, though no one had knocked on her door in the middle of the night yet.

The newspapers were arranged in small, overlapping piles on a low shelf just inside the window, below the rack of magazines. From there, as she pretended to make her selection with her back turned to the newsagent, she could get a closer look at the man as he went past. She bent and pretended to leaf through the stack, as if she were scanning the front pages for the best headlines, when suddenly he appeared right outside. He didn't walk past as she had expected. Instead, he patted his pockets, turned and came inside.

Sue kept her back to the counter and examined the *Radio Times* and *Woman's Own* in the rack above the papers.

'Afternoon, Greg,' she heard the woman say. 'In for some baccy, I suppose?'

'Yes, please.' The man's voice sounded muffled and Sue couldn't hear him clearly.

'Usual?'

'Aye. Oh, and I'll have a box of matches, too, please, love. Swan Vestas.'

'Finished for the day?'

'Aye. Just got back from the Leeds and Bradford run. Can't leave the poor beggars without their fish and chips, can we?'

The newsagent laughed.

Sue gripped the rack of magazines to keep herself from falling over. Her heart was beating so fast and loud that she thought it would burst. At the very least, both the newsagent and the man in the shop must be able to hear it. Her face was flushed and her breath was hard to catch. Everything seemed to swim and ripple in front of her eyes like motes dancing in rays of light: the magazine covers, the grim terraced houses across the street. And all the while she struggled to stay on her feet; she couldn't let these two people see that there was anything wrong with her. They would rush over to help, and then . . .

Sue held on and fought for control as the voice, the horrible, familiar voice that had been whispering hoarsely in her nightmares for a month, carried on making small talk as if nothing terrible had ever happened.

40

KIRSTEN

When Kirsten stood on the platform and watched the Intercity pull out at 12.25 on 3 January, she felt frightened and desolate. Despite an awkward beginning, Christmas at Brierley Coombe that year had turned out to be the best time she had enjoyed since the assault. She had been glad to have Sarah around, especially as a counter to all the uncles, aunts and grandparents who had treated her as if she were a half-witted invalid.

The village itself looked like a Christmas-card illustration. The snow that began on 22 December went on for almost two days and settled a treat, particularly out in the country, where there was little traffic and no industry to spoil it. It lay about two feet thick on the thatched roofs, smooth and contoured around the eaves and gables; and in the woods, where Kirsten often took Sarah for early-morning walks, the snow that rested on twigs and branches created an image of two worlds in stark contrast, the white superimposed on the dark.

They went into Bath once more to do some shopping at the Boxing Day sales and have drinks with Laura Henderson, whom Sarah liked immediately. One night they shocked the locals in the village pub. Sarah wore her FISH ON A BICYCLE T-shirt, and everyone looked embarrassed. There she was: the careless tangle of blonde hair, the pale complexion and exquisite features that looked as if they had been expertly worked from the finest porcelain, then smoothed and polished to perfection, and, to cap it all, that great advertisement for the redundancy of the male sex scrawled across her chest.

Nobody bothered them, like the Lancashire lads in Bath had, but the village men glanced over and muttered nervously among themselves, some of them smiling superciliously. It was the most uncomfortable evening of the holiday for Kirsten. Her enjoyment of crowded pubs didn't seem to have lasted long. She could relax with Laura and Sarah, but the proximity of men still made her tense and angry. And when they looked over with those superior smiles on their faces, her cheeks burned with fear and anger. After all, a man had taken what other men wanted from her. Somehow, she reasoned, they were all implicated in that.

On New Year's Eve, Kirsten's parents went to a party. Kirsten and Sarah were invited, but neither of them fancied spending the evening with a bunch of drunken old stockbrokers, their bored wives and yuppie offspring, so they decided to stay at home and celebrate by themselves.

The cocktail cabinet was well stocked, a log fire blazed in the hearth, and they turned out the lights and lit candles instead. The open curtains of the French windows revealed the snow-covered garden and trees. Kirsten brought some of her records and tapes down from her room to play on her father's stereo, and everything seemed perfect. They sat on the thick rug in front of the spitting fire, listening to Mozart, with the cognac bottle beside them.

'What are you going to do?' Sarah asked as she poured out their second drinks.

'With my life, you mean?'

'Yes.'

'I don't know. I haven't made any plans.'

'You can't just stay here for ever, you know.' Sarah looked around the room, where the candles and fire tossed shadows like dark sails in a storm, and out of the windows at the fairy-tale garden in the snow. 'Nice as it is, it isn't real life. Not yours.'

'And what is my life?'

'For Christ's sake, you got a First, a good one. You're not going to waste your education, are you?'

Kirsten laughed. 'Listen to yourself. You sound like a bloody guidance counsellor or something.'

Sarah bit her lip and looked away.

'I'm sorry.' Kirsten reached out and touched her shoulder. 'I didn't mean that. It's just that I haven't thought about it. I suppose I've put the future off and I resent being made to dwell on it.'

'Why don't you go back to university, do your MA? It needn't be up north if you don't want. There's plenty of other places would be glad to have you.'

Kirsten nodded slowly. 'I won't say it hasn't crossed my mind. But I couldn't start till the next academic year. What would I do in the meantime?'

Sarah laughed. 'How the hell should I know? What do you think I am, a guidance counsellor? But seriously, you could get a job, something in Bath. Just to keep you going and take you out of yourself. You've got too much time to brood on the past hanging around this village. What about a bookshop, for example? You'd probably like that.'

'But what would my mother think?' She put on a finishing-school accent: 'I mean, it's *awfully* common being a shopgirl, dear.'

Sarah laughed. 'Is that why she's so frosty towards me? Maybe I should tell her my father owns half of Herefordshire. Think that would help?'

'I'm sure it would. She's such a snob.'

'Seriously though, Kirstie, you've got to do something, get out of here. What about Toronto? You could go out there and join Galen.'

Kirsten topped up both their drinks. It was eleven-thirty. Mozart's *Requiem* had just ended and the world outside was silent and still.

'Well?' Sarah repeated. 'What about it? Or is it over between you?'

Kirsten stared into the fire. Flames licked the wood like angry tongues. If I don't tell her now, she thought, I probably never will. She looked at Sarah, so lovely in the winter firelight with red and orange and yellow flames dancing in her eyes and flickering over her face. Her skin looked almost transparent, especially where the fire seemed to shine a delicate coral through her nostrils and over her cheekbones. And she had it all: not just the looks, but a whole body. She could make love and have orgasms and have children.

'What is it?' Sarah asked softly.

Kirsten realized that a tear had trickled from the corner of one eye. Quickly, she wiped it away. She would have to stop this crying business. Once was all right, it had helped drain her of tension, but it mustn't become a habit, a weakness.

Over another cigarette, she finally told Sarah all about the damage to her body. Sarah listened in horror and couldn't find anything to say. She poured more cognac. They leaned back against the sofa, and Sarah put her arm around Kirsten and held her close. There were no more tears. They sat like that, content and silent for a while, sipping Rémy. Finally, Sarah swore softly: 'Shit, it's ten past twelve. We've forgotten the new year.'

Kirsten looked up and the spell was broken. Her back ached from the position she'd been sitting in. 'So it is. Never mind. I'll get the Veuve Clicquot and we'll have our own new year a bit late.' She stood up, rubbed her aching muscles, and went into the kitchen.

And so they had poured champagne, sung 'Auld Lang Syne' and wished each other a Happy New Year at twenty past twelve.

And now Sarah was gone. Kirsten walked aimlessly around Bath, its streets quiet with post-seasonal depression, and thought over what Sarah had said about the future. She decided that she would resume her studies, or at least apply for next year. It would be a good cover, and it would keep her parents off her back.

In the meantime, she was going to attempt to find out who had crippled her. It might take months, she realized, but at least now she had discovered that the knowledge was there, locked inside her. Of course, she must take care that no one suspected what she was really up to; she had to appear as if she was simply getting on with her life and putting the past behind her. She didn't know yet what she was going to do if she did discover anything, but she had to find the key, unlock the voice, and then . . . First, though, she had a lot of thinking and a lot of planning to do.

41

SUSAN

By the time the man had left the newsagent's, Sue had managed to get her breathing under control. She bought her papers and a packet of cigarettes, then walked back out into the drizzle.

He had reached the end of the street and turned left, down the lane towards the water. Without really considering what she was going to do, Sue started following him. She half expected him to turn into the council estate, assuming that was where he lived, but he didn't. Instead of walking down to Church Street, however, he turned right along a narrow road that ran parallel to it.

There were no houses on the right-hand side of the street, just a stretch of waste ground that sloped up to the southern edge of the council estate, almost hidden beyond the convex swell of the land. On the left stood a row of small, detached cottages. They were nothing much really – just red brick with slate roofs – but each had its own front and back gardens. Their rear windows would also look out over the harbour towards West Cliff, and a good view always costs money.

Sue had tried to hang back a reasonable distance behind the man, and she didn't think he had spotted her. Beyond the row of cottages lay another open tract of weeds and nettles, where the street itself petered out into a narrow dirt path that veered left, eventually to join

Church Street by the Esk. It might be difficult to follow him over open land, Sue thought. Although she looked ordinary enough in her long navy-blue raincoat and hood, if he turned he might just recognize her from the shop. And then he would wonder what a tourist was doing following him through such an unattractive part of town.

Before she had time to decide whether to go on or turn back, however, she saw him walk down the path to the last cottage in the row. She paused, taking cover behind a parked van, and watched him put the key in the lock and enter. So that was where he lived. She wondered if he lived alone. If he really was the man who had attacked her, and she had been certain as soon as she heard his voice that he was, he probably did.

Then she thought of Peter Sutcliffe, the Yorkshire Ripper who had lived with his wife, Sonia, throughout the period he had killed and butchered thirteen women. And hadn't there been two or three others who had survived his attacks? Sue wondered what had become of them. Anything was possible, but somehow she couldn't bring herself to believe that the man she was after shared his life with a woman.

When he had disappeared inside the cottage, Sue turned and walked back down the lane to the road. There was nothing more she could do at the moment. A little careful planning, at least, was called for now. She couldn't just go barging in and kill him; she had to lure him to an isolated open place after dark. Because she had been attacked in just such a place, she felt that she would have more chance of succeeding somewhere similar when the tables were turned. He was stronger than her, so she would have to use cunning. She couldn't see it happening in a house or on a street. But she knew where he lived now, and that was comforting knowledge. It gave her an advantage.

As if to mark her entry into tourist Whitby, the drizzle stopped and the clouds began to break, allowing a few feeble rays of sun through here and there. She was on the narrow, cobbled part of Church Street again, north of Whitby Bridge. The world went on as normal there: families and courting couples wandered down the road as usual, pausing to look in the windows of the jet shops and the little gift shops that sold flavoured fudge or sachets of Earl Grey tea and Colombian coffee.

It was one-thirty, and Sue hadn't eaten yet. She was also eager to read the papers. She went into the Black Horse, bought a half of lager and ordered a steak and kidney pie. The place was moderately busy, mostly with young couples eating lunch, mackintoshes strewn on the seats beside them and umbrellas propped up against the wall. She managed to find a small corner table and sat down to read the papers while she ate.

There was nothing about the Student Slasher in the *Independent*. It had, after all, been almost a week since he had last struck. Unless the police caught him or found an important clue, there would be nothing more about him until he had slashed and strangled his next victim. Sue meant to see that that never happened. She glanced quickly at the headlines – war, lies, corruption, misery – and then turned anxiously to the local paper.

The news was on the front page, staring her right in the face:

CRIMES LINKED?

Police in Whitby are attempting to establish whether there is any link between the murder of Whitby man, Jack Grimley, and the serious wounding of an Australian national, Keith McLaren, whose unconscious body was discovered by a wildlife worker in some woods near Dalehouse late last night. Mr McLaren, suffering from serious head injuries, is presently in a coma in St Mary's Hospital, Scarborough. Doctors refuse to comment on his chances of recovery but one hospital spokesman admitted there is a strong risk of permanent brain damage. When asked if the attacks could have been carried out by the same person a police spokesman told our reporter, 'It is too early to say. We are looking at two different cases, both with similar head wounds, but so far there is no evidence of a connection between these two men.' Police are still anxious to interview anyone who might have seen Grimley after he left the Lucky Fisherman last Thursday. They are also interested in discovering the identity of a woman seen with McLaren in Hinderwell last Monday afternoon. She is described as young, with short light-brown hair, wearing jeans, a grey jacket and a checked shirt. Police are eager that anyone who can identify her come forward at once.

Sue put the paper down on the table and tried to control her shaking hands. He wasn't dead! Keith wasn't dead. She should have known she hadn't hit him hard enough. Instead of finishing the job, she had been frightened by that damn dog and hurried away without making sure. Perhaps she had felt sorry for him, too, and that had made her soft. But it had never entered her mind that she might not have killed him. What could she do now? What if he were to come round and tell the police who she was? They already had a description of Martha Browne.

Sue pushed the rest of her pie aside and lit a cigarette. She had no appetite left. It was time to get a grip on herself. She went to the bar, bought a double brandy, then settled down to re-read the article carefully. She must be careful not to panic, not now that she had the scent of her true prey. She had to think clearly. The description of the girl was vague, for a start, and it certainly didn't resemble the way she looked now. But would the proprietor of the Abbey Terrace guesthouse remember her? And what about Grimley's pals in the Lucky Fisherman? She had been dressed much the same that night, she recalled, as when she had walked in the woods with Keith. Would the men remember seeing her sitting with the Australian, glancing over at Grimley as if she knew him? And had anyone seen her with Keith in Staithes? She had been wearing her new outfit at first, before she had changed in the toilet, so what if someone could connect the one girl with the other?

The police could be getting very close indeed, she realized. She would have to act quickly. There was no sense in staying around to get arrested for killing Jack Grimley when she had now caught up with the man she really wanted. Time was definitely working against her, its winged chariot snapping at her heels. And what about Keith? He might recover consciousness at any moment. Would he still be able to identify her, or would his memory of the incident be gone, as hers had been for so long? She didn't know. All she knew was that she had her man in sight, and she had better find a way of luring him into the open soon, or the whole mission would be at risk.

A tweedy woman who had just come to sit at the next table gave her a curious look. It was probably time to change her haunts. She had been to this pub and the nearby cafe far too often.

She sipped some more brandy; it warmed her throat and settled her fluttering stomach. Should she go to the hospital in Scarborough, creep into Keith's room and put the pillow over his face? Could she do it? Did she have the nerve? But she remembered that her attacker had tried to get to her in a similar situation and he hadn't succeeded. There would be police guards; security would be far too tight for her to be able to get through to him. No, that was out of the question. All she could do was hope that he wouldn't recover.

There was still the holdall back in her room. She hadn't got rid of it yet. That was something she could do while she worked out a plan to deal with 'Greg'. Then she would have to leave town quickly, no foolish hanging around to wallow in the outcome of her actions. She would have to read about and savour her success at a distance, like everyone else.

42

KIRSTEN

With Sarah gone, Kirsten had only her fears and a growing sense of mission to keep her going. In late January, the killer claimed his fourth victim, a second-year biology student called Jane Pitcombe. Carefully, Kirsten cut out her picture and all the details she could find and put them in the scrapbook she had started to keep track of the victims.

Also that month, she told Laura Henderson that she wanted to stop the hypnotherapy sessions as they were becoming too painful for her. In reality, she was worried that she would give away to Laura whatever she discovered and that the police would find the killer first. She had come to realize shortly after Sarah left that she wanted him for herself. It was the only way to heal her wounds and put the spirits of Margaret, Kathleen and Jane to rest. It wasn't difficult to convince Laura to stop the hypnotism; after all, the police had got as good a description of the killer as they were likely to.

It was important to try to keep everyone happy, so to this end she finally read Galen's letters and wrote him a long, cheery but noncommittal reply. She apologized for not writing sooner, but said she had just come through a lengthy period of depression. She also told him she was going to resume her studies, probably back up north. Canada just seemed too far away from home for her to consider yet. She was sure he would understand.

February, bleak and cold, came and went. Kirsten spent much of the time in her room brooding on the dark places in her mind, trying to find ways to make the cloud yield up its secrets. This was her main problem. Without Laura's hypnotherapy, she couldn't get at her censored memories. She bought a book on self-hypnosis and practised with some success. She could relax easily enough and induce a light trance, but she couldn't get beyond the fishy odour. Nonetheless, she intended to keep at it until she dispersed the cloud.

Towards the end of that month and until well into April, she found some solace in *The Cloud of Unknowing*, the fourteenth-century masterpiece of Christian mysticism, which she picked off her shelf to help her set her mind on university studies again. Yet Kirsten very much doubted that she read it the way its author intended. The words seemed to address her own problem in a startlingly direct way, and the irony wasn't lost on her:

> When you first begin, you find only darkness, and as it were a cloud of unknowing. You don't know what this means except that in your will you feel a simple steadfast intention reaching out towards God. Do what you will, this darkness and this cloud remain between you and God, and stop you both from seeing him in the clear light of rational understanding, and from experiencing his loving sweetness in your affection. Reconcile yourself to wait in this darkness as long as necessary but still go on longing after him whom you love.

It was a kind of inversion of what Kirsten felt – certainly it wasn't God she was seeking, nor did she love the object of her quest – but the words gave her sustenance, nonetheless, and helped her through the darkness, both internal and external.

The book also helped describe what she was experiencing in a way that even Laura Henderson hadn't been able to get at:

> Do not think because I call it a 'darkness' or a 'cloud' it is the sort of cloud you see in the sky or the kind of darkness you know at home when the light is out . . . By 'darkness' I mean 'a lack of knowing' – just as anything that you do not know or may have forgotten may be said to be 'dark' to you, for you cannot see it with your inward eye.

It was exactly like the dark bubble, or cloud, she felt in her mind. It came between her and the Devil, the man who had maimed her, and it wasn't so much an object or an element as a feeling, a sense of something impenetrable anchored deep in her mind.

The book offered more in the way of practical advice, too, and Kirsten began to wonder how she had ever sustained herself for so long without it. Especially the fifth meditation, which read:

> If ever you are to come to this cloud and live and work in it, as I suggest, then just as this cloud of unknowing is as it were above you, between you and God, so you must also put a cloud of forgetting beneath you and all creation. We are apt to think that we are very far from God because of this cloud of unknowing between us and him, but surely it would be more correct to say that we are much further from him if there is no cloud of forgetting between us and the whole created world.

Kirsten had to distance and detach herself from the everyday world if she wanted to follow through with her purpose. There was no use clinging to sentimental notions of good and evil. She had to learn to exist in a detached, rarefied world where the object of her quest had supreme importance and everything and everyone else was lost, for as long as it took, in a cloud of forgetting. But nobody must know this. She had to appear to be making progress as far as family and friends were concerned.

The book was arranged into seventy-five short numbered chapters, or meditations, and it was not the kind of text one could read for hours on end. Kirsten read a chapter a day, occasionally skipping a day to read a novel, so she managed to stretch the book out for over two months, as winter turned into spring.

Soon, bluebells and forget-me-nots grew in the woods again, and dandelions and buttercups gilded the open fields. The bitter air warmed and released the scents of the countryside from its wintry grip: grass and tree bark after rain; wild garlic rubbed between the fingers; damp earth recently ploughed over. As she walked and took it all in, Kirsten remembered last autumn, when she had felt dead inside and nothing could touch her. Now that she had a purpose, a sense of mission, she could enjoy the world again.

The book continued to convince her of the holiness of her task and seemed to promise success. When, on the final page one fresh, bright morning in mid-May, she read that 'it is not what you are or have been that God looks at with his merciful eyes, but what you would be,' she knew without doubt that she would succeed. 'All holy desires grow by delays; and if they fade because of these delays then they were never holy desires.' Tenacity. Determination. They were the qualities she had to nurture in order to prove her desires holy. Her need would not fade; it was with her, part of her, day and night.

Throughout this period, she still continued to visit Bath and see Laura, too, though not as frequently as before. Once a fortnight seemed enough for what they had to talk about. The main topic towards the end was Kirsten's feelings about being a 'victim'.

Some schools, Laura explained, hold that there are people who are born victims, who somehow attract killers. When the circumstances are right, they will get what they were born for. Things happen to us because of what we are, some psychologists maintain, and because of this, some of us keep making the same mistakes time after time – marrying the wrong man or woman, for example, or seeking out situations in which we are abused, asking for trouble. It wasn't masochism, Laura said, but something rooted deep in a person's unconscious that led him or her to keep making the same wrong choices.

Did Kirsten think she was one of those people? Did she feel guilt over what had happened to her? Did she feel as if she had asked for it?

The whole subject puzzled Kirsten at first. For a long time, she had simply assumed that it had been her bad luck to be in the wrong place at the wrong time, the unfortunate victim of a random assault. It had never, in fact, occurred to her that she might have been asking for it. That was the rapist's common defence, wasn't it, that his victim had been asking for it because she had dressed in a certain way or smiled at the wrong time? Kirsten couldn't accept that.

If she had given in to Hugo's advances that night and gone home with him, none of this would have happened. If she hadn't had to get home reasonably early and sober to pack for the next day, then she might have stayed at the party longer and walked across the park with a group of drunken friends. If she hadn't walked across the park that night but had taken the well-lit roads around it, if she hadn't strayed from the path to sit on the lion like a silly girl . . . and so it went on, nothing but a lot of ifs. And on the plus side, if that man hadn't been walking his dog at precisely the right time, then Kirsten would have died like the later victims had.

But the more she talked about it with Laura, the more she realized that things could only have been different had she been a different kind of person. Those schools were right, in a way. The roots of what happened were tangled up with who she was. She could easily have given in to Hugo, for example. He was attractive enough, and plenty of her friends would have done so; indeed, most of them had, at one time or another. But no, she wasn't 'that kind' of girl. And she did habitually cross the park alone after dark, no matter how often people expressed concern. Also, it would never have occurred to her not to give in to that childish impulse to ride the lion unless she had been with company. In other words, maybe she did think of herself as a born victim and she just hadn't admitted it before. But she didn't tell Laura this. She could sense that Laura was testing her, trying to find out how sensitive she was, so she gave what she thought were the right answers. Laura seemed relieved.

But Kirsten continued to question herself. Why did she cross the park by herself in the dark, for example? Was she looking for something to happen? She certainly hadn't been making any kind of a feminist gesture. When women want to make a point about their right to walk the streets and parks in safety, they do so in large, well-publicized groups – the sensible way. But Kirsten often did it alone. Why? Was she inviting destruction?

Somehow, a simple chain of causality wasn't enough to explain what had happened to her. She had been living in a dream ever since the attack had occurred simply because she had accepted it in such a shallow way and had never really contemplated the deeper implications. That was no acceptance at all. *The Cloud of Unknowing*, her last talks with Laura Henderson: both of these gave a shape and depth to her quest that she had never imagined possible before; they concentrated her resolve and acted like a magnet forming a rose-pattern from iron filings.

It all meant something – everything happened for a reason – and the more she thought about it, if there was a part of her deep inside that made her the victim – just as hatred twisted deep inside the man made him a killer – then the person who had found her must have been destined to be her saviour. He had found her for a purpose, she now realized. She hadn't died like the others; she had been delivered from that. And this was when the compelling idea of fate, destiny and retribution started to occur to her. If she had been a victim not by blind chance but for a reason, then she was still alive for a reason. She bore her stigmata for a reason. She carried within her the means of destroying this evil force. In a sense, she was his nemesis. And that was destiny, too.

She never told Laura all this; like the true nature of the cloud or bubble in her mind, it would have been too difficult to put into words. Besides, she wasn't at all clear about it herself at first. It didn't evolve as a fully fledged theory, like a Pallas Athene sprung from the head of Zeus, but the ideas took shape over time. It was something that she thought about a lot in the spring months of May and June while she re-read old novels, ploughed through Julian of Norwich's *Revelations of Divine Love*, and considered which university to apply to and which area of study to concentrate on. It would probably be best, she decided, to apply to several places – say the north, where Sarah suggested they share a flat together, and to Bath and Bristol, where her parents wanted her to go. Then, when the time came, she could see how she felt and make her choice.

In early June, the killer, the man the press were now calling the 'Student Slasher', claimed yet another victim: Kim Waterford, a petite brunette with a twinkle in her eyes that even the poor-quality newspaper photograph couldn't dim. Well, he had dimmed it, hadn't he? Now her eyes would be dull and lifeless as dead fish. Kirsten pasted the picture and articles in her scrapbook and worked even harder at self-hypnosis.

One glorious day in late June when Bath was filled with tourists again and boaters splashed and laughed on the Avon outside the half-open window, Laura smiled at the end of the session, offered Kirsten a cigarette and said, 'I think we've gone as far as we can go together. If you need me, I'll be here. Don't hesitate to call. But, really, I think you're on your own now.'

Kirsten nodded. She knew she was.

43

SUSAN

Still clutching her holdall in the carrier bag, Sue returned to the shops again that afternoon and spent a few pounds of her fast-dwindling funds on some dark grey Marks & Spencer slacks and a blue windcheater with a zip-up front. She spent a good while in front of the toilet mirror on her make-up, changing the emphasis a little here and there, and found that it was possible to fasten her wig back in a ponytail without revealing any of her own hair. Her glasses also went well with the new outfit. Now she looked just different enough not to spark any memories among those who might have noticed her ghost-like presence. She was no longer just the plain, primly dressed, 'nice girl' in the raincoat; nor was she the short-haired tomboy in jeans and a checked shirt. She looked more like a family holidaymaker taking a break from her parents' company for a while. The new clothes would also be more suitable for hanging around in the woods watching over the factory, if it came to that.

She was annoyed about the holdall. When she had got to Saltwick Nab, she found that the tide was coming in, not going out. She would have to go back later in the evening, or perhaps it would be easier to throw it from the top of West Cliff or somewhere closer. There would be too many people around in that area, though. Someone might see her. She shoved the raincoat and hood along with everything else in the holdall and took it back to her room. At least it was coming in useful now she had more stuff to get rid of.

She thought about Keith a lot too. Lying in that hospital in Scarborough with tubes and needles stuck in him, just as she had lain over a year ago. She had dismissed the idea of trying to get to him – security would be too tight, and she wasn't sure she could go through with it in cold blood – but she couldn't stop worrying. The police might be looking for her at that very moment. All the more reason to hurry up.

At a quarter to five, she dropped in at Rose's Cafe. The stringy blonde behind the counter showed no interest in her beyond taking her money. Sue needed some idea of what her man's hours were. When could she expect to find him walking alone in the dark? When did he make his deliveries? When did he sleep? She assumed that he had either made a morning delivery that day, or had set off the night before and stayed over. If the latter, then the odds were that he would be at home tonight. It annoyed her that she couldn't find out for sure. She certainly couldn't ask anyone. No doubt the drivers worked very irregular hours, taking loads when they were ready and standing in for mates who were ill or had driven too many hours. All she could really do was watch a little longer, and she didn't know how much time she had left.

Over the next two days, the weather, though still chilly, continued to improve. Sue took to hanging around the area by the factory almost constantly. All the time she felt as if she were looking over her shoulder for the police, when she was the one who should be doing the watching. She read the papers every morning, but they reported no change in Keith's condition or in the state of the police investigation. In a way, though she still felt nervous and paranoid at times, she took heart that nothing had happened yet. Surely they must have reached a dead end or they would have been on to her already? Nothing could stop her now. She was meant to succeed. Her task was holy.

She kept a low profile in Rose's and the Brown Cow, but found that now she had the man in sight, she could even recognize his squat, dark figure from the woods above the factory. She also investigated another pub, called the Merry Monk, at the bottom end of the council estate, and found that from one of its small windows in a dark corner she could just about see across the waste ground down to his cottage at the end of the row. As she had expected, his comings and goings were irregular, and as far as she could make out, he lived alone. She would have to know her opportunity when it arose and grab it without hesitation.

First, she wanted him to *know* that she had found him. When she finally lured him to his death, she wanted him to know who was doing it, and why. He would be asking for it. But she had to do this without causing undue danger to herself. Also, though she was certain this time, after her mistake she wanted more confirmation. She needed proof. If she killed or wounded another innocent man in the area, her chances of success would be practically nil. Slowly, as she watched him, she began to form a plan.

She almost bumped into him on her way back to town from Rose's Cafe at five-thirty-five on her second day of full surveillance. He was walking the other way, back towards the factory. She averted her face, but for a moment she could have sworn that he noticed her. He didn't know who she was – she would have felt that kind of recognition jolt her like an electric shock – but perhaps he connected her with the woman he'd seen yesterday in the newsagent's. Or perhaps, given what he was, he looked at all women that way. Sue hurried on with her head down and didn't stop until she got to the end of the street. From there, hidden by the wall of the corner house, she saw him in the distance by the loading bays talking to a man in a white smock and trilby, probably a foreman, who gave him some papers. Her man got in his van and drove off.

Sue carried on walking down the lane. She hadn't got far before he passed her, then he turned right, towards the junction for the main Scarborough road. It didn't mean that he was going to Scarborough, of course, as it was one of the few ways out of the town and could lead to York or to the Leeds area. But one thing was for certain: he was out on a job and he wouldn't be home for a while. Sue hurried down to the main road, but he was nowhere in sight. She walked north a little way on the pavement, then doubled back on the dirt path that eventually curved around past his cottage.

Sue's heart felt as if it were in her throat as she approached the cottage. Coming from that direction across the waste ground, she couldn't be seen from any of the other houses on the row. Luckily, too, there were no buildings on the other side of the street, only the scrub ground that sloped up to the council estate. She could be seen from her little window in the pub, but it was still early in the evening for drinkers, and there was no reason why anyone enjoying a pint and a chat in the Merry Monk should make the effort of looking out of that particular window, especially as it meant pulling the curtain aside a little. Even if they did, what they saw would mean nothing to them.

She had thought of waiting until dark, but that meant she would need a torch, which would, in the long run, give her much more risk of being spotted. No, this was better: a blind approach at a time when most people would be busy preparing their evening meals anyway. She had already noticed that he kept his curtains closed whenever he was out, and that would keep her hidden, should anyone pass by, while still giving her enough light to search by.

There was only one small window in the side of the house that faced the waste ground, and that was too high to reach. A kitchen extension built on the back, which also shielded her from the neighbours' view, looked more promising. The back door itself was solid and locked, and the curtained window that probably led into the living room or dining room also proved impossible to open. The kitchen window looked like a better possibility. The wood was old and the unfastened catch had been painted over in the open position long ago.

Sue wedged the heels of her hands against the cross-bar and pushed up. At first nothing happened and she thought that perhaps the window too had been painted shut. But the paint was cracked and peeling on the outside, and before long it began to shudder upwards. Sue paused after she had made a space big enough to enter, but there was no sound; nobody had heard her. Nimbly, she slipped in over the kitchen sink and closed the window behind her. The palms of her hands felt sore and sweaty from the effort.

She had no idea what she expected to find – walls daubed in blood, perhaps, or heads on spikes and violent red graffiti scrawled over whitewashed walls: 666 and THE WHORE MUST DIE – but she wasn't prepared for the sheer ordinariness of the place. The only uncurtained window was the one through which she had climbed, and that let plenty of light into the kitchen. Everything was in its place; the washing-up lay in the draining rack; glasses and plates shone like new. The surfaces were all clean, too, and the room smelled of lemon washing-up liquid. A refrigerator she could see her reflection in hummed; cans of soup and tins of spaghetti stood in an orderly row on a shelf above the dining table, with its salt and pepper set out neatly on a mat at its centre. Even the small cooker was spotless.

The living room, where light filtered in pale blue through the thin curtains, was just as tidy. Magazines stood in the vertical rack by the hearth, corners and pages aligned so they looked like one solid block as thick as a telephone directory. A pipe rack hung above the mantelpiece, and the air was acrid with the smell of stale smoke. In the corner near the window was a television on a stand with a video on the shelf beneath it and, next to that, a cassette storage rack with a varnished wood finish – and not a speck of dust in sight. What did this man watch? Sue wondered. Pornography? Snuff movies?

But when she examined the cassettes, she saw they were all ordinary enough. He had labelled each one in clear print, and most of them were simply tapes of recent television programmes he must have missed while out driving: nothing more interesting than a couple of episodes of *Coronation Street*, no doubt taped while he was out on a delivery, a BBC2 wildlife special, a few American cop programmes, and two movies rented from a local shop: *Angel Heart* and *Fatal Attraction*. They weren't exactly *Mary Poppins*, but they weren't hard-core pornography either.

An old sofa sat in front of the fireplace, its beige upholstery protected by lace antimacassars, and one matching armchair stood at a precise angle to it. Like the rest of the house, the room was small and spotless, and as far as Sue could make out in the faint light, the walls were painted light blue, rather than papered. The only thing that struck her as at all odd was the complete absence of photographs and personal knick-knacks. The mantelpiece was bare, as were the solid oak sideboard and the walls.

There was, however, a small bookcase by the kitchen door. Most of the titles were on local history, some of them large illustrated volumes, and the only novels were used paperbacks of blockbusters by Robert Ludlum, Lawrence Sanders and Harold Robbins. Bede's *History* was there, of course. Sue picked it up, and noticed that the old paperback had been well thumbed. One passage, in particular, had been heavily underscored. Sue shivered and put the book back.

Upstairs revealed nothing different about the owner of the cottage. In the bathroom, every fixture, fitting and surface looked in shining pristine condition, and in the bathroom cabinet, various pills, potions and creams stood in orderly rows like soldiers at attention. There was only one bedroom: his. The bed was made, covered in yellow nylon sheets, and there was nothing in the drawers and cupboards but carefully ironed shirts, a couple of sports jackets, one pressed suit, and neatly folded underwear and socks. The place seemed to have no personality at all. Was he really her man? Surely there ought to be *some* sign beyond the book.

Back downstairs, Sue looked for a cellar door but couldn't find one. Perhaps it was just as well, she thought. She was feeling edgy being there at all; if she found a body in the cellar she didn't know how she would react. But that was silly, she told herself, just nerves. He didn't take the bodies home with him.

She opened the doors of the sideboard and found a little port, sherry and brandy, along with glasses of various shapes and sizes, place mats and a white linen tablecloth. In one of the top drawers were the everyday odds and ends one needs around a house: fuse wire, string, candles, matches, penknife, extra shoelaces, pencil stubs.

When she opened the second drawer, though, Sue's breath caught in her throat.

There, laid out neatly in a row on a lining of faded rose-patterned wallpaper, were six locks of hair, each bound in the middle by a pink ribbon. Six victims, six locks of hair. Sue felt dizzy. She had to turn away and support herself by gripping the back of an armchair. When she had fought back the vertigo and nausea, she turned to look again at the sight she found so gruesome in its simplicity and ordinariness. Nothing too grotesque for this man: no severed breasts, ears or fingers, just six locks of hair laid out neatly in a row on a lining of faded rose-patterned wallpaper. And, further back in the drawer, a pair of scissors, a roll of pink satin ribbon, and a long knife with a worn bone handle and a gleaming stainless-steel blade.

But it was the hair that really captured Sue's attention. Six locks. One blonde, three brunettes, two redheads. She reached out and touched them, as she would stroke a cat. She could even put names to them. One of the red locks, the darkest, was Kathleen Shannon's; the blonde was Margaret Snell's; the curly brunette lock had belonged to Kim Waterford; and the straight, jet-black strand was Jill Sarsden's. None of them was Sue's. He must have been disturbed before he got around to taking it, she realized. No doubt it was the last thing he did, take a souvenir. And the police had never said anything about it – which meant either that they didn't know, or that they were keeping the knowledge up their sleeves to deter copycats and check against phoney confessions, and, of course, to verify the true one, if it ever came.

Well, Sue thought, here was an oversight she could rectify easily enough. She pushed back her wig, picked up the scissors, and carefully snipped off a lock about two inches long, exactly the same length as the others. She then bound it neatly with a piece of ribbon and placed it in line with the rest.

Now, she thought, pleased with herself, just wait till he notices that. She was convinced that he drooled over his trophies every day, and what a bloody shock he'd get when he found another lock of hair there. Not only would he know there was someone on to him, he would probably know who it was. And that was just what Sue wanted.

The house was silent except for the sound of Sue's heart beating, but she still felt uneasy. It was time to get out before he came back. She slid the drawer shut and hurried back to the kitchen window.

44

KIRSTEN

That summer, Kirsten took long, brooding walks in the woods and reckless drives in the countryside. Close to the end of the university term, about the same time she had been attacked a year ago, the killer found his sixth victim – the fifth to die – in a quiet Halifax nursing student called Jill Sarsden. Kirsten pasted the photo and details in her scrapbook as usual.

At home, she pretended all was well. The dark cloud still troubled her, bringing painful headaches and bouts of depression that were difficult to hide. But she managed to convince Dr Craven that she was making excellent progress since discontinuing the analysis, and the doctor's opinion helped to reassure her parents. If she was occasionally quiet and withdrawn, well, that was only to be expected. Her parents knew that she had always valued her solitude and privacy anyway.

In her room each night, she kept at the self-hypnosis, but got no further. The directions she had read in the book were simple enough: roll your eyeballs up as far as you can, close your eyes and take a deep breath, then let your eyes relax, breathe out and feel yourself floating. She had even delved back into earlier memories of pain as practice – the time her finger got trapped in a door when she was six; the day she fell off her bicycle and needed stitches in her arm – but still she couldn't get beyond the odour of fish without feeling overcome by a sense of choking panic.

One hot, bright day in late July, she stopped in a Cotswold village for a cold drink. Walking back to the car, she noticed a craft centre in an old stone cottage and decided to have a look inside. The cottage had been extended at the back and part of it converted into a glass-blowing studio. Kirsten watched entranced as the delicate and fragile pieces took shape from molten glass at the end of the tube. Afterwards, as she browsed around the shop, she noticed a row of solid glass paper-weights, like the one in Laura's office, with colourful abstract designs trapped inside them. The rose pattern appealed to her most, and she bought it, feeling great satisfaction at the smooth, slippery weight in her palm. And it gave her an idea.

That evening in her room, she prepared for self-hypnosis again, doing breathing exercises and relaxing each muscle in turn. When she was ready, she sat before her desk, where the paperweight lay between two candles, drawing and twisting their light into its curved scarlet petals. Her book had mentioned that there were many ways of self-hypnosis, and she had chosen the method said to be the most effective. But whether there was something about the connection with her early sessions with Laura, or something special about the paperweight itself, Kirsten found she had much more success this way. Though the first attempt led to no great breakthrough, she got a strong feeling that she would soon find what she wanted if she persisted.

It happened a week later. She had been taking herself further and further back from the attack and moving forward slowly. This time she started with her preparations for the evening: a long bath, the lemon-fresh scent of her clean comfortable clothes, the pleasant walk to the Ring O'Bells with Sarah. As usual, she drew back at the oily rag and the fishy smell, but this time she heard his voice. Not all the words – just fragments about a 'dark one' and a 'song of destruction' – but it was enough. With her training in linguistics and dialect, Kirsten could place the accent easily enough.

When she came out of the light trance, her heart was thumping and she felt as if she had just been dropped into an icy bath. She breathed deeply, fully alert now, and poured herself a glass of water. The raspy voice still sounded clear in her mind. He was from Yorkshire. She couldn't be certain, but she didn't think he had a city accent or the broad speech of the Dales and the Pennine Moorlands. When she added this new knowledge to the salt smell of raw fish that had covered his fingers and palms, then she knew he was from the Yorkshire coast – a holiday resort or a fishing village perhaps. The more she thought about it, replayed the voice and remembered her lessons, the more sure she became.

She jumped up and pulled down the old school atlas from her bookshelf. From what she could see, the coastline stretched from around Bridlington Bay in the south to near Redcar in the north. County boundaries were no sure guide, though, especially as they had been changed in the seventies. She didn't think he was from as far north as Middlesbrough, where a Northumbrian strain subtly infused the local speech, but she would have to include the Humberside area as far south as the Humber estuary. That left more than a hundred miles of rugged coastline. It was useless, she thought. Even if she were right, she would never be able to find him in such a large area. She dropped the atlas on the floor and threw herself onto the bed.

The next day, she tried the same self-hypnosis technique again, and again she heard the voice, the flat vowels and clipped consonants. She felt something about the words this time, something that rang a bell deep inside her mind. Try as she might, though, she couldn't identify them. He had been reciting a poem or a song of some kind. She had read somewhere that such killers sometimes do that, talk while they work, often quoting fragments of the Bible. But she didn't think it was from the Bible. He had said something about 'leaving a feast' because someone had asked him to sing a song and he couldn't. She knew the words; she had heard them before at some time in her studies, but she couldn't for the life of her remember where.

She slept badly that night, haunted by the fragmented speech and the raspy tone of his voice, but in the morning she felt no closer to her goal. She didn't know how it could help, but she needed to know exactly what he had said. She had to *think*, to work at it. The source was old – certainly pre-Renaissance by the sound of it – and that probably meant something from medieval literature. People were always singing and attending feasts then. There was only one thing to do: read.

And so she set to reading medieval literature on warm days in the garden: Sir Gawain, Chaucer, Piers Plowman, anthologies full of religious lyrics. She read them all to no avail. All she got for her pains was that awful feeling of trying to find a quotation you have on the tip of your tongue but can't pin down, or the frustration of looking for a phrase in Shakespeare when you can't even remember what play it comes from. Outwardly, Kirsten seemed fine, preparing to go back to university, optimistic about her future. She even told her parents that she was considering the restorative surgery that the doctor had mentioned might be possible. But inside she was seething with anger and frustration.

One golden day in late August she sat out on the back lawn under the copper beech with hardly a breeze to stir her hair from her brow. She had given up on medieval literature as a source and gone back even further, to Anglo-Saxon, which she had studied in her first year. So far, she had read translations of *Beowulf* and 'The Seafarer' and was now working her way through Bede's *An Ecclesiastical History of the English Nation*. It was an old translation that she had bought in a second-hand bookshop, attracted by the worn blue binding, the gilded page edges, and a pleasantly musty smell that reminded her of the local library. Inside the flyleaf, in faded, copper-coloured ink, was written, 'To Reginald, with Love from Elizabeth, October 1939. May God go with you.'

Despite the translator's flowery language, the Venerable Bede came through as far more human to her than many of his austere colleagues in the early church, and she could picture him out on the lonely island of Lindisfarne poring over illuminated manuscripts as he suffered through a wild Northumbrian winter. About two-thirds of the way through the book, she came to the passage about England's 'first' poet, Caedmon, who had been unable to sing. Whenever the harp was passed around at dinners, and everyone was expected to contribute a song, Caedmon always stole away.

One evening, after he left a feast to care for the horses in the stables, he had a vision in which a man came and spoke his name and asked him to sing. Caedmon protested, but the stranger paid no attention to his excuses. 'Yet shall ye sing to me,' he insisted. When Caedmon asked what he should sing about, the man replied, 'Praise ye Creation.' And Caedmon found his inspiration.

There was no blinding flash of light, but as Kirsten read, the dark cloud that had lodged itself in her mind since the attack seemed to disperse. In addition to her own silent voice, she could hear another voice reading along with her a perversion of Bede's words: 'And, lo, I asked, "Of what shall I sing?" and the Dark One told me, "Sing of Destruction".' It was the story *he* had told her as he beat her and slashed at her in the park that night. The summer garden turned to mist around her like a place filmed through a greasy lens, and her book slipped onto the grass. She took a deep breath and closed her eyes. After-images of light and leaves danced before her eyelids, then the memories flowed back unbidden.

She could see his face now, in shadow, with the moon over his shoulder catching one lined cheek, as he smeared the smell of fish all over her lips and nostrils. He stuffed a piece of oily rag in her mouth and it made her feel sick. Then he started slapping her, back and forth across her face, and talking in that raspy sing-song voice about how he had left the Feast of Whores one night and had a vision of the Dark One, to whom he confessed his impotence. The Dark One, he said, gave him the power to sing to women. That's what he was doing with his knife; he was singing to her, just like that old poet from his town, who had suddenly been blessed with the gift of poetry late in life.

The images went on. She could easily recall every painful moment of consciousness now. But she held herself back and pulled out with a sharp gasp when the unbearable image of the knife blade flashing in moonlight took shape.

When she had breathed in the warm air and run her fingers over the tree's smooth bark to bring herself back to earth, she remembered that he had actually said, 'just like the old poet from my town'. She could play the words back now as if they were on a tape inside her mind. She picked up the book and found that, according to Bede, Caedmon came from a place called Streanaeshalch. Of course, that would be the Anglo-Saxon name; Bede often used the Roman or Saxon names. Flipping through the index, Kirsten found it in no time: 'Streanaeshalch: *see* Whitby.' So he came from Whitby. It made perfect sense. It all added up: the fishy smell, the accent, and now the reference to Caedmon, poet of his town.

He had had no reason to assume that Kirsten would survive the attack; her continued existence had not been his intention. Hadn't Superintendent Elswick said something about him trying to get to her at the hospital, too? That must have been because he was worried that she might remember what he had said in his ritual chant. And as time went by and nothing happened, he must have realized that she had lost her memory and that he had nothing more to worry about. Then, he had continued blithely with his mission, singing his song with a knife on a woman's body.

So now she knew. What was she to do next? First, she hurried inside to find one of her father's old *AA Members Handbooks*. He usually kept a couple along with the telephone directory in the bureau drawer in the hall. She turned to the maps at the back and found Whitby. It was on the coast between Scarborough and Redcar, and it didn't look too big. She ran her finger down the Ws in the gazetteer: Whimple, Whippingham, Whiston – there it was, 'Whitby, population 13,763.' Bigger than she thought. Still, if the man she was after had such rough hands and smelled of fish, then she would probably find him around the docks or on the boats. She thought she would be able to recognize him, and now the voice would confirm it.

And she had guidance in her mission – Margaret, Brenda, Kim and the rest – they wouldn't let her fail, not now she had come so far. There was a *holiness* about what she had to do, a reason why she, out of all of them, had been saved. She had been chosen as his nemesis; it was her destiny to find him and face him. She couldn't picture the actual occasion of their meeting, what would happen. It would be in the open and it would take place at night; that was all she knew. As for the outcome: one of them would die.

But even a nemesis, she thought wryly, has to plan and deal with practical realities. The AA handbook also gave information about distances from London, York and Scarborough, and listed market days. There followed a selection of hotels, most of which would probably be too expensive for Kirsten. No matter, she could go into Bath and buy a local travel guide that would probably list bed and breakfast accommodation.

Excited and nervous at the prospect of the hunt, Kirsten settled down to make preparations. She would visit Sarah first and go to Whitby from there. She wouldn't take much with her, just a handy holdall, jeans, a couple of shirts, and whatever she needed to do the job. It would have to be something small, something she could conceal in her hand, as she knew she might have to act quickly.

Kirsten shuddered at the thought and began to doubt herself. Then she reminded herself again of all that she had suffered and survived, and the reason for that. She had to be strong; she had to concentrate on practical matters as far as she could and trust to instinct and fate to take care of the rest.

Two days later, after she had bought a Whitby guide and written to Sarah, she informed her parents that she had decided to go back up north to university. They both expressed concern and displeasure, but that was balanced by relief that she seemed to have come out of her long depression and decided to get on with her life.

'I won't say I'm happy you're going away,' her father said with a sad smile, 'but I will say I'm happy that you've decided to go. Do you know what I mean?'

Kirsten nodded. 'I suppose I must have been a bit of a pest. I haven't been very good company, have I?'

Her father shook his head quickly as if to dismiss her apology. 'You know you're welcome here,' he said, 'for as long as you want to stay.'

All the time, her mother sat stiffly, twisting her hands in her lap. She'll be glad to see the back of me, Kirsten thought, but she'll never admit such a horrible thought to herself. Her mother's life, Kirsten realized, was dominated by the need to keep all unpleasantness at a distance, look good in the eyes of her neighbours, and savagely maintain the borders of her closed and narrow world.

'I thought I'd go up before term, just to get my bearings again. I think it'd do me good to get out and about a bit. Sarah and I might do some walking in the Dales.'

'The *Yorkshire* Dales?' her mother said.

'Yes. Why?'

'Well, dear, I'm just not sure it's a very suitable environment for a well-brought-up girl such as yourself, that's all. It's so very . . . well, so very bleak and muddy, I hear, and so uncivilized. I'm not sure you even have the proper clothes for such an excursion.'

'Oh, Mother,' Kirsten said. 'Don't be such a snob.'

Her mother sniffed. 'I was only thinking of your comfort, darling. Of course, I dare say your friend is used to such a . . . a rough life. But not you.'

'Mother, Sarah's family owns half of Herefordshire. She's not quite the bit of rough you seem to think she is.'

Her mother looked at her blankly. 'I don't know what you mean, Kirsten. Breeding shows. That's all I'm saying.'

'Well, I'm going, anyway. And that's that.'

'Of course you must go,' her father said, patting her knee. 'Your mother's only concerned about your health, that's all. Make sure you take plenty of warm clothes and some sensible hiking boots. And stick to the pathways.'

Kirsten laughed. 'You're almost as bad,' she said. 'Anyone would think I was off to the North Pole or somewhere. It's only a couple of hundred miles north, you know, not a couple of thousand.'

'All the same,' her father said, 'the landscape can be quite treacherous in those parts, and it does rain an awful lot. Just be careful, that's all I'm asking of you.'

'Don't worry, I will.'

'When are you planning on going?' he asked.

'Well, I'll have to wait till I hear from Sarah first and make sure she can put me up and get some time off, but I thought I'd go as soon as I can.'

'And you'll be coming back before term starts?'

'Oh yes. That's not until the beginning of October. I'll come back and pick up my books and stuff. I'm hoping I can find a flat up there first, too. Perhaps Sarah and I can share.'

'Do you think that's wise?' her mother asked.

'It'll be better than being on my own, won't it?'

Her mother could offer no argument against that.

'So,' her father said, 'you're off on an adventure. Well, good for you. You must have known there were times when your mother and I . . . we . . . we didn't know what the future was going to bring.'

'I'm all right, Daddy,' Kirsten said. 'Really I am.'

'Yes, of course. Will you be seeing Dr Masterson at all while you're up there? About the . . . you know?'

Kirsten nodded. 'Probably,' she said. 'It won't do any harm to ask about it, will it?'

'No, I don't suppose it will. I'm afraid I won't be able to give you a lift up there. We've got a very important project on at the moment and I just can't take time off. Perhaps you could rent—'

'That's all right,' Kirsten said. 'I was planning on taking the train. I have to learn to get around on my own.'

'Well, that's fine, as long as you feel comfortable with the idea. You'll be needing some money, won't you?' he said, and went over to the top right-hand drawer of the sideboard to fetch his cheque book.

45

SUSAN

Sue got out of the house easily enough without anyone seeing her and went to celebrate her first housebreaking with veal scaloppine, garlic bread and a bottle of Chianti at the expensive restaurant on New Quay Road. After that, she stopped off at her room, then walked about a mile along the coast and threw her holdall, weighted down with heavy pebbles, into the sea. She stood and watched as the tide first threw it back, then sucked it out again and swallowed it. Even if it did turn up somewhere, she thought, it wouldn't be of any interest to anyone.

Now it was time to put the final stage of her plan into operation. First, let him sweat for a while.

And sweat he did. The first time Sue saw him on the day after she had broken into his cottage, he looked harried and preoccupied as he walked in to work. It was raining, and he kept his hands deep in his pockets and his head down, but his glittering eyes swept the street and the windows of the houses all around him. He must have noticed her sitting in the front of Rose's Cafe, Sue thought, but his eyes just flicked over her as they did everything and everyone else. He was nervous, on edge, as if he was expecting an ambush at any moment.

After he had gone by, Sue turned back to the local newspaper. There was no change reported in Keith's condition and the police seemed to have got nowhere in their search for Jack Grimley's killer. So far, so good. It would soon be over now.

Near lunchtime on the second day, from the same vantage point, Sue saw him slip into the newsagent's. Quickly, she left her tea and crossed the street to go in after him. He wouldn't recognize her. This time, she was dressed differently; also, she wore glasses, and her hair was tied back in a ponytail. He glanced around with a start at the bell when she entered, her head lowered, then turned his gaze back to the newsagent.

'All right today, love?' the woman asked. 'You look a bit peaky.'

'Not enough sleep, that's all,' he mumbled.

'Well, you take good care of yourself, you never know what germs are going round these days.'

'I'm all right,' he said, a little testily. 'Just tired, that's all.' Then he paid for his tobacco and left without even glancing at Sue, who bent over the newspaper and magazine section as before. She picked up the local paper and the *Independent*. When she took them over to the counter to pay, the woman clucked her tongue and said, 'I don't know what's the matter with him. Show a bit of polite interest and he damn near bites your head off. Some people can't even be bothered to be civil these days.'

'Maybe he's worried about something,' Sue suggested.

The woman sighed. 'Aye,' she said. 'We've all got plenty to worry about, haven't we, what with nuclear war and pollution all over t'place. But I still manage to find a smile and a good morning for my customers.' She went on, almost to herself, as she counted out Sue's change, 'Not like Greg Eastcote, that isn't. Usually such a pleasant chap.' Then she shrugged. 'Ah, well, maybe he is just tired. I could do with a bit of a lie-down myself.'

'I'm sure that's it,' said Sue, folding the newspapers under her arm and walking over to the door. 'He's just tired.'

'Aye. No rest for the wicked, is there, love? Bye now.'

As Sue walked along the street, Eastcote's van passed her by and took the same route out of town as it had before. Another delivery. Whether he would be back later or would be staying out overnight, she had no idea. She could imagine, though, that he would be loath to leave his cottage empty for very long. In fact, if she were in his shoes, she would make sure she was back before dark. After all, he didn't know that she had broken in during daylight.

She wondered what he had made of the extra lock of hair. Did he know it was hers? Surely he must suspect? Or perhaps he thought he was being haunted, that the supernatural was responsible for the sudden appearance of a seventh lock? Like the seventh daughter of a seventh son was supposed to be powerful in magic. One thing she did know: he had seen her, as one would notice any stranger in the street, but he didn't know who she was. Maybe when he got over the shock, he would start to think clearly again and count the times he'd glimpsed her from the corner of his eye; perhaps he would connect the girl in the navy-blue raincoat with the girl in glasses and a ponytail. But by then it would be too late.

Sue walked by the river towards town. The good weather seemed to have made a return. It was a beautiful day, with plenty of that intense blue sky you sometimes get at the seaside, and just enough plump white clouds drifting over to give a sense of depth and perspective. Beyond the greenish shallows, the sea reflected the sky's bright ultramarine. Sue stood on the swing bridge and looked around at the harbour. It was like another world to her now, after so long spent in the other, dingier part of town.

The tide was well out, and some of the light boats rested almost on their sides, with their masts at forty-five-degree angles to the slick mud. To Sue's left, beyond the high harbour wall, stood the buildings of St Ann's Staith, a mixture of architectural styles and materials: red brick, gables, chimneys, black and white Tudor-style fronting, even millstone grit. Further along, towards the sheds where the fish were auctioned, the jumble of buildings rose all the way up the hillside to the elegant white terrace of hotels that formed East Terrace.

People walked by, carefree and smiling: a courting couple, the man with his arm so low around the girl that it was practically in the back pocket of her tight jeans; two elderly ladies overdressed in checked tweeds and lace-up shoes, one carrying a walking stick; a pregnant woman, glowing with health, her husband walking proudly beside her.

All this normality, Sue thought. All these ordinary people going about their business, enjoying themselves, eating ice-cream cones and bouncing garish beachballs in the street, and they have no idea about the monster walking among them.

They have no idea that Greg Eastcote murdered six women and maimed one, that he slashed at their sexual organs with a sharp, bone-handled knife, and just to make sure they were dead, he strangled them. When he'd done that, when he'd finished his crude surgery, he carefully cut off a single lock of hair from each bruised and bleeding body, took it home with him, tied it up in a pink ribbon and placed it neatly in his sideboard drawer. Six of them all in a row. Seven now.

According to the press clippings that Sue had saved, he hadn't raped any of his victims. Clearly he was incapable of that, and the rage he felt towards women for causing his condition partly explained his actions. But only partly. There was an enormous chasm between his motives and his deeds that nobody could fathom. In a vision, the Dark One had appeared to him in a perversion of the Caedmon story and told him to sing his own song. And so he had. Only his accompanying instrument wasn't a lute, it was a knife, and the tune it played was death.

Sue wanted to jump up on the bridge rail and shout all this out to the complacent holidaymakers heading for the beach or the amusement arcades. They would shove their coins into slots, listen to the bingo caller, or sit on the beach in the sun on striped deck-chairs, newspapers shielding their faces, edging back every so often as the tide came in closer. Then, late in the afternoon, they would go to one of the many fish and chip restaurants and eat.

None of them knew about the man with the oily smell of fish on his fingers – probably the last thing his victims smelled – the Ancient Mariner eyes and the raspy voice. She wanted to tell them all about Greg Eastcote and the atrocities he had committed against women, all about the blood, the pain, the utter degradation and humiliation, and the way she had been imperfectly sewn back together again. All the king's horses and all the king's men . . . That man there, the balding one with the crying toddler in his arms, she wanted to assure him that she was here to restore the balance. But she wasn't crazy; she knew she couldn't say anything. Instead she just watched the people passing back and forth over the bridge for a while, wondering whether they were truly innocent or just indifferent, then she went to find a quiet pub.

She soon found a place on Baxtergate. Three bored-looking punks with green and yellow hair sat in the lounge playing the jukebox, but through a corridor by the side of the bar, separated from the lounge by swing doors, was a much quieter room, all dark varnished panels, hard chairs and benches. Sue realized that not only hadn't she looked at the papers yet, she hadn't even eaten since her meagre and greasy breakfast at Mrs Cummings's. The tea was so bad at Rose's that she hadn't felt inclined to find out what the food was like. All the pub served was cold snacks, so she ordered a crab sandwich and a half of lager and lime.

When she had eaten, she sat back with her drink and lit a cigarette, turning to the local paper first to see if there was any news of Keith. A brief report told her that police were continuing their inquiries into the suspicious death of Jack Grimley and the 'brutal assault' on a young Australian tourist, who was still in a critical condition at St Mary's Hospital, Scarborough. Apparently, Keith had not yet regained consciousness.

Then, under the heading HAVE YOU SEEN THIS GIRL? she suddenly noticed an artist's impression of her. She hadn't spotted it at first because it looked nothing like her. Perhaps there was a faint resemblance to Martha Browne, but even that would be pushing it a bit. The shape of the head was all wrong, far too round, and the eyes were too close together, the lips too thick. Still, it was enough to make her pulse race. It meant they were on the right track and they were getting closer. All the caption said was that police were anxious to talk to this girl, who had been seen with the Australian in Hinderwell, as she 'may have been the last person to see him before the attack.'

Sue folded the paper and turned to the crossword, but she found herself too preoccupied to concentrate on the clues. She knew that the police in general told little of what they knew to the papers. If she read between the lines, it seemed likely that they had also found the bus driver who had picked her up near Staithes. But all he could tell them was that she had got off at Whitby bus station. After that, Martha Browne had disappeared for ever.

Could they also track her to the lodgings on Abbey Terrace? Certainly if they traced Keith's movements, as they would surely be doing, then the odds were that they would check the register there, get a better description of her from the owner or his wife, and mount a full-scale search for 'Martha Browne'. Why, she wondered, were they taking so long? They must have found out where Keith had been staying in Staithes quickly enough. From there, it surely wouldn't have taken them long to work their way back to Whitby, unless there was no evidence among his belongings to say where he'd been – no journal, no brochures, no postcards unsent. What if they did know and every policeman in Whitby was on the lookout for her already? Nervously, she glanced over at a young couple by the bar, but they were only interested in one another.

Still, she told herself, she had no real cause to worry. Martha Browne no longer existed. She could have gone anywhere from Whitby bus station – Scarborough, York, Leeds – and why not on to London, Paris or Rome? Surely nobody would expect her to hang around in the area after she had attacked Keith McLaren? Even if they did know who they were after, they wouldn't centre their search in Whitby. She had told Keith that she came from Exeter, but she couldn't remember what she had written, if anything, in the register at the guesthouse. She wondered how long it would take the police to discover that Martha Browne had never existed in the first place. And what would they do then?

Of course, she knew that all this was nothing but speculation. Even if they could link her to Keith via Abbey Terrace, the Lucky Fisherman and Hinderwell, they still couldn't prove that she had done anything wrong. She could say that Keith had wanted to lead her into the woods but she had refused and left him, taking the bus back to Whitby. It probably wouldn't come to that, but if it did, she knew they couldn't prove anything. If the worst came to the worst, she could say he had tried to rape her and she had defended herself, then got scared and run away.

The only real problem was that it would look very odd indeed if they found her and discovered that Martha Browne and Sue Bridehead were the same person, and what's more, that she was really Kirsten, the only surviving victim of the Student Slasher. That would certainly look incriminating, especially when they found his body. But would it be enough to convict her of anything? Perhaps. Still, she had known from the start that the whole business was fraught with risks, though she hadn't expected it to turn into such a mess.

There was also a chance that the police might find out

about the wig and clothes she had bought in Scarborough, but that was very unlikely. She had purposely chosen large, busy department stores, and none of the shop assistants had paid her very much attention. Since she had been in, they would have served hundreds of other customers. Then she remembered the scrawny woman with the large head, the smoker she had startled in the ladies' toilet. She might remember. But so what? All she knew was that Sue had gone to the toilet in a Scarborough department store. Nothing unusual in that. There had been another woman who had spoken to her too that day. She remembered putting on make-up next to a woman who joked about her husband saying she always took so long to go to the toilet. But none of it mattered. She had spoken to lots of people during her time in Whitby, as anybody would.

No, there was nothing to worry about. Besides, she had divine protection, at least until she had fulfilled her destiny. Her spirit guides would hardly allow her to fail after she had got so far. Nonetheless, it was wise to be cautious, get it done quickly and leave town. There was no sense in jeopardizing the main reason for her visit just for the pleasure of toying with her prey a bit longer and watching Greg Eastcote grow more paranoid day by day. She wasn't in this for cruelty, for pleasure. Besides, he would be growing more and more cautious. Best get it done tonight, then, if she could.

The Student Slasher seemed to have disappeared completely from the pages of the *Independent*, as Sue had suspected he soon would. And he wouldn't appear there alive again. With luck, when she had killed him, the police would search his house and find the seven locks of hair. They would check the dates and places of his overnight deliveries, and they would find out who he was and what he had done. Also with luck, they would probably assume that a victim had got the better of him this time, and they wouldn't employ all their resources trying to find out exactly who she was.

After lunch, Sue returned to the factory area. Eastcote could be on a short local run and might come back at any time. She watched from the woods, lying on her stomach, then at evening opening-time she went to the Merry Monk and took her usual table by the window. By pulling back the curtain just a little when nobody was looking, she could see straight down the convex slope of waste ground to Eastcote's cottage. She would wait for him to come home, then she would somehow lure him away. He hadn't struck in his own town before, perhaps due to caution, but this time he wouldn't be able to resist.

Shortly after seven, Sue saw him arrive home. The lights went on behind the pale blue curtains in the cottage. Uncertain how to draw him out, she finished her drink and left the pub. Instead of returning to the lane, walking downhill and turning right onto Eastcote's street, she walked straight across the waste ground, from where she could easily be seen. Sunset was almost over now, and the western sky glowed in even striations of deep violet, scarlet and purple. A jet's trail snaked right across the western horizon, losing shape quickly, and one or two clouds blushed in the last light. Nettles and thistles stung Sue's legs as she brushed her way through the weeds, but the pain felt distant, unreal.

She could knock on his door, or telephone perhaps. But she hadn't seen a phone when she had been inside his house. Knocking on the door was too risky. He might react quickly and drag her inside. Instead, she just walked slowly down to the street and paused when she got to the end of the low garden wall. The curtains were still drawn. She thought she could see a shadow move behind them. She stood for a few moments, certain that they were looking at one another with only the thin blue curtains between them, then moved on, taking the dirt path across the scrub land that led down to the main road. As she walked, she felt a strange drifting sensation, as if she was floating an inch or two above the grass.

Sue stopped and just stood there, about a hundred yards from his house. It was uncanny, the certainty she felt that he had been aware of her standing outside his cottage and that he would open his door and look. And he did. She stood there in the middle of a piece of waste land, nettles, weeds and thistles all around, silhouetted by the sunset. He walked to the end of his garden path, turned his head in her direction, and slowly opened the gate.

46

KIRSTEN

Kirsten stared out of the window at the landscape beyond her reflection. The rounded green hills of the Cotswolds soon gave way to the fertile Vale of Evesham, where barley and wheat looked ready for harvest in the fields, and apples, pears and plums hung heavy on their trees in the hillside orchards.

Then came the built-up landscape of the Midlands: cooling towers, the sprawling monotony of council estates, allotments, greenhouses, a red-brick school, a football field with white goal posts. When the train crept into Birmingham and she could feel the huge city pressing in on all sides, she began to feel nervous. This was, after all, her longest journey in ages, and she was making it alone. For over a year she had been living in a soft, comfortable, familiar world, shuttling between the Georgian elegance of Bath and the bucolic indifference of Brierley Coombe.

Now it was grey and raining and she was in Birmingham, a big, rough city with slums, skinheads, race riots and all the rest. Luckily, she didn't have to get off the train there. She hoped Sarah would be at the station to meet her when she arrived at her destination.

After a twenty-minute stop, the train pulled out and lumbered past twisting concrete overpasses into another built-up area: the derelict warehouses with rusty zigzag fire escapes, and the messy factory yards stacked high with crates and pallets that always seemed to back onto train tracks in cities. It ran alongside a busy commuter road, a dirty brown canal, and a dark brick embankment wall scrawled with graffiti. Next came a few green fields with grazing cows, and then the train settled into a steady, lulling clickety-click through Derbyshire into South Yorkshire, with its slag heaps and idle pit wheels, a landscape in which all the green seemed to have been smudged by an inky finger that was now running in the rain.

Kirsten closed her eyes and let the rhythm carry her. She would stay with Sarah for a day or two perhaps, until she felt it was time to go. Despite what she had told her parents, she had not suggested that Sarah take time off work. Kirsten would say she was going to the Dales walking for a few days alone. If that sounded odd – after all, she *had* spent the last year in the countryside, much of the time alone – then it was too bad. But Sarah would take her word. It was surprising how eager people were to believe her about anything after what had happened to her.

The rain had stopped when Sarah met her at the station later that evening. They allowed themselves the luxury of a taxi to take them back to the bedsit. All the way, Sarah chatted about how glad she was that Kirsten had decided to come back, and how they would look for a flat together as soon as Kirsten had got her bearings again. Kirsten listened and made the right responses, glancing left and right out of the window like a nervous bird as familiar sights unfolded around her: the tall, white university tower, the terraces of sooty red-brick student housing, the park. Washed and glistening after the rain, it all took her breath away with its combination of familiarity and strangeness. For fifteen months it had been simply a landscape of the mind, a closed-off world in which certain things had happened and been filed away. Now that she was actually riding through it again in a taxi, she felt as if she had somehow drawn her surroundings from deep inside herself, from her imagination. She was no longer in the real world at all; she was in a painting, an imagined landscape.

It was getting dark outside when they arrived at the flat. Kirsten followed Sarah up the stairs, remembering with her body rather than in her mind how often she had made this journey before. Her feet remembered in their cells the cracked linoleum they trod, and her fingertips seemed to hold within them the memory of the light switch she pressed.

When she entered her room itself, she had that sensation, however mistaken, of being at a journey's end. It was something she had felt so often before, arriving home after lectures or tiring exams. She remembered the occasional day spent ill in bed with a cold or a sore throat, when she would read and watch the shadows of the houses opposite slowly crawl up the far wall and over the ceiling until the room grew so dark that she had to put the reading lamp on.

She dropped her holdall in the corner and looked around. Some of her belongings were still in their original places: a few books and cassettes in the main room and mugs and jars in the little kitchen alcove. All Sarah had done was clear space for her own things. There was no problem with clothes, of course, as Kirsten had emptied the cupboard of most of hers, but Sarah had filled one cardboard box with some of Kirsten's books and papers to make room for her own on the shelves and the desk.

'Well?' Sarah said, watching her. 'Not changed much, has it?'

'No, it hasn't. I'm surprised.'

'Does it upset you, being back here again?'

'No,' said Kirsten. 'I don't think so. I'm not sure. It's just a very odd feeling, hard to explain.'

'Well, don't worry about it. Just sit down for now. Do you want some tea? Or there's wine. I got a bottle of plonk. Thought you might like that better than going out on the first night.'

'Yes, that's great. I don't much fancy going out. I'm a bit tired and shaky. But some wine would be nice.'

Sarah took the bottle from the small refrigerator and held it up. It was a pale gold colour. 'Aussie stuff,' she said. 'A Chardonnay. Supposed to be good.' She picked up two glasses from the dishrack and searched for the corkscrew in the kitchen drawer. Finally, everything in hand, she filled their glasses and brought them through. 'Cheese? I've got a wedge of Brie and some Wensleydale.'

'Yes, please.'

Sarah brought in the cheese with a selection of biscuits on a Tetley's tray, liberated from the Ring O'Bells. They toasted the future and drank. Kirsten helped herself to some food, then picked up a book she noticed lying on the floor by the armchair. It was a thick biography of Thomas Hardy. 'Is this what you're reading right now?' she asked.

Sarah nodded. 'I'm thinking about doing my PhD in Victorian fiction, and you know how I love biographies. It seemed a pleasurable enough way of getting back into academic gear.'

'And is it? I mean, Hardy's hardly a light, cheerful read, is he?'

Sarah laughed. 'I don't know about a pessimist, but he was certainly a bloody pervert.'

'How?' asked Kirsten. 'I've only read *Far from the Madding Crowd* for that novel course in first year. I don't even remember much about that except some soldier showing off his fancy sword-play. I suppose that was meant to be phallic?'

Sarah laughed. 'Yes, but that's not what I meant. All writers do that kind of symbolism thing to some extent, don't they?'

'What *do* you mean?'

'Well, for one thing,' Sarah went on, 'do you know he used to like attending public executions when he was in his teens? Especially when women were being hanged.' She reached for the book and turned the pages slowly as she talked. 'There was one in Dorchester and he told someone about it when he was much older . . . ah, here it is . . . 1856. Martha Browne was the woman's name, and she was hanged for murdering her husband. She caught him with another woman and they got into a fight. He attacked her with a whip and she stabbed him. Hanging her was the Victorians' idea of justice. Anyway, Hardy went along and wrote about it.' She pushed the book under Kirsten's nose. 'Just look at that.'

Kirsten read: 'What a fine figure she showed against the sky as she hung in the misty rain, and how the tight black silk gown set off her shape as she wheeled half round and back.'

'I mean, really,' Sarah went on, 'the poor woman was swinging at the end of a bloody rope and Hardy makes out as if she was entering some kind of wet T-shirt contest. Would you credit it?'

Kirsten read over the description; it was certainly tinged with eroticism.

'Am I right?' Sarah asked, pouring more wine. 'Don't you get the feeling that Hardy got some kind of kinky sexual pleasure from watching the woman get snuffed?' She put a hand to her mouth quickly. 'Oh. I'm sorry, love. I . . . I put my foot in it. Must be the wine going to my head. I mean, I wasn't thinking. I didn't mean to . . . you know.'

Kirsten waved her hand. 'It's all right. I'd rather you say what you like than walk around handling me with kid gloves. I can take it. And anyway, you're right, it *is* sexual.'

'Yes. And what's more, did you notice how he turns her into some sort of convenient image for a poem. As if her life was only important because he got a charge from watching her get hanged. She wasn't even a person, an individual, to him.'

'I wonder what she was like,' Kirsten said abstractedly.

'We'll never know, will we?'

'I suppose not. But it's not as odd as all that, is it? The way Hardy uses her, I mean. We all tend to see other people as bit players in our own dramas, don't we? I mean we're all self-centred.'

'I don't think so. Not to that extent.'

'Maybe not. But you might be surprised.' She held her glass out and Sarah emptied the bottle. Kirsten was beginning to feel a little tipsy. After the journey and the disorienting effect of coming back to her old room, the wine was affecting her more than it usually would. Still, it wasn't an unpleasant sensation. She helped herself to another chunk of Wensleydale.

Sarah shook the wine bottle, grinned and jumped up, ruffling Kirsten's short hair as she passed by. 'Fear not,' she said. 'I suspected we might need more than the usual amount of alcoholic sustenance. How about some music? All right?'

Kirsten shrugged. 'Fine.'

Sarah turned on the cassette player and disappeared behind the curtain into the kitchen. She must have been playing the tape earlier because one song was just fading out, and then 'Simple Twist of Fate' began to play. It was the second track on Bob Dylan's *Blood on the Tracks*, Kirsten remembered, and it used to be one of her favourites; now, as she listened to Dylan's hoarse, plaintive voice while Sarah was busy opening the second bottle, she realized that the strange lyrics didn't mean what she used to think they did. Nothing did any more.

Sarah returned with a larger bottle, lifting it up with a flourish. 'Da-da! More your cheaper kind of plonk, really, but I'm sure at this stage it'll do.'

Kirsten smiled. 'Oh, it'll do fine.'

'What did you mean,' Sarah asked when she had filled the glasses and sat down, 'when you said I'd be surprised? What would I be surprised by?'

Kirsten frowned. 'I was thinking of the man who attacked me,' she said. 'I wasn't a person, an individual, to him, was I? I was just a convenient symbol of what he hated or feared.'

'Would it have made any difference?'

'I don't know. Would it have made any difference if it had been someone I knew? I can think of one way it would have: I'd know who it was.'

'And?'

'I'd bloody well kill him.' Kirsten lifted her glass of wine too quickly and spilled some down the front of her shirt. She patted herself on the chest. 'Doesn't matter' she said. 'It'll dry.'

'An eye for an eye?'

'Something like that.'

Sarah shook her head slowly.

'I'm not crazy, you know,' Kirsten went on. 'I mean it. Oh, there've been times . . . Sometimes I think it's some sort of contagious disease he gave me, like AIDS, only in the mind. Or like vampirism. Can you imagine all those ripped-up women coming back from the grave to prey on men? Of course, I didn't die, but maybe a part of me did. Maybe I have a little bit of the undead in me.'

'That's cuckoo talk, Kirstie. Or drunk talk. You're not going to convince me you're turning into some sort of vampire version of Joan of Arc.'

Kirsten looked hard at her and felt the focus blurring. My God, she thought, I'm losing it. I almost told her. She laughed and reached for a cigarette. 'You're right,' she said. 'I'm not. It's all academic anyway, isn't it?'

'Thank God for that,' Sarah said. The music stopped and she got up and turned over the tape.

As the two of them chatted, Kirsten glanced out now and then at the windows of the bedsits and flats over the street, just as she had in years past. At some point, she noticed 'Shelter from the Storm', another of her favourites, was playing, and her eyes burned with tears. She held them back.

Around midnight, Kirsten began to yawn in the middle of one of Sarah's stories about a retired brigadier-general who had strayed into Harridan by mistake.

'Boring you, am I?' Sarah asked.

'No. I'm just tired, that's all. It must be the wine and the travel. How about sleeping arrangements?'

Sarah yawned too. 'Look, now you've got me at it. How about I take the chair and you have the bed?'

'Oh no, I couldn't do that.'

'It *is* your room, after all. I've just been caretaking.'

'It *was* my room. No, I'll put a couple of cushions on the floor and sleep there.'

'But that's stupid. You'll be so uncomfortable. Hell, it's a three-quarter bed, let's share it.'

Kirsten said nothing for a moment. The suggestion made her feel nervous and shy. She knew that Sarah wasn't offering any kind of sexual invitation, but the thought of her own patched-up body next to Sarah's smooth, whole skin made her cheeks burn.

'I haven't brought a nightie,' she said.

'Not to worry. I've got a spare pair of pyjamas. Okay?'

'All right.' Kirsten was too tired to argue, and the idea of sleeping in what had once been her own bed was inviting. When she stood up, she felt herself sway a little. She really had drunk too much.

They prepared themselves for bed and drew the curtains. Kirsten watched Sarah pull her T-shirt over her head and struggle with her tight jeans, then stand there naked and unselfconsciously brush her blonde hair in front of the mirror. Her breasts bounced lightly with the motion of her arm, and below her flat stomach, the spun-gold hair between her legs caught the light.

Kirsten undressed last, in the dark, so that Sarah couldn't see her scars, and when she slipped between the crisp sheets, she found herself staying as close to the edge of the bed as possible to avoid any unconscious contact.

But she needn't have worried. Sarah lay with her face turned to the wall below the window, and soon her breathing settled into a slow, regular pattern. Kirsten listened for a while, feeling slightly dizzy and nauseated and cursing herself for almost telling Sarah everything she knew, not to mention what she intended to do about it. Eventually, she drifted off to sleep and dreamed of Martha Browne, that unknown woman in black swinging back and forth at the end of a rope in the misty Dorchester rain over a hundred years ago.

The next day, Sarah went into the bookshop, and Kirsten spent the morning revisiting her old campus haunts: the coffee lounge where she had met friends between lectures, the library where she had worked so hard for the final exams. She even wandered into an empty lecture theatre and imagined Professor Simpkins droning on about Milton's *Areopagitica*.

Though she had avoided it on her way over, taking the roads instead, Kirsten walked back through the park. As her feet followed the familiar tarmac path through the trees she felt nothing at all, but when she reached the lion, its head still spray-painted blue and the red graffiti still scrawled all over its body, her hands started shaking. Unable to stop herself, she walked over to the sculpture.

It was a little after twelve. Children played on the swings and seesaw nearby. The clack of bowls came from the green behind the low hedge, and one or two people sprawled out on the grass, listening to portable cassettes or reading. But Kirsten still felt extreme unease, as if she had somehow stumbled on a taboo place, an evil spot shunned by natives. She couldn't help herself when she sat astride the lion, drawing amused glances from two students playing cards on the grass nearby. It

all happened so quickly. The fishy smell began to suffo-
cate her and the world darkened at the corners of her
vision. Then she saw him and heard his raspy voice and
saw the blade flash in the moonlight. She leapt off and
hurried on her way, trembling.

As she walked on down the avenue of trees, she
cursed herself for giving in to fear. She would need all
the courage and strength she could get for what she had
to do, and jumping at shadows was a poor start. Still, she
told herself, somehow shadows were more frightening to
her now than substance. That must be a good sign. It
was time to go.

First she went back to the flat and left a note for
Sarah, then she went into town. After shopping for one
or two essentials she needed for her trip, she headed for
the bus station. About three hours later, Martha Browne
arrived in Whitby on a clear afternoon in early
September, convinced of her destiny.

47

SUSAN

Like some shadowy female figure out of Hardy standing on a blasted heath waiting for her lover, Sue stood on the waste land in the thickening darkness and watched Greg Eastcote shut his garden gate and take the path towards her.

Before he had got far, while Sue was still about sixty yards ahead, she turned her back to him and started walking along the rough path. When she got to the main road, there were few people about, but the street was well lit. Sensing him behind her, rather than seeing him, Sue continued along until she had passed the intersection with Bridge Street, where the road narrowed. This was the tourist area again, the cobbled street of gift shops, the Monk's Haven, the Black Horse. At this time of evening though, all the shops were closed. Polished jet gleamed in its gold and silver settings in the windows, and the enamel trays that had been covered with coffee- or mint-flavoured fudge all day lay empty. All the happy holiday families were back at the guesthouses watching television, or they had managed to put the kids to bed and gone out to the pub for a quiet pint alone. Only lovers and vampires walked the streets.

Hands in the pockets of her windcheater, Sue walked on purposefully. She had known where she was heading all along, she realized, but she had known it in her instinct and her muscles, not in her conscious mind. He was still behind her, moving more cautiously now, not hurrying to catch up with her. Perhaps he was getting worried. When she got to the steps, she turned and started climbing, counting by habit as she went. It was dark and deserted up the hill, with no street lights to light her way. But St Mary's was floodlit, like a beacon, and high above the church a waning three-quarter moon shone in the clear sky, surrounded by stars. At the top of the hundred and ninety-ninth step, where Caedmon's Cross stood silhouetted against the bright sand-coloured church, Sue turned through the graveyard of nameless stones. She could tell he was following her, that he would soon appear at the top and look around to see which way she had gone. She slowed down. She didn't want to disappoint him.

In the light of St Mary's, she followed the path through the graves around the seaward side of the church and across the deserted car park, where the world turned dark again. She found the coast path and stopped for a moment by the gate. Yes, he was there, just coming out of the cemetery and looking in her direction.

She turned back to the path and hurried on. She was high on the cliff now, the sheer part known as the Scar, walking in the general direction of Robin Hood's Bay. The raised boardwalk underfoot creaked in places, and she had to slow down in case of missing boards. A barbed-wire fence came between the path and the drop, but it had collapsed here and there where erosion had eaten the rock away.

Now that she was further away from the church's interfering floodlights, the moonlight shone more clearly, dusting the grass on one side and the sea on the other with its ghostly silver light. Sue thought she might lead him as far as Saltwick Nab and down the steps, out towards the knuckled rocks that pointed to the sea. But he was getting closer. She could hear his footsteps on the boardwalk, and when she half-turned her head, she could see him outlined faintly by the moonlight.

He was walking faster. She would never make it that far before he caught up with her, and she didn't intend him to attack her from behind. As she walked, she reached her hand into her shoulder bag and felt for the paperweight. There it was, smooth and heavy against her sweating palm.

He was almost so close now that she could hear his laboured breathing. The climb up the steps must have tired him. When she could bear it no longer, Sue stopped abruptly and turned to face him. In the moonlight, she could just about make out his features: the low, dark brow, wide, grim-set mouth and the eyes glittering like stars reflected on the water's surface. He had stopped, too. Only about five yards lay between them, and at first nobody said a word; neither of them even seemed to be breathing. Sue found that she was shaking. Suddenly, she remembered with perfect clarity all the pain she had suffered the last time she had seen this ghostly face in the moonlight.

Finally, she found the courage to speak, 'Do you remember me?'

'You,' he said, in that familiar raspy whisper. 'You were in my house.'

'Yes,' she said, gaining strength as they talked, feeling the hardness of the solid glass in her hand.

'Why? What are you trying to do to me?'

Sue didn't answer. Now that she had found him, she had said all she wanted to.

'Why?' he repeated.

She noticed that he was moving towards her very slowly, closing the gap as he talked.

'You know what you are,' she said, bringing her hand out of the shoulder bag. Then she took a sudden step towards him and shouted, 'Come on, then! Here I am. Come on, do it. Finish me!'

She could see the confusion and horror on his face as she continued moving towards him. 'Come on. What's wrong with you? Do it!'

But he kept on backing away as Sue edged closer, paperweight out in her hand now. He stretched out his arms before him as if to ward her off, and immediately she knew. She knew that he needed surprise to succeed. He was a coward. And what must she look like, she wondered, coming towards him with a fist of thick glass held out and all the rage of a ruined life in her face and voice? It didn't bear thinking about. The miserable bastard was terrified and his fear unnerved her for a moment.

He must have sensed her confusion like an animal scents its prey, for he began to smile as he slowed his retreat. In a moment he would start walking towards her again. But he had already gone too far. On his next slow step backwards, one of the rotten boards shifted under him and he wobbled at the edge. He waved his arms like a semaphorist, a look of terror on his face, and Sue almost reached forward to help him. Almost. But he regained his balance and again she saw that *other* face, the one his human mask barely hid. She took a pace forward and kicked out hard at him. Her foot connected with his groin and he tottered back towards the edge of the cliff with a scream.

The fence was low there, only about a foot or so off

the ground, and the post stood at an odd angle, crooked, pointing out to sea. As he fell backwards, his clothing snagged on the rusted barbed wire and he managed to turn himself around. He was half over the edge but his hands clawed at the thick tufts of grass. The more he struggled, the more the wire seemed to wrap him up, and when she moved closer, Sue could see blood seeping through his clothes. He grunted and snatched at the sods as he tried to stop himself from slowly sliding over. Sue knelt down and smashed at his hands with the paperweight. The fence post twitched like a dowsing rod as he howled and struggled, snatching at the barbed wire now, anything to get a grip, his hands coming away crushed, ripped and bloody. Only his head and shoulders showed above the edge now. The wire had torn one sleeve right off his jacket and its barbs stuck in the skin beneath. The post was almost out of the ground, pointing out to sea, and the more he struggled the more he slipped.

At last he managed to find a foothold in the cliff face just below the edge, but his hands were so badly damaged that all he could do was push himself up with his feet and flail his arms about. The barbed wire tied him to the edge but his feet pushed him away. Sue stood up, raised the paperweight and hit him on the side of his head. The jolt ran all the way up her arm. Blood filled his eye. She hit out again, this time catching him over the ear. He screamed and put one hand to the wound. The post broke free of its shallow pit and shot over the cliff side, taking him with it. Sue knelt right at the edge and saw him twist around in the wire like an animal in a trap before he tore free and plunged.

Far below, the sea lapped and spumed around the rocks at the base of the cliff, and the body, arms and legs whirling, hit them with a thud louder than the breaking waves themselves. Sue could see him down there, slumped and broken over the sharp dark rocks, where the foaming waves licked at him like the tongues of madmen.

It was done. Sue looked back towards the distant church and thought of the normal, day-to-day world that lay below it in the town. What would she do now that it was over? Should she follow him? It would be so easy just to relax and let herself slide over the edge to oblivion.

But no. Suicide wasn't part of her destiny. Her own death had been her stake, what she had risked, but it was not part of the bargain if she won. She had to accept her fate, whatever it might be: live with the guilt, if such she felt, or pay for her crimes if she was caught. But there was no giving in to suicide. She was free of her burden now, come what may.

She had no idea if the police were close to discovering her identity. Perhaps they were already waiting back at Mrs Cummings' to arrest her. And then there was Keith McLaren, still in a coma. What if he woke up and remembered everything? On the other hand, he might have brain damage or amnesia. If so, was it possible that he would spend his days trying to piece together the fragments of his memory by himself, and, if he succeeded, would he hunt down the woman who had so suddenly and without provocation wrecked his life? She didn't know. She might have created another like herself, someone with a bit of the undead in him.

But no matter how bleak some of the possibilities seemed, she felt free at last. More than that, she was Kirsten again. Even imprisonment would be a kind of freedom now. It didn't really matter what happened because she had done what had to be done. Now she was free.

Certainly her best bet would be to get out of town and back to Sarah first thing in the morning and destroy anything that might link her to the place. That's what she would do. Perhaps she could also tint her hair and make sure she looked like none of the girls who had been in Whitby.

All Kirsten really wanted to do at the moment, she realized, looking towards the church, was crawl into one of those box pews marked FOR STRANGERS ONLY, kneel and offer a prayer of sorts, then curl up on the green baize and sleep. But the place would be locked up for the night.

As she got to her feet, the paperweight slipped out of her sweaty palm, bounced on the springy grass and fell over the edge. She leaned forward to watch and saw the glass shatter against a rock in a shower of white powder like a wave breaking. Free of its cage, the rose seemed to drift up on a current of warm air. Its crimson petals opened, pale in the moonlight, then slowly it floated back down and a departing wave carried it out to sea.

afterword

'8th September 1987
Coast road, Whitby–Staithes. Rolling farmland, patchwork of hedged fields (cows grazing) light brown after
harvest & wheat-coloured barley etc. End abruptly at
cliffs, pinkish strata, sea clear light blue, sun glinting
silver on distant ship. Flock of gulls on red-brown field.
Clumps of trees in hollows. Cluster of village houses,
light stone, red pantile roofs: ". . . arrived at the small
coastal town at 11.15 a.m. in early September, her mind
made up." '

Such were the humble origins of *Caedmon's Song*, I discover, looking back over my notebook for August 1987,
to March 1988. I wrote the book in the late eighties, then,
after my first four Inspector Banks novels. I remember I
needed a change; a novel in which the police played a
subsidiary role. Ever since reading about the Yorkshire
Ripper, I'd had an idea for a story about someone who
had survived a serial killer's attack setting out for
revenge.

The idea lay fallow, as these things often do, until one
September day in 1987, when we crested the hill into
Whitby, shortly before the above-described trip to
Staithes, when the original opening revealed itself. There
lay Whitby, spread out below. The colours seemed
somehow brighter and more vibrant than I remembered:

the greens and blues of the North Sea, the red pantile roofs. Then there was the dramatic setting of the lobster-claw harbour and the two opposing hills, one capped with a church and a ruined abbey, the other with Captain Cook's statue and the massive jawbone of a whale. I knew immediately that this was where the story had to take place, and that it began with a woman getting off a bus, feeling a little travel-sick, trying the place on for size.

When I heard that Macmillan planned to publish this novel in 2003, I toyed with the idea of rewriting it and updating it. After all, isn't it every writer's dream to get another chance years later at improving something one wrote in one's early days? But the more I thought about it, the more I realized that it just wouldn't work, that the world has changed so much since 1987, and that the events in *Caedmon's Song* couldn't happen in a world with mobile phones, e-mail, a McDonald's or Pizza Hut on every corner, and the current techniques of DNA testing. Genetic fingerprinting existed back then, as Joseph Wambaugh's *The Blooding* demonstrates very well, but it was still in its infancy. Besides, I was supposed to be leaving the police behind. Given the advances in forensic science since 1987, it seemed that if I were to update the book for 2003, it would be almost impossible to keep them in the background. Whitby has changed, too, especially the footpath along the top of the cliffs which plays such an important role in the book.

In the end, I settled for correcting a few minor points, changing a character's name, getting rid of an obtrusive comment about Margaret Thatcher. That sort of thing. In all other respects it's the original novel, now a period piece of sorts, a slice of late twentieth-century history, set in a time when you could smoke anywhere, get bed and breakfast for £9.50 a night and *Crocodile Dundee* was all the rage!